First Romance

First Romance

Stories of Young Love

Cathay Books

This compilation first published in 1987 by Cathay Books,
59 Grosvenor Street, London W1.
© Copyright 1987 this compilation The Hamlyn Publishing Group Limited,
Bridge House, 69 London Road, Twickenham, Middlesex, England.

Illustrations by Tony Masero;
© Copyright The Hamlyn Publishing Group Limited 1983, 1984, 1987.

ISBN 0 86178 487 1
Printed and bound in Yugoslavia.

Cover illustration by Martin Salisbury.

Contents

WHAT THE EYE DOESN'T SEE

Maureen Spurgeon

MY GRANDPA'S ALWAYS GOING ON about life playing funny tricks on people. Reckon I know what he means now – even though I still can't believe how it all happened. Maybe, that's why I'm writing it down, you know? To get everything clear in my mind.

To start off, I'd best tell you, my name's Cindy Parsons, and my folks – that includes Grandpa – run the General Store out at Longville West.

Now, I wouldn't call Longville a bad place to live. Early morning, with the sun coming up over the hills, it's real pretty, specially when it's spring time, and you can smell the fruit blossom just as soon as you wake up. And even the traffic on the freeways leading to the big cities out in the distance seems like something out of a fancy travel brochure.

No, I'd say Longville is more slow and sleepy than anything else. The sort of place where everyone knows everyone – or, nearly everyone. And, being in the General Store, we all hear most of what's going on.

'See another of John Pullen's cows had twin calves,' Mamie Fraser might say, stomping in from the yard like a man in her great thick boots and leggings. 'And wouldn't I just like to know how he does it!'

That was generally the cue for Mr Butler, out from Shuman's Ridge, to pipe up with something like, 'My old pa always swore by a spoonful of treacle before sun-up! Never had no twin calves, but milk yield went up a-plenty!'

7

That sort of talk would remind my daddy that he'd got some of the new churns they'd ordered, or a stock of grain, spare parts for tractors, and the rest, leaving me to count up the weeks to the next Hoe-Down, which was about the only reason I ever had to change out of jeans and a shirt.

Sometimes, helping Grandpa to sort the mail, I'd find myself staring at letters from exciting places I'd only heard about, and wish I was one of the birds from the outback that Mam sometimes liked to watch, flying away somewhere a whole lot different to Longville.

'You ain't saying much lately, Cindy,' Grandpa noticed one morning, before the bus left for school. 'Something troublin' you?'

Grandpa probably guessed how I felt. After all, I'd had plenty of dismal spells before, but I reckon he thought it might help if I could manage to talk things over.

I was just making up my mind whether or not to say anything at all, when the shop bell jangled, and in came Herbie Graham, whistling nothing in particular, like he usually did, and letting the door bang hard enough to set the candy jars rattling – as he always did. 'Morning, Mr Parsons,' he chirped gaily, thumbs in the bib of his dungarees. 'Morning, Cindy.'

'Morning, Herbie.' Guess I wasn't quite as cheerful as Herbie looked.

'Morning, Herbie. What can I get you?' Grandpa asked.

'Some of your best home-cured sausage for Frank Lawson's breakfast, and mind there's no teethmarks in it this time, his wife says.'

'Teeth marks!' Grandpa's face was bulging so much, I half expected him to burst like a big, red balloon. 'See here. If you're hinting we got mice in this store, I'll have you know. . . .'

He stopped, looking all around, and then at me. And I looked at him. We'd both heard it at the same moment – a kind

8

of scratching, scrabbling noise. And, then – 'Eeeee, eeeee,' squeaking like the soundtrack from some horror movie.

Grandpa didn't say a word. He started to pull out sacks and stuff, then looked in all the boxes, rummaged in the mailbags, even pulled out the drawer of the cash register, while I squeezed myself against the wall, wondering whether to jump up on the counter, or make a dash for the back door.

'Eeeee, eeee,' the mouse sounds went on, near enough driving me loopy.

'Thought you were going to say there's no mice in this store, Mr Parsons!' exclaimed Herbie, with a long whistle. 'Ho-ly Moses!'

I could have kicked myself for not seeing he had to be laughing inside, from his canvas shoes, right up to the roots of his carroty hair.

'Herbie Graham!' I said, in what I meant to be an accusing voice. 'You ought to be ashamed of yourself!'

'C'mon, Cindy – it's only a joke!' He took one hand out from under his dungarees and held a flat sort of plastic tub towards me. 'Look – that's all it is – like a miniature recorder that works off a battery. Press the button yourself!'

'No, thanks!' I snarled at him. 'You've made me late for the school bus, already.'

'I'll run you down to the stop in the truck, Cindy!' Grandpa volunteered – and then he started chuckling. 'Hey, now that's a smart gadget, Herbie. I wondered what was in that mail-order parcel for you, last week.'

'About time you learned to spend your money on something useful,' I couldn't help butting in, still mad at the way he'd fooled us. 'Supposing anyone else was coming into the store, and heard them mouse-squeaking noises?'

'All the more to share in the joke!' Herbie laughed, making me grit my teeth hard. 'You – you ought to have seen your faces!

Herbie took one hand from his dungarees and held out a flat sort of plastic tub.

'Not still annoyed at me, are you?' he asked anxiously, hurrying after me towards the door. 'Your Grandpa's taken it all in good fun – and – and everyone knows this General Store's the best in the whole place.'

'Because it's the *only* one in the whole place,' I reminded him, stamping my foot. 'Herbie – can't you ever open your big mouth without putting your foot in it?'

I didn't wait for an answer – just raced out into the yard, and sat in the truck, waiting for Grandpa. Just think of all the super boys who could have come to live in Longville West, I fumed. And I had to be lumbered with a dope like Herbie!

'I shouldn't be too tough on him, Cindy,' advised Grandpa, as we drove to the bus stop. 'Herbie's a good boy, cheerful and willing, Frank Lawson says. He don't mean no harm with them jokes and tricks, an' all. Don't forget, he's got no family,' he added, glancing at me sitting there without saying anything. 'Mr and Mrs Lawson took him in when he got too old for the orphanage. Says plenty for him, that he's settled down, learning a good job in Frank's garage business, with nobody behind him.'

Well. . . . maybe that was true, I agreed, as the school bus came in sight. But, Herbie Graham. I might have said 'Yuk!' right out loud, if my friend Liz hadn't pulled open the door for me to get in and sit beside her on the front seat. I could see she was busting to tell me something.

'Cindy, you'll never guess! Darren Francis – he asked me for a date last Friday! We went to the drive-in movie, over at Clarkson!'

'That's nice, Liz,' I murmured politely.

'Clarkson's where they've opened a new leisure centre. Not only swimming, basketball, and all that, but square dancing and disco music, as well. You ought to come, Cindy.'

'Thanks, Liz,' I said, making sure I kept looking out of the window. 'But I wouldn't want to spoil things, tagging along with you and Darren. He's your boyfriend, not mine.'

'Just as you like.' Liz shrugged her shoulders, and went on talking. Can't say I listened much, though.

Altogether, it wasn't the sort of day I'd want to remember for a lifetime, and that was before I discovered Grandpa had told Mam and Daddy about Herbie's daft joke. They kept chatting and laughing about it non-stop, like he was the local celebrity, or something.

'Wish I'd been there, hearing you say we had no mice in the store, Pop!' Mam gurgled, wiping tears from her eyes. 'The tricks that boy gets up to!'

'Remember how he planted the minister's best panama hat on top of the belltower, last summer?' grinned Daddy. 'The minister never did get to know how come so many folks came to church, that day!'

I just couldn't stand much more of it, so I went outside, thinking I'd maybe stroll through Longville and watch the sun go down, seeing as there was nothing much else to do.

And, guess who I saw, running across the ridge, and waving his arms like some half-broken Aunt Sally left over from a fair?

'Hey, Cindy!' Herbie was bawling. 'Wait a minute! I want to ask you. . . .'

'Can't stop now, Herbie!' I shouted back, making a beeline for the tool store. 'I've got to do some – er – some urgent stocktaking.'

That meant I had to spend the rest of the evening sitting on an old barrel with my chin in my hands, and looking up at the sunset through the window. What a pest that boy was!

Liz came up with the next bit of excitement when I met her again on the school bus. Mind you, at first she was rambling on about Darren, the good times they were having, and how marvellous he was – making me real jealous, I can tell you – when something else she said made me prick my ears up.

'I know you said you didn't fancy coming to the leisure centre, Cindy. But there's this friend of Darren's, a sort of quiet type, you know? Darren used to go to school with him, till he left and moved on, almost a year back, I think.'

From the way Liz was talking, it all sounded more than a bit interesting. 'This friend, Hank. He's got a great personality. Good-looking, too.'

'So, why hasn't some girl at the leisure centre snapped him up already?'

Liz frowned, looking 'real puzzled-up', as Grandpa always says when Mam can't work out the accounts too easily. 'Don't know, really. Most of them have tried, but he don't seem all that keen. 'At least,' she corrected herself, 'not about any of the girls who are keen on him. And that goes for most of them.'

It was getting to sound better all the time. But, there just had to be a snag, somewhere.

'So, what makes you think I'd be any different?'

'Oh, Cindy! Darren happens to be Hank's *friend*,' Liz pointed out, real patiently, like she was talking to some kid in the nursery class. 'He seemed to like the idea of a foursome, when I asked Darren to mention about you being a girl who wanted to see around the place, but didn't have anyone to go with. Just a hint, sort of. Go on, Cindy, be a pal,' she urged, seeing that I was still thinking it was all just too good to be true. 'You could easily come back home with me after school tomorrow, and we'll see you get a lift into Longville afterwards.'

I could feel her eyes watching me anxiously, while I weighed everything up, choosing between the latest weather forecasts, Grandpa's stamp collection, and reports on how great Herbie Graham was – once you got to know him – on one hand. And, going to Clarkson Leisure Centre, with the prospect of meeting a super new boyfriend, on the other!

What was I waiting for?

13

As I told myself all through supper, even if this super-guy didn't turn out to be all that Liz had said, a wasted evening wasn't something I couldn't afford, anyway!

The candy-pink dress with the lacy frills Aunty Em had sent me last birthday – I could wear that with my new flattie shoes. They'd pack into my schoolbag, without too much trouble, along with my best bracelet and spare pair of tights.

Even having to go and serve Herbie in the store didn't stop me wondering what my dreamboat would be like. Whether he'd think I was his kind of girl, and if we'd take to each other. I was sure I'd like him. I already liked his name – Hank. He sounded so sort of rugged, a real heart-throb.

'For the third time, Cindy,' Herbie was saying, stressing every word, 'I'd like a pair of brown laces, a sachet of shampoo, and, he took a deep breath, 'a bottle of that after-shave lotion that's advertised outside!'

'Don't drink it all at once!' I teased him, trying not to burst out laughing at the thought of someone like dear old Herbie actually using after-shave.

'Hey – y'know, that's bad!' he grinned, stuffing everything into a crumpled paper bag, then shuffling away from the counter, looking like he felt sorry about the mice joke.

When he banged the back of his head against a pile of kidney beans, I just had to smile. Having a new boyfriend was making me feel quite warm-hearted.

Everything seemed to get off to a good start as I stepped inside the Clarkson Leisure Centre. Light and roomy, with cloak-rooms, showers, dance areas. Quite a change from the poky little church hall at Longville West!

Liz showed me around, while Darren went to let Hank know I'd arrived. By this time, I was really quaking inside, and seeing Darren hurrying back alone didn't make me feel any easier, even though he was grinning from ear to ear.

'Hear that cheering?' He jerked his thumb backwards. 'Hank's only set up a game of old-fashioned ninepins in the badminton hall, because tonight's match has been cancelled, and he didn't want anyone disappointed! That's the sort of guy he is – always brim full of ideas, no matter what!'

Me? I couldn't understand why he didn't have his own fan club, judging by all the clapping and laughing going on, as well as girls standing around and screaming out things like: 'Good shot, Hank!' and calling out his name, like he was a pop star.

Hank! My date! I couldn't wait any longer to meet him. Even before Darren started leading the way, I was squeezing nearer the front, just as fast as I could.

And that's when I caught sight of his carrot-coloured hair.

'Hank!' Darren called. 'Like to meet Liz's friend. You know, the girl I was telling you about?'

'Herbie!' I cried out, and watched him spin round, and I could see his smart new jeans and tunic shirt. Strange, I'd never seen how handsome he was.

'Cindy!' he yelled back, rushing over to give me a hug, and not caring too much about being in the middle of a game, or whoever happened to be watching.

I couldn't help hugging him in return. 'So, you're Hank! I might have known!'

'That's only a nickname from my schooldays,' Herbie chuckled, squeezing me closer. 'And, you're the girl who didn't want to come into Clarkson's on her own. Maybe, if you hadn't run away from me the other evening, I'd have brought you here, myself!'

'Never heard you being the quiet, retiring type, either!' I told him, so glad to see that he was smiling right back at me.

We hadn't really noticed Liz and Darren, standing by. 'You two know each other?' Liz was asking, looking from Herbie to me, then back again.

'You could say that,' I began, glancing up at Herbie, and seeing just a flicker of what I'd call serious thought pass over his freckled face. 'Only,' I added, more quietly, 'maybe not quite well enough.'

That made Herbie give a burst of hearty laughter. Laughter I thought I was tired of hearing. 'But, we've got all the time in the world to put that right! What do you say, Cindy?'

I looked up at him again, glad to feel his arm resting lightly around my shoulders. 'All the time in the world, Herbie,' I agreed simply.

And I couldn't help thinking how pleased Grandpa would be!

THE REAL THING

Joyce Wilson

THE SCHOOL CRUISE for Redthorpe Comprehensive had been arranged for the second half of September so that Class 1A would be back in time for mock O level exams. With the real examinations almost a year away, in the following June, they had been told that it was the ideal time for a break, and on their return they would all have to settle down.

Not that it was much of a holiday, Kathie thought, as she stared out of the window of the stateroom that now served them as a classroom. The paying passengers who had all the smaller cabins on board were strolling about the decks, admiring the wide blue of the Mediterranean, or lazed in folding chairs, sipping long cool drinks against the unaccustomed heat.

Even the dolphins, twisting and diving around the great white ship, seemed to be saying, 'Look at us, aren't we lucky,' to the rows of students who had to stay in and write up their notes on their most recent port of call, in Sicily. Now *The Raleigh* was going full steam ahead for the Greek islands, and that afternoon the lectures on the antiquities they would soon see would begin.

But before that came the one thing Kathie really liked about the cruise – the chance to swim in the ship's sea-water pool, with its gentle imitation waves, its sharply clean smell, and its beautiful setting of coloured tiles, white tables, and red parasols.

This was the one place in which Kathie felt able to breathe.

No one else on the cruise knew that since her parents had died in a freak avalanche in the French Alps and she had been trapped in the caravan behind the buried car, that she had suffered from claustrophobia, the fear of being shut up in a small, enclosed place – such as a ship's cabin. Luckily for her, they all shared the larger staterooms, which had been turned into dormitories, and she had also learnt to combat her phobia – knowing that the real threat came from her own fear of panicking.

In the pool that afternoon, she met Grant, the boy who lived next door to her and her Aunt at home. She and Grant had practically grown up together, but since they had gone into separate, top classes at school she had become somewhat shy with him. They were both good swimmers, and raced each other several times the length of the pool, somehow avoiding the flailing arms and elbows of the crowd. Afterwards, they sat on the side, their feet dangling in the water. It had become suddenly unbearably hot and humid, as if a storm threatened.

'You can expect a surprise in your dormitory tonight,' Grant told her. 'Don't let on. We've got plans for a midnight picnic. Can you organize some music?'

Her eyes widened, and she looked round to make sure no one else had heard. There were very few private passengers at the pool, as the heat had become overpowering. Only a fat man in a white suit and straw hat with a bright red band sat slumped at one of the tables.

'I told the others you were someone we could trust,' Grant persisted. She knew from the years in which they had grown up together how persuasive he could be when it came to a prank. But he had never led her into any real trouble.

'All right,' she said, and dived neatly into the water, followed closely by Grant. As they both surfaced, he grinned at her, and she realized how much she had missed his company since they came on board.

That afternoon, they could hardly keep their eyes open in the ship's cinema which was used as a lecture room, as slide after slide of ruins and relics came up on the projection screen.

One rather pretty, ancient vase in black and white ceramic, a pattern of dolphins – Kathie's favourite animal – on its graceful curved surface, made her look twice. It was on show, the lecturer told them, in the museum at Mylos, the tiny Greek island which was their next port of call.

'In fact it's the most valuable thing the islanders possess,' he droned on. 'At least two thousand years old, it brings the tourists in droves.'

'Is that its real size, Sir?' A voice at the back from a boy they all knew liked to lead a teacher off the point.

'Oh no, it's much smaller, perhaps thirty centimetres.'

'And what would it be worth, Sir, in sterling?'

'If you ever have the good fortune to become a millionaire, Bates, which from your present record I would say is highly unlikely, then you would still be hard put to it to find the spare cash for a relic like this. It's quite without price. Something the Americans would give their souls to own.'

With a click that told Bates the conversation was closed, the lecturer moved on to the next slide.

That night, the sea began to grow rough, and in her narrow berth, Kathie fought rising fear. Surely the boys would not bring their picnic to the girls' quarters if the weather got worse? But it was exactly midnight when there was a heavy thump at the door, and a large hamper slid into view.

Half an hour later, one of the girls took a third slice of chocolate gateau and announced she was going to be sick. Within ten minutes she was joined by three others, and as *The Raleigh* heaved through the dark tumble of the waters, the whole party writhed on the bunks or – in the boys' case – disappeared back below decks.

But something about the emergency had calmed Kathie's nerves. She was very pleased with herself when she realized that she did not suffer from seasickness. As for Grant, one of the annoying things about him was that he could eat as much as he liked and feel no after-effects. Now she was glad to have someone so reliable around.

'We'll have to go to the sick bay and get help,' she said.

'I'll come with you. In this storm you'll need someone.' He took her hand, and she was strengthened by his closeness.

She did not tell him that she felt better out in the long corridors or on deck, if there was a storm. But as they left the stateroom and made their way to the steps that led to the main body of the ship, *The Raleigh* swung wildly in a sudden gust, and she clung to Grant as the ship's lights flickered.

They had turned into a section where the paying passengers had their cabins, when the lights failed altogether. Her heart in her mouth, Kathie stood very still. Whatever happened, she knew she must not give in to her rising terror. She felt the narrow walls of the corridor close in on her in the dark. She heard her own breath coming in fast, frightened panting sounds like that of an animal at bay.

Turning helplessly, her arms outstretched like a blind girl, Kathie found a door. Her fingers touched the handle, and instinctively she put her whole weight against it.

'Kathie,' Grant whispered, 'don't go in there. There'll be people. Stay with me.'

He was too late. The door fell open, and Kathie stood in the middle of a small, private cabin as the lights came on. Grant was in the doorway. They blinked at each other. Then Kathie saw that Grant was staring with disbelief beyond her, in the direction of the narrow berth. On the white coverlet, half wrapped in newspaper, was the exact replica of the vase they had seen in that afternoon's lecture. The same colours, the size the teacher had mentioned, the dolphin motif.

'It can't be!' Kathie whispered.

'We've got to get out of here,' Grant said, and grabbed her arm just as a voice came from somewhere along the corridor. 'Mr Skyros, are you all right, Sir?'

They almost leapt out of the cabin, and round the corner of the corridor – into the arms of the fat man in the white suit whom Kathie had noticed at the pool. His face was green, and he clutched his white straw hat to his stomach.

'Excuse me,' he said as he pushed past them and into the cabin, shutting the door with a bang.

'I think he's too ill to notice anything,' Grant said. 'Come on.' And they raced in the direction of the sick bay, the vase for the moment forgotten as they remembered the seasick friends they had left only minutes ago.

In the strange calm after the storm, they disembarked for their day in Milos. Kathie and Grant spent the day together. They exchanged smiles, congratulating each other wordlessly, on the way in which they had got the ship's doctor to deal out tablets to the casualties of the midnight feast, without telling on them to their superiors.

The museum in which the famous vase was housed was oddly disappointing, Kathie thought. No more than a dusty cave cut into the rock, it contained a few other relics in glass cases but the only exhibit of any importance was displayed quite openly in the centre of a large white natural rock, surrounded by a very low metal grid.

Guarding the whole of the exhibits was a small fat man who served as both guide and ticket collector. Kathie nudged Grant as she read the name tag he had pinned on his crumpled lapel: Skyros M.

'It's a very common name,' Grant said. 'Doesn't mean a thing.'

Outside in the glare of the afternoon, as they took a break

and drank Coca Cola at a cafe table in the small village square, Kathie narrowed her eyes and watched the Mr Skyros from *The Raleigh* advance upon them.

'Don't look now,' she said through half-closed lips to Grant. 'I don't think he remembers us. But look where he's going!'

Speechless, they watched the fat man mop his brow and replace the straw hat as he entered the museum guarded by his namesake. If he was up to no good, they could do nothing about it. He would be sure, then, to recall the brief meeting with them the night before – when they had been out of bounds and on their secret mercy dash. That was the last thing they wanted.

'He's probably only calling on one of a thousand cousins,' Grant said, but his voice lacked conviction. Under the man's jacket his inner pocket had bulged suspiciously. Unless he was carrying a packed lunch with him at this late hour, Mr Skyros was up to no good.

But ten minutes later they stood together in the village street and burst out laughing. The main shop spilled its wares on to the stony roadway. Its shelves, from the display at the front to the dark recesses at the back, consisted of one item only. In rank upon rank, a thousand replicas of the Mylos vase, in actual size and colour, stood challenging the tourist to buy.

'If he is going to exchange his vase for one in the museum,' Grant said to Kathie, 'there's no way of telling.' But not many hours were to pass before he would be proved wrong.

There was a gala on board ship that night. The guests were all to wear fancy dress, and the passengers were to mix with the schools. The theme of the evening was Greece, and there would be a prize for the best outfit. For the remainder of the day there were not many sheets left on the berths, and by nightfall, *The Raleigh's* corridors seemed to be haunted by innumerable Greek maidens and boys in white tunics.

Somehow, Kathie was delayed in the dormitory, and found herself alone. She left hurriedly, trying to catch up with the others, and quite by chance took the same route she and Grant had used the night before to reach the sick bay. As she passed the cabin which Mr Skyros used, she paused. The temptation to see if he still had the Mylos vase was very strong. But it was against her nature to pry. The incident during the storm had been an accident, after all.

She began to walk on, but something warned her that she was in danger, and she turned – too late – to find herself staring into dark eyes in a sweating face, and the strong hands of Mr Skyros held her arms in a vice-like grip.

'I saw you watching me at the pool, young lady. And then, last night during the storm – what were you doing so close to my cabin? And why were you in the square at Mylos this afternoon just when I arrived?'

She gulped silently, too scared to answer, even had she known what to say. If Skyros was so annoyed at being watched, then he did have something to hide. At last she managed to gasp, 'You're wrong, quite wrong Mr Skyros.'

'So! You know my name. Now you can explain why you should go to the trouble of finding out my name?'

As he spoke, he released one of her arms, and she tugged away from him. But he was too quick for her. With his free hand he had already opened the door of his cabin, and he grabbed her again with the other hand, pulling her in after him and standing between her and the door.

She was aware of only one thing. That on the bed, just as she had seen it the night before, the Mylos vase lay in its strangely mundane coat of newspaper. Then, her fear of being locked in with this man was too much for her, and she fainted.

When she regained consciousness, the first thing she saw was a tab of gold braid on a broad, white shoulder. *The Raleigh's*

Kathy turned to find herself staring into dark eyes, and the strong hands of Mr Skyros held her arms in a vice-like grip.

captain, for some strange reason, had been called to Mr Skyros's cabin to a foolish girl who had chosen to faint for no reason at all.

Behind the captain, in the doorway, stood Mr Skyros himself, perspiring even more profusely than usual, and mopping his brow. For once the straw hat was not in evidence. Beside him, white-faced and very quiet, was Grant.

Then, the captain helped Kathie to walk to the narrow berth and sit down. He pushed aside the vase in its wrapping, as she heard Grant's voice. 'I think I can explain, Sir.' He sounded very, very polite. Kathie knew that was going to be the moment that ruined their lives.

'It's the Mylos vase, you see,' Grant went on. 'There on the bunk. We – we have reason to believe that it has been recently stolen. The original is here. The museum now has a cheap copy.'

Kathie thought that Mr Skyros would explode. 'And what part do you think I have played in this – this comedy – young man?'

He and the captain waited for Grant's reply. Grant looked round the cabin, and took a deep breath. But the captain held up a warning hand. 'I think I know what you are about to say, my boy. And I'd like you to think very carefully before you go on. In fact, I am ready to take you into my confidence, rather than have any more trouble. *The Raleigh* has always been a very happy ship.' He looked at Mr Skyros as if seeking his approval for what was to follow.

Kathie and Grant eyed each other miserably. The whole thing had got out of control, but they had no choice now. They had to listen to what the captain had to say.

'You see,' he told them, 'in some ways you are not so far from the truth. But you have things a little muddled. I have known since Mr Skyros boarded my ship at Marseilles that he had the Mylos vase in his possession. Unfortunately, he would not put it into my strongroom, as I would have wished. No – it was not a cheap copy you saw here last night. It was the actual, original Mylos vase. It was stolen a year ago from the island museum, and Mr Skyros's brother, who is the controller –'

'And the guide, and the ticket collector,' Grant muttered under his breath, causing the captain to give him a warning look.

'Mr Skyros's brother has entrusted him to find it, and to bring it to its true home – without a word to the public, or worst of all to the press. It has been, you see, a matter of family honour. So very important to the Greeks.'

Grant looked at the brother of the Mylos museum's controller doubtfully. He looked at Kathie. She shrugged, as if to say there was nothing more to be done. The story at least had the merit of explaining why someone had brought a Mylos vase on board the ship and taken it all the way to the island where there were a thousand exact replicas to be bought. Only was that worth doing if the true original was the one *The Raleigh* had carried from Marseilles.

And yet . . . Kathie and Grant seemed to be reading each other's thoughts. If none of this were true, if Mr Skyros really had set out to exchange the vase in the museum with a copy, with his brother's connivance, then this story of a theft a year ago would be just what was needed to gain the captain's trust. After all, the priceless vase – if it was the one now resting on the bunk beside Kathie – still had to be transported to where it could fetch the highest price.

'Captain,' Grant said softly. 'Did I hear you tell one of the passengers that your next cruise takes you to America?'

'That is so,' the Captain replied. 'But I fail to see what that has to do with it. And now, I'm afraid I have wasted too much of my evening. If you will forgive me?'

He got up and took Kathie's hand as if to lead her to the door. Mr Skyros moved quickly to one side, stepping into the cabin with undue haste for someone who has just settled a trifling misunderstanding.

But Grant was quicker. He stood between the Greek and the berth. 'I learnt that any American collector would pay a fortune for this vase,' he said in a conversational tone.

The Greek shrugged, trying to edge past the boy now.

It was Grant who reached the vase first. Then, snatching it out of its crumpled wrapping, he held it high above his head, as if defying anyone to come near. At that moment, he looked like some young terrorist threatening to hurl a bomb into their midst. But Kathie knew him well enough to read in his face that he was bluffing.

The others were not so sure. The captain seemed frozen to the spot, and Mr Skyros was evidently on the verge of a heart attack.

'Don't worry, Mr Skyros,' Grant assured him, but still not moving. 'After all, you say this is only a copy of the vase. But why bother to bring it away from the island if that is the truth? And what if I drop it? No! Don't move! If I break it, Grant continued, 'there are several other copies on board you know. Some of the others bought them as souvenirs. I'm sure we could soon buy you another.'

Kathie's eyes sparkled in answer to the slow grin that had spread on Grant's face. Now he looked like an athlete holding a golden trophy above his head for the lap of honour. 'There is one sure way of finding out if this *is* the real thing. . . .?

Then, as Grant brought his arms down in a sudden lightning move, feigning a drop, Mr Skyros gave a hoarse cry of rage and threw his considerable bulk across the narrow cabin, his plump hands outstretched in a desperate effort to save the Mylos vase.

The Raleigh's captain looked down with cold eyes on his grovelling form. Then, he pushed Kathie and Grant before him through the cabin door, locking it behind him. He took the precious vase from Grant, and said, 'Thanks to you two, the world won't have to know I've been made a fool of. This is going straight to the strongroom, and then I shall contact the Greek police. I'm sure they'll be interested in what I have for them.'

Kathy and Grant grinned at each other. Then, together, they went to join in the gala festivities, feeling rather pleased with themselves.

WHEN LOVE COMES AROUND

Maureen Spurgeon

HE WAS PASSING Widow Barker's cottage, when Betsy first saw him, breeches tucked up past his knees, and shoes slung around his neck. She guessed he was looking around for somewhere to 'set a spell', as Miss Hooker would have said, when her feet were aching towards evening-time at Hampton's Flour Mill, and they all felt every bit as tired as the stranger appeared to be.

'A pedlar,' Betsy murmured, watching him sit on a flat stone bleached white by the sun. 'Yet – he don't seem like no traveller, for all his back-pack and dusty feet.'

Should she wait until he'd moved on, she asked herself, her heart beating strangely. Or, walk along the other side of the track, like she hadn't seen him?

Miss Hooker was always most particular about who her girls spoke to, specially when Confederate rebels were still said to be making their way through the state, ready to take sides against the Yankee army.

He opened his pack and unwrapped a hunk of cheese from a piece of calico, smiling contentedly and looking all around, while Betsy shifted uneasily from one foot to another.

Miss Hooker always hollered if any of the girls were late back for supper. Even if they'd only been to see their one relation, as Betsy's Cousin Cassie was, and had to run back the long way round because the steamboat ferry was late crossing the river.

She stepped forward. The young pedlar-man was now

laying back, hands underneath his head, and the setting rays of the sun were making shadows across his tanned face.

'Go right ahead!' he called out lazily, lifting his head. 'I ain't gonna bite you!'

'Oh – I – I weren't thinking of anything like that,' Betsy said hastily.

'Then, why were you watching me from that clump of sycamore trees? Think I didn't see you?'

'N–no.' She twisted Cousin Cassie's lace handkerchief in her hand, trying to think of what to say, while all the time his clear grey eyes danced with laughter.

'Must be something for you to act this way!' He paused, his head cocked to one side, like a curious bird. 'Like me to see you safely home?'

'No!' Betsy cried again, this time in panic. 'No! Miss Hooker, she's overseer at the flour mill where I work, says we have to act respectable, or we lose our place at the boarding house!'

'And that means I daren't get home late!' she called back, running along the narrow track as fast as she could in her best shoes. 'Good – goodbye, then.'

'Hey! You come and see me at the County Fair, you hear? I'll be down by the creek from tomorrow, helping to get everything set up. The name's Matthew Hadley.'

He shouted out something else which Betsy couldn't rightly hear, holding her breath to see the wooden latch on the back door rising slowly.

'Betsy!' hissed a voice, and a hand gripped her wrist. 'Betsy Clair. Are you asking for trouble?'

'Oh – am—am I glad to see you, Alice-Mary!' she burst out, pressing the lace handkerchief against the bodice of her dress. I – I feared for a moment it'd be Miss Hooker.'

'Mighty lucky for you, Mr Hampton called in, wanting some changes in our prayer meetings. If she'd seen you, walking and talking to that pedlar. . . .'

Betsy gave a gasp, clutching tightly at the rough timber of the handrail that led up the stairs to the dormitory. 'How come you know, Alice-Mary? I tried to dodge past him.'

'Maybe. But I could see from the top window the way he was smiling at you. And you didn't seem none too keen to send him packing, neither!'

'Why, that's plain imagination!' Betsy was surprised how sharply she spoke, still more surprised at the idea that what Alice-Mary had said might be true.

The County Fair, he'd said. If she got to the mill just past sunrise and missed out on a bowl of broth and bread at noon, she'd be finished before dusk. Then, maybe, nobody would notice her slipping away.

'Betsy Clair! How many more times do I have to tell you? Stop staring out of that darned window!'

'S – sorry, Miss Hooker.' Betsy started guiltily at the sound of the woman's harsh voice.

'I should hope you are!'

Even her face was hard, Betsy thought, her hair scraped back into a knot, making her cheeks tight and sharp-looking. Yet her hair was a nice colour. Same colour as Matthew's eyes.

'Betsy, have you gone plumb crazy?' demanded Alice-Mary in a hoarse whisper when the last candle had been snuffed out. 'Throwing yourself away on a pedlar. I ask you!'

'I am not throwing myself away!' Betsy whispered back. 'I'm only asking you to leave the back door open tomorrow evening, same as I've done for you, when you've been out meeting Jacob Simms!'

Alice-Mary sat up in bed, tossing her head in the shaft of moonlight filtering in through the window. 'Jacob's father happens to be a schoolteacher! He's the steady type, a boy even Miss Hooker would take kindly to, some day!'

'Besides,' put in Laura, on the other side of Betsy. What makes him so special? You've never paid much attention to the boys around here, not even Mr Hampton's two sons, well set-up as they are!'

'All right!' Betsy snapped, in a voice that none of the other girls had ever heard before. 'Don't leave the door open! Don't help me!'

She was glad there was no answer, praying she could keep back the tears that were already pricking her eyelids, at least until everyone else was asleep.

Maybe Alice-Mary and Laura were right. Maybe, she was crazy. But, then, she could never have known how happy she would be to see the look of glad surprise on Matthew's face, his hands reaching out to greet her.

'I–I was hoping all along you'd get here,' he told her, again and again, stroking her hair. 'Somehow, I knew you wouldn't turn away from me.'

'Matthew!' was all Betsy could say. 'Oh, Matthew!'

Even squeezing through the basement window with the dread of tearing her new muslin dress had been worth it, to see him just for an hour. Hampton's Flour Mill and Miss Hooker were far, far into the distance.

'Seems a long time till tomorrow night, Betsy,' Matthew said quietly, as they began walking back towards the boarding house. 'Can I see you again?

'The County Fair's only here for two days,' he pleaded, seeing her glancing up anxiously at the attic window. 'Then, I'll have to be away!'

'Away? Oh, no, Matthew – no! You can't.'

He pressed a finger lightly against her trembling lips. 'Betsy, I've got to take the next steamboat ferry. I–I'll soon be starting a job that pays money I wouldn't be able to earn around these parts. But, I'll come back, real soon,' he continued, stroking a tear away from her cheek. 'You see if I don't!'

Betsy nodded her head, not trusting herself to speak, even though she could hear her voice repeating his name. 'Matthew. Matthew.'

Miss Hooker was leading evening prayers by the time Betsy crept in through the cellars, and up the back stairs, hoping she wasn't panting loud enough for anyone to hear. But Miss Hooker kept her eyes tight shut, her bony hands clasped together.

'So, Lord, we ask Your blessing on our brave young men, fighting for President Lincoln. And we pray that they may soon return, glorying in justice and freedom, to their loved ones. Amen.'

'Amen,' the girls chorused soberly, gathered around the big table in the common room.

'Amen,' said Betsy, with such feeling that they all opened their eyes to look at her.

'Well, girls,' said Miss Hooker, gathering up the prayer books and becoming her own, brisk self again. 'That's all the extra prayers Mr Hampton asked us to say, following the news that General Sherman is leading his men further south to defeat the Confederates. Church services will be held tomorrow to pray for the General's success, and you may have an extra hour's recreation to attend!'

'Suppose you'll be meeting Matthew, instead?' Alice-Mary sneered in the washroom afterwards. 'You have to say goodbye before the County Fair moves on.'

'We–we won't be saying goodbye,' Betsy told her quietly, pressing her hands against the bottom of the china bowl. 'At least – not the way you mean.'

'What?' Alice-Mary spun round in amazement. 'Betsy, you can't promise yourself to a pedlar! He's a traveller, meeting lots of girls.'

'And you can't know too much about him,' Ellen pointed

out. 'Never thought you'd give your heart for nothing more than a meeting with a stranger.'

Yet, Betsy kept saying to herself, all through the long, lonely night, Matthew was the only one she'd ever want to be with. It was as if she'd known him, for always. How could anyone understand?

In the months that were to follow, Betsy was never to remember quite how beautiful the river looked at twilight next evening, with all the lights from the fair splashing on the ripples like frail waterlilies.

It was the picture of Matthew she kept in her mind, his grey eyes laughing as he tried to make her smile. Then serious, as he took her hand. 'I–I want you to have this ring, Betsy. Just so's you can have something to remember me by, for always.'

'Matthew,' she faltered, half sad at the thought of losing him, half glad at having something so pretty threaded on to her finger. The single yellow stone caught the pale light of the fading sun.

'It – it fits like it was made for me, Matthew. Oh, it's just beautiful! Beautiful!'

'Been carrying it around in my pack, ever since an old woman gave it to me for good luck, just afore she died. Reckoned it was a blessed stone, she did, bringing a great love between two people. That's why I've been saving it for someone special, Betsy. I knowed you was that someone, first time I ever saw you.'

Betsy began to weep softly, leaning her head against his shoulder, and twisting the precious ring around on her finger, Matthew holding her very close.

'That woman said love was like a ring, Betsy. Never ending – yet, which of us can say where it first began?'

'I'll wear your ring always, Matthew! Always!'

'Then that's how long our love will last, Betsy.'

34

'I'll wear your ring always, Matthew! Always!' Betsy said.

The hooting of the steamboat grew louder, as it made its way further upstream.

'Nearly time for you to go,' Betsy sobbed, leaning her head against his chest. 'Oh, Matthew – how can I watch you walk away from me?'

'By believing that I'll come back again, one year from today. I promise, Betsy.'

They clung together, listening to the hooting of the steamboat getting nearer. Until, at last, Matthew drew away, taking both Betsy's hands in his. 'Time I was going, Betsy,' he whispered, lifting her fingertips to his lips. 'See you at next year's County Fair.'

One last kiss, and he was walking slowly across the wooden bridge, looking back at her in the same way as when she had first seen him, just three days ago. Three days, And now, he was leaving, her tears making it seem that he was just melting into the blurred outline of the steamboat, chugging its way around the bend in the river.

She turned away, a soft yellow sheen catching her eye as she lifted a hand to brush away her tears. 'I–I'll not weep,' she scolded herself, looking down at Matthew's ring. 'He said he'd be back. He promised. And, what is but one year, when we shall have a lifetime together?'

That thought was to comfort Betsy all through the dark winter months, then into spring. She seemed untouched by everyone's rejoicing at General Sherman's victories in the south. Surely, she pleaded within herself, surely it could not be long before Matthew returned to her?

And if Miss Hooker slapped her for daydreaming, and the other girls cast doubtful looks, what did they know? She only had to look at her ring's clear, yellow stone, to see Matthew's face reflected there, far away, yet so near to her.

Time seemed to drag so slowly by, it was quite a shock when

she overheard Mr Hampton telling Miss Hooker, 'Don't seem possible the County Fair starts tomorrow. Best let the girls know they can have an extra halfday, Sunday.'

'The County Fair!' Betsy echoed silently, her heart singing. 'The County Fair!'

A few lingering hours, and she'd see Matthew walking back over the bridge, holding out his hand towards her. Matthew.

At first light, she was sitting by the river, watching the sun bathing the pale sky with stripes of pink and gold. It was going to be a beautiful day. Men led their horses along the bank, nodding and smiling to each other as they fixed the tether-ropes, barely noticing the girl with the ringlets tied back in a blue ribbon to match her dress, and whose eyes never left the bridge, the whole day long.

'He'll come back to me,' she kept saying. 'The girls at the flour mill were wrong about Matthew. I–I know they were.'

She twisted the ring absently, feeling the stone with her fingers. 'He – he must be here, soon. He would never forget me, not when he gave me his solemn promise.'

Hour by hour, minute by minute, the air grew colder as daylight began fading, until the bridge itself was nothing more than a dark shape, slowly spreading itself out into the blackness that was lightened only by the silvery thread of the river flowing silently past.

Betsy gave a great, shuddering sigh, and covered her face with her hands, rocking herself back and forth as her sobs mingled with the quiet noises of the dark night. 'He – he'll never return, now. Never. Oh, Matthew. How – how could you do this to me? How could you leave me so alone?'

Only the wind sobbing through the trees, and the rain pattering down on the leaves disturbed the sound of her tears. She tried with all her might to picture the face of Matthew in her ring, – until there was nothing but the chill darkness, closing in all around her.

Now, the rain had stopped. Fingers of sunlight dappled the surface of the river, as Anna lifted her tear-stained face to the damp, morning air.

'Hey!' called a voice, just behind her. 'Remember me?'

She brushed a strand of hair away from her face, and looked round. 'Yes, I–I do. Aren't you in my history class at high school? Tim – er – Tim. . . .'

'Tim Warren – yes, that's right! And your name's Anna – I know that!'

He took her hand, looking steadily into her face as he helped her to her feet. 'What I don't know is – why were you crying? What's wrong?'

Anna gave a watery half-smile, dabbing at her eyes. 'Can't say I rightly know, that's what's so strange. I just happened to notice this, stuck in the mud right here, where that old wooden bridge used to be. I thought it was an old nickel-piece, till I looked again.'

'And that's when I wanted to cry, Tim. Soon as I knelt down to pick out the ring, I–I couldn't help feeling cold – and then, sort of sad, and all alone, like there was nobody out here who'd ever care about me – you know?'

She giggled nervously. 'Guess you'll think that sounds kinda stupid.'

'I wouldn't say that,' Tim answered slowly. 'But, if it makes you feel any better, well,' he stretched out his hands, 'I'm here, same as I've been ever since you moved into the house on the next block, a month or more ago. So, there's no fear of you being lonely, is there?'

'No.' A smile flitted across her face, before her lips quivered once more. 'B–but the girl who owned this ring. I–I'm sure she wasn't so lucky, Tim. I–I can't explain, I know I can't.'

He grinned, and patted her on the back. 'Slip it on to your finger as a souvenir of this year's County Fair, and bring it into class, next time. Remember Mr Simms telling us how

Confederates picked out yellow-stone from the river bed in this State, to wear as a symbol of their grey and yellow colours? Some girl must have had a rebel for a sweetheart!'

But Anna was looking down at the ring with a new interest, her lips now curved into a wide smile. 'It's sparkling, Tim! The ring – it's sparkling, winking at me, like it's come alive again!'

She hesitated, then turned to face him. 'And, Tim – I've got the strangest feeling that someone, somewhere is very happy, too.'

Her words trailed away at the sound of footsteps pounding across dry earth, jumbling with the burst of sound from the fair. Two figures moved swiftly towards each other, first hugging, then kissing, until the blue of the girl's dress melted into the colour of the sky, and her ringlets blended with the boy's dark hair into a patch of bright mist that faded away to nothing.

The words they spoke carried clearly above the gay tunes of the carousel. 'I came back, Betsy, just like I promised. And now, we can be together, at last.'

'For always, Matthew. Always.'

Anna blinked hard, glad to feel the sun on her face, and hear the river lapping lazily against the mossy bank.

'Wake up, dreamy!' Tim took hold of her arm, making the yellow-stone ring glint brightly on her finger. 'Time we were joining in the fun!'

Together, they walked into the sunshine.

THEATRE OF DREAMS

Jane Butterworth

'PENNY FOR YOUR THOUGHTS, NICOLA.'

Jeff's voice made me jump. I'd thought I was alone in the theatre as I stood in the middle of the stage imagining myself taking countless curtain calls, nodding and smiling at my adoring public who were on their feet, applauding. And now Jeff had spoilt it all.

I turned towards him, the spell broken. 'Just daydreaming,' I said.

'You'll dream your life away,' he said with a laugh. 'You've always got your head stuck in the clouds.'

'Well, why not?' I replied irritably. 'Otherwise life wouldn't be worth living.'

He put an arm around my shoulders and gave me an affectionate hug. 'Come along home. Everyone else has gone. I'll walk home with you. You need an early night because we've got a busy day tomorrow. The Ariel Touring Company are arriving.'

We walked home through the dark, quiet streets, scarcely speaking. I was very tired – I always was nowadays, because I worked so hard. But I still sometimes wondered in despair, if I'd ever make it to the top.

I'd always wanted to be an actress. Ever since I was a kid, when I used to dress up in my mum's clothes and act out stories for her and Dad, I'd dreamt of the day when I'd do it for real. Nothing my parents or my teachers could do would put me off.

After I left school, with hardly an exam to my name, my despairing parents suggested I wrote to some theatres to see if they'd give me a job. Eventually, the Theatre Royal wrote back, and when I went to see them they offered me the lowly and underpaid job of Assistant Stage Manager. I jumped at the chance – I was confident it would lead to better things. How many great actresses started off as an ASM? And the Stage Manager told me that after a while I'd be able to do a bit of understudying and then perhaps a walk-on part – which could lead to a bigger role.

But to date, it just hadn't been like that. I'd been working there for months now, and I'd made lots of tea, swept the stage daily, fetched and carried for everyone – but I hadn't done any acting. The Royal never even had any well known actors. It had its own resident company which performed most of its repertoire, and although, occasionally, we got a touring company, no one famous ever came.

But still I went on dreaming. One day I might understudy the leading lady. And the day she's off sick with flu and I walk on stage saying her lines, is the day a famous impresario is sitting in the front row.

Jeff and I had reached my house and he gave me a quick peck on the cheek. 'See you tomorrow,' he said. I nodded. Even Jeff was dull! It had seemed so exciting to have a boyfriend who also worked in the theatre and I was so happy when he first asked me out. But Jeff was only an electrician and he could have been working in Woollies for all he cared about the theatre. Oh, I was being unkind, because dear old Jeff was the kindest boy I'd ever been out with. It's just that I wanted excitement, adventure, and fame – and I knew he wasn't the one to give it to me.

But we dated together regularly – well, we went out on our one day off a week. But we got little time together other than that, because we both worked such anti-social hours when performances were in progress. Sometimes, we'd go and see a late movie after we'd finished at the theatre, but I was usually so tired by then I'd fall asleep. So, more often than not, I just went home to bed.

Jeff would sometimes tease me gently about my ambition, and tell me that it was an overcrowded profession and why didn't I get a proper job. Although that made me mad, I never let on. I was just determined to show him, no matter what, that I had talent, I had good looks, and that sooner or later someone would discover me.

The next day, when I arrived at the theatre, I found everything in turmoil and everyone in a state of great excitement.

'Oh Nicola, thank goodness you're here!' Steve, the Stage Manager, came hurrying towards me. 'Someone from Ariel has just phoned. The stuffed parrot which is absolutely essential to the play has been stolen, and they said could we get hold of another one. Could you go round every antique shop in town and try to get hold of one. I don't know what we're going to do if nobody's got one. We can't possibly open!'

Grumpily, I marched towards the stage door. Goodness knows where I was going to get a parrot from! I caught sight of Jeff halfway up a ladder, tinkering with the lights, and he gave me a cheery wave.

'Why's everyone so excited?' I asked Terry, another ASM.

'Haven't you heard?' she asked excitedly. 'Frank Fenton's joined the cast of the play Ariel are bringing here. Isn't it exciting?'

'Frank Fenton,' I said wonderingly. He was a very well known actor, particularly on television. He always seemed to be starring in plays or series. Mind you, I hadn't seen much of him lately. He was an attractive man, if you liked older men. He was tall with dark hair slightly flecked with grey, and a beautiful, rich actor's voice. 'But why? What's happened?'

'Apparently, the actor playing the part of Justin, which is the lead, was rushed to hospital last night with appendicitis, and since Frank's a friend of the director and he was out of work at the time, he offered to step in for the rest of the tour,' Terry said excitedly. 'It's terrific, isn't it? We might even get London critics up here!'

Bother the London critics, I thought. If Frank Fenton was coming here that would be the nearest I'd ever been to a well known actor – an actor who knows influential people in the business – and I had to spend the day rushing around looking for a stuffed parrot!

But I was lucky. The third shop I visited had a stuffed parrot on a stand, exactly what was wanted for the second act. They were only too pleased to lend it to us. I set off back to the theatre with the parrot under my arm, humming. Suddenly, things weren't so bad after all.

When I got back to the theatre, the company had arrived and they'd started a technical rehearsal to check the lights and sound cues. This was the time in a theatre I really enjoyed – when it was full of noise and bustle, and people rushing around in a panic. It was so exciting.

'Oh you darling,' Steve said gratefully, when I presented him with the parrot. He gave me a list of props to check off. I was very careful to do that properly now, ever since in a play we'd done a couple of months ago, the leading lady opened a drawer to take out a gun during a crucial scene and the gun wasn't there. I'd forgotten to put it there.

Suddenly, a hand landed on my shoulder, and I spun round in alarm. Then my heart nearly fell through the floor, because I was looking up into the unmistakable face of Frank Fenton.

He looked older and greyer than he did on the television, but he was still very attractive, and he was smiling at me.

'You're the ASM, aren't you?' he asked.

'Nicola Patterson,' I said, my heart thumping.

'Well, Nicola,' he said, giving me a charming smile, 'perhaps you'd be kind enough to fetch me something to eat? I haven't had anything since first thing this morning, and I simply don't think I can make it through the day if I don't have food.'

'Of course,' I said, leaping to my feet. He really did just ooze with charm. If he'd asked me to dance barefoot on hot coals I'd probably have done so.

'Good girl,' he murmured, and handed me a list and a fifty pound note.

What didn't he want – bottles of wine, cooked chicken breasts, smoked salmon, cheesecake. If he ate like this everyday it was a wonder he kept his slim figure. Eventually I bought everything he wanted, and presented it to him while he took a break from rehearsing.

'Thanks so much,' he said, giving me a smile and passing his long slim hand gently across my cheek. 'Come now, won't you join me?'

I stared at him. Me sit down to dinner with Frank Fenton? 'I'd love to,' I said promptly.

We sat side by side in a dark corner of the auditorium, while various members of the stage crew passed by and gave us curious glances. But not even Steve dared tell me to get back to work, because Frank Fenton was really somebody!

While we ate, he talked almost non-stop. He told me about his triumphs on the West End stage, every film he'd ever made, and all about his television successes. He told me about the time he toured Russia with Chekhov's *The Seagull*, which was a bit like taking coals to Newcastle, and how the Russians loved him so much they mobbed him with roses after the performance. By the time he'd finished, I felt quite exhausted.

'I'd like to be a famous actress, Frank,' I said as soon as I could get a word in edgeways.

While we ate, Frank talked almost non-stop.

'Would you darling?' he said, elegantly wiping his mouth on a large silk handkerchief. 'Well, the best of luck to you.'

'I don't suppose . . . I don't suppose you could introduce me to anyone in London, could you? Agents, people like that,' I asked, hardly able to believe my own temerity.

He turned and stared at me and gave a wide smile. 'Why, of course! You're a pretty little girl and you've got a nice voice. Next time you're in London, you look me up at the Actors Club and we'll see what we can do.'

I was just about to continue this, when I saw Steve glowering at me from the stage.

'I must go,' I said hastily, and Frank gave my hand a squeeze.

'I'll see you again,' he whispered.

I was so happily wrapped up in my own little world, that I was hardly aware of what was going on for the rest of the day. I was aware of Jeff giving me some nasty looks, but I didn't care. By the time we packed up, it was late but I wasn't tired. I was walking on air. Frank Fenton fancied *me*. Why else would he have singled me out for attention?

I searched around for Frank as I was leaving, to say goodbye, and was disappointed to find he'd gone. So I didn't object when Jeff said he'd walk me home.

'Why were you spending so much time with that creep Fenton?' he asked moodily. 'Everyone says he's a real con man. He gets everyone running around after him, and he's so lazy he won't lift a finger. He's a real bighead, too, always boasting about what he's done and how good he was in it. Everyone says he gets all the silly girls running after him.'

Furiously, I flashed back, 'You're only jealous. He's a very nice man, and what's more he says he'll help me get an agent in London.'

Jeff raised his eyebrows. 'I bet he says that to everyone,' he snorted. 'You don't believe all that old flannel, do you?'

I poked my tongue out at him and we walked the remainder of the way home in hostile silence.

After that, things weren't the same between Jeff and me. I felt very cool towards him and although he was still friendly, he didn't suggest walking me home again.

The play opened the following night and was a success, and I struck up a relationship with Frank Fenton. I willingly fetched and carried for him. I'd dash out in between acts to fetch his dinner. I'd buy him bottles of wine and keep them on ice until he fancied them. I'd order him boxes of cigars, press his costumes, clean his shoes and buy his newspapers. In return, he was expansive, friendly, and promised that he would take me out to dinner when we met up in London.

I was also beginning to feel very attracted towards him. I knew all the other girls thought he was attractive too, and I was proud when he slipped his arm through mine, or kissed me when I gave him a special cup of coffee while everyone else had watery tea.

The week flew by, and soon it was the last performance. I stood watching him take his final curtain and imagined the day when I would be his leading lady and stand beside him bowing.

'Oh Frank, take me back to London with you,' I said when he was sitting in his dressing-room taking off his make up. 'I'll miss you so much.'

'Oh Nicola, I'll miss you too,' he said as he wiped his face clean with a tissue I handed to him. 'But you look me up one day in London, okay?'

'You could take me to London when you go tomorrow, and introduce me to agents,' I said eagerly. 'I wouldn't be any trouble. Please Frank.'

'Oh . . . well, if you're here tomorrow morning when I go,

we'll see about it.'

'Oh thank you, thank you,' I said. I didn't bother to think about anything else, I was so happy. I rushed out of the theatre thinking that I was on my way at last.

Jeff stopped me as I was going home. I had hardly spoken to him all week and felt a bit guilty.

'Nicola,' he said, 'I heard what you and Frank were saying as I was passing by his dressing-room. He doesn't want you, and you can't go running off to London. That's not the way to become an actress.'

I shook his hand off my arm. 'What do you know about it?' I said fiercely. I left him standing there looking anxiously after me.

The next morning I was up early. I packed my case and stole out of the house before Mum and Dad were up. I'd give them a ring when I got to London to explain.

The theatre was silent and deserted when I arrived, except for Bert, the stage door keeper. I went inside and sat on the edge of the stage to wait. I didn't like theatres when they were empty – they were depressing.

I waited . . . and waited . . . and waited. An hour ticked by. Where on earth was Frank?

Then I heard dootsteps and swung round to see Jeff.

'Hello Nicola,' he said quietly. 'You're still here, then.'

'He's late,' I said fearfully, unwilling to admit that he might not be coming.

'He's not coming Nicola. After you'd gone last night, I heard him tell Sally Tresswell that he was returning to London last night instead of this morning. He offered her a lift home and invited her out to dinner. Ring his hotel if you don't believe me.'

I swallowed hard. Sally Tresswell had been his leading lady.

'He never meant to help you. I've been asking around about him and apparently he's an awful liar and is always spinning stories so pretty girls like you will run after him and wait on him just like you did. He does it the whole time. He's no good.'

My face went a dull red. I'd been a fool chasing after a man like him. And all the time I could have been with dear, faithful Jeff. I wouldn't blame him if he never spoke to me again.

'There's no short cut to stardom,' he carried on. 'If you stick it out here for a bit you'll get leading roles eventually, and then you can go to London for auditions. In the meantime, let's go to a film tonight, shall we?'

I stared at Jeff's faithful face. 'I'm sorry Jeff,' I murmured. 'But yes – let's go out tonight.'

ANNIE IN THE OUTBACK

C. J. White

ANNIE AND HER FATHER were having a furious argument. 'It's not fair, Dad – if I was a boy you'd let me stay here on Windrush Farm with you.'

'Now Annie, don't say such things. You know you've always had your own way, but now it's time for you to go and train for a career. You'll enjoy a secretarial college in Melbourne once you get there. You can stay with your aunt Lilian during term-time and come home to the farm for holidays. It'll be much better for you to be mixing with people of your own age. And once you get to the city you'll see what you've been missing.'

'But all I want is to help on the farm like I've always done. I hate the idea of living in a city, and I've managed all right getting my education by correspondence course, haven't I?'

Her father didn't answer.

'Well, I refuse to go to secretarial college and that's that,' Annie continued.

'Now don't you be so cheeky. I won't have any more arguing from you.'

Her father stormed out of the farmhouse. Annie was blazing mad. How could he suggest that she went to stay in the city? She knew he felt he'd let her grow up into too much of a tomboy, and after all, it had been difficult for him, being a single parent. Her mother had died when Annie was two years old, and her father had brought her up himself with help from Mary, their Aborigine housekeeper who lived with her own family nearby. Even though Annie felt lonely sometimes, she didn't want to live anywhere else.

She decided to try and forget about their argument, so she saddled her horse and went for a long ride up to the hills and Mount Sturt. On her way back she called in to see her one local friend, Dawn, Mary's fifteen-year-old daughter, who was watching over her little brothers and sisters.

She felt a bit guilty when she saw Dawn, who hated the outback and would have jumped at the chance of going to live in the city. She helped Dawn to bathe the two youngest children and get their supper ready, then Mary arrived back from Windrush Farm.

'Your father's worried about you – he thinks you might have run away and left him! You'd better go home and show him that you're not angry with him after all. You know you mean the whole world to him.'

'But if that's true, why does he want to send me away?' It seemed so simple to Annie.

'You know he's only thinking of your own good. He's getting old, and farming's a hard life – anything could happen to him. He wants you to have a life of your own, and also he probably wants you to meet the right kind of man and settle down and have your own family. There's no young men for you to mix with around here,' said Mary.

'That doesn't bother me,' replied Annie. 'Anyway, I'd better get back. See you tomorrow.'

Over supper Jack Kirby was quiet.

'I'm sorry about earlier, Dad,' Annie said. But I can't bear the thought of leaving Windrush Farm and you.'

'Well, I've had another idea,' her father said. 'It's a difficult decision, but I think it might be the right one. I've been thinking about this all day. We'll sell the farm . . .'

'Dad, you can't be . . .' Annie began.

'Just listen to me for a minute. We'll sell the farm and we'll both go to Melbourne and buy a house there. Let's face it –

we'll have to sell up eventually anyway because it's no life for
you living on the outback looking after an old man. If you'd
been a boy . . .'

'What do you mean? I can be just as good at managing this
farm as any man. You've been teaching me all you know, and
I'm expert at doing the accounts. . . .'

'That's all very well now, but in a few years you can bet
you'd be hankering after a different life. Anyway, in a few days
it'll be time for the shearing, and Bill Smart will be bringing his
gang over to give us a hand. He's always fancied buying this
farm, so I'll see what kind of price he's got in mind.'

Windrush Farm had a large flock of Merino sheep, and
there were too many for Annie and her father to round up and
shear themselves. Every year Bill Smart, who had his own
sheep station near Lake Yantara, came to help, with some of
his hands and anyone else who happened to be around.
Although it was hard work and a long drive for him, he
enjoyed seeing his old friend Jack Kirby again and watching
Annie grow up from year to year, and he usually stayed a few
days.

Annie and Mary spent one entire day cooking, making pies
and pastries, stews and puddings, for they knew the shearing
gang would have mammoth appetites. They also laid in
plentiful supplies of drink, knowing the amount the men could
put away once they started swapping reminiscences.

Late one Monday afternoon, the Land Rover engines could
be heard approaching. Annie and her father rushed out to
meet the men, who started whooping and shouting as soon as
they were within earshot. One man Annie hadn't seen before
was sitting next to Bill in the leading Land Rover.

He was young, she guessed about twenty years old, and Bill
introduced him as his nephew. 'I thought Annie would enjoy
having someone her own age around to keep her company for
a few days. In actual fact, Stewart here is at agricultural

college, and he's got one more year to go, so now we're showing him what farming is really like!' explained Bill.

'Come on in – it's good to see you all again,' welcomed Jack Kirby.

After a noisy supper, full of laughing and good humour, Annie went out to sit on the verandah as she liked to do in the evening. Before long, a figure appeared in the doorway.

'Do you mind if I join you?' asked Stewart. 'They've started talking about old times in there, and I'd rather sit out here with you and look at the hills.'

'Yes, it's the nicest time of evening just now,' she replied. 'How do you like it out here?'

'I think it's one of the most beautiful places I've ever seen. If I could have my dream farm, this would be it.'

She started to tell him all about her father's plan to sell up and move to the city.

'But how could he?' Stewart was incredulous. 'It would be bad enough to have to leave here in the first place, but to go to the city . . . It's noisy, crowded, full of traffic – and there's not that many jobs going either. You're much better off out here where you can earn your own living rather than being at the mercy of employers all the time.'

'You'd better tell that to Dad!' Annie laughed. 'I don't need any convincing.'

Over the next few days the men worked from dawn to dusk, with Annie working alongside them, and by the fourth day their job was done for another year.

Mary had prepared a special supper for their last night, and they were going to have a barbecue in the back yard. However, there was a total fire ban that day so, in the end, the food had to be cooked indoors.

Annie felt sad that this jolly gang of people would soon be leaving, and she might never see Stewart again. Her father had

53

been right – it was nice to meet a young man of her own age. He was quiet and thoughtful with a great sense of humour, and Annie had enjoyed every moment she'd spent in his company, even if it was working furiously alongside him with the other shearers all around them. She felt that if only Stewart were going to be living locally then she'd enjoy getting to know him better.

'How do you fancy a swim in the river, Annie, to wash off the day's grime?' he suddenly asked.

'Great idea,' Annie replied. 'I don't think the food will be ready for a while, and anyway there's more than enough for everyone.' The delicious smell of grilling meat was giving her a hearty appetite, but the cool river was a very tempting prospect.

They quickly saddled up Annie's and her father's horses and raced over to the river which was in a beautiful cool spot amid the dry dusty fields.

They tethered the horses, got changed behind the bushes, then jumped into the water. Although the river was low and a bit muddy, it was still blissful after the sticky heat and sweat of the day.

After splashing about for a little while, Annie climbed out and lay on the bank, looking up at the sky which was changing into reds and oranges in the sunset. Stewart clambered out and lay beside her.

'I'll be really sorry to go tomorrow, Annie,' he said. 'And not just because it's such a perfect spot here. I've never met a girl quite like you before – we seem to have so much in common, and I can tell just what you're thinking half the time. It's uncanny. I can't bear the thought of not seeing you again. If only I was rich I'd buy Windrush Farm so you and your father didn't have to leave.'

Annie could hardly believe what she was hearing. She had felt as soon as she met Stewart that they were somehow in tune,

Annie had felt as soon as she met Stewart that they were somehow in tune.

but she had never dreamt that he felt the same. She couldn't say anything for a moment – she felt too choked up.

'What are your plans for the future,' she managed to say eventually.

'Well, I've got one more year to go at college. Then I'll look for a job as a farm manager somewhere . . . hey look, what's that on the horizon, on the slopes of Mount Sturt,' he suddenly cried, jumping to his feet.

'It looks like smoke . . . oh no, it must be a fire. You know how dry the grass is at the moment,' Annie said, grabbing her clothes. 'It's quite near Mary's house. Dawn's younger sister Tracey is babysitting – I'd better rush over there before the fire gets to them.'

'Right – you do that and I'll ride back to the farm and warn the others. If we act quickly we should be able to put it out before it does too much damage.'

They threw on their clothes, grabbed the horses and galloped off, each in opposite directions.

Annie was thankful it was a still evening. At least there wasn't a wind to blow the fire over a great distance. Bush fires were a constant hazard in that part of Australia, where the scrub became as dry as tinder in the long hot summers. She and her father had dug a system of firebreaks – stretches of ploughed earth – over which, hopefully, the flames couldn't leap.

Annie prayed that the fire wouldn't spread too far. She galloped furiously towards Mary's house, the smell of smoke bitter in her nostrils. The flames were still a fair distance from it, but when she rushed indoors she found Tracey and her brothers watching television, completely oblivious of the danger they were in. She lifted the children up on to the saddle, two in front and one behind her, and told them to hang on tight as she returned to the farm as quickly as she could.

Before long she saw the men coming in the opposite

direction. They were in every vehicle the farm possessed, with oil drums full of water and fire-beaters. Stewart was following, galloping furiously, still on Annie's father's horse. He grabbed one of the children and sat him on the saddle in front of him, and he and Annie carried on back to the farm.

'Your father's radioed the fire-fighting service. They're sending out some planes and say they'll have the fire out in no time,' Stewart told her.

'Luckily it doesn't seem to be spreading too fast,' Annie said, relieved.

'And thank goodness it's not heading towards the farm-house. It looks like it'll miss Mary's house too.'

The children were crying and frightened, and as they approached the farmhouse they saw Mary and Dawn standing on the verandah with binoculars. Mary was overjoyed to see her children safe.

Because the fire service had been alerted so rapidly, they were able to put out the fire before it had done too much damage.

'Thank goodness you two spotted the smoke,' said Annie's father over the remains of supper. 'If it hadn't been for your quick action we might have been in serious trouble. In fact, Stewart, it's a shame you don't live round here. We could do with someone like you to help us out, couldn't we Annie?'

'But Dad, a few days ago you were talking about selling the farm,' she replied, puzzled.

'Well, I've been discussing it with Bill while he's been here, and though he's happy to give me a fair price for it, I've realized that I couldn't bear to leave. What we need is a trained farm manager to take over from me and look after the place as I get older. I've been very impressed by Stewart here – and, well, I was wondering if you'd be interested in the job?'

'Quite frankly, Sir, I'd like nothing better than to work here with you and Annie. As soon as I've finished my training I'll be out here like a shot.'

'That's settled then,' said Jack Kirby.

'You've forgotten one thing,' Annie reminded him. 'What about me?'

'If I might make a suggestion . . .' began Stewart.

'Of course, go right ahead,' said Annie's father.

'Why doesn't Annie go to agricultural college too? You want her to have some kind of decent education, and there's lots of girls at my college.'

Annie's father couldn't believe his ears. 'Girls at agricultural college?'

'Yes, Dad, you're living in the past century,' Annie told him.

Stewart continued. 'She could learn the ropes, then before we know it, she'll be ready to take over from both of us!'

The look on Annie's face showed that she thought it was a marvellous idea. 'Oh Dad, please . . .' she begged.

'Well, of course I'll have to think about it. But I suppose you could keep an eye on her during her first year there, to make sure she's all right!'

Stewart smiled at Annie. 'If she doesn't mind, I'll be more than happy to do so!'

Annie smiled back. 'Does that mean I can go then, Dad?'

'You know I never could refuse you anything you wanted. OK, you can go. We'll write to the college tomorrow.'

Annie could hardly contain herself, she was so happy. At last she was about to have everything she wanted – company of her own age, the prospect of seeing more of Stewart, a happy future . . . and Windrush Farm.

RHYME – OR REASON?

Maureen Spurgeon

'THANKS FOR LENDING ME YOUR SPARKLY TOP for tonight's invitation dance, Tracey!' Anyone could hear how delighted the girl was. 'You're a real sport!'

'Well, don't forget, you promised me some of your new nail varnish. And my dad says he'll be fetching us home – all right?'

'Enough room for me, Julie?' queried a third voice. 'Then Mum says I can stay till the end.'

'Stop worrying, Lisa! You can always squeeze in the back with the rest of the rubbish, can't you?'

It wasn't the type of joke to win any prizes for a flash of brilliant comedy. But they laughed loudly enough to give Jane the perfect excuse to shut her bedroom window with an impatient slam, hoping they'd hear it in the street below.

She glared outside for only a moment, before her mother hurried in, tying the belt of her overall with a firm tug.

'Jane! What was that bang, just now?'

'Nothing. Only the window.' Jane was wishing she hadn't shut it quite so hard now. 'I – er – wanted to close it, and it sort of jerked back.'

'Lucky for you the glass didn't break!' observed Mum with a suspicious snort. 'If you've got nothing better to do than mope around with a gloomy look on your face, you can give me a hand clearing some stuff out of our bedroom. Your dad's finally decided to start decorating, this weekend.'

'Great,' Jane commented absently, in a tone of such dismay that her mother looked round sharply, wagging a finger at her.

'Now, I've told you before, it's no good sitting around feeling sorry for yourself because you've got nowhere to go. It isn't as if you need to look a mess, with nothing nice to wear.'

Jane didn't answer. She knew all her mum's little speeches by heart.

'Nothing nice will ever happen just by you waiting for it. I don't know what's wrong with you, I'm sure.'

Jane could have replied that she didn't know, either, but, as she had to confess, that wasn't strictly true. All right, she admitted. So, she could go along to the under-eighteens invitation dance at the community centre that evening. Practically every girl she'd ever known had been talking of nothing else for days, until she was sick and tired of hearing about it.

But, nobody had actually asked her to go. Nobody had said, 'Jane, like to make up a group, along with us?' or, 'Jane, you're coming to the invitation dance, and no excuses.' She might have gone then. Same as she might have gone to the summer Fun Weekend at the sports centre, or joined in the sponsored crazy golf competition.

'Then, what would happen?' Jane burst out, picking at her fingernails. 'I'd be left sitting in a corner, that's what. Trying to look happy with a drink and a bag of crisps for company, while everyone else was laughing and dancing with their boyfriends.'

Nibbling at her thumb could not stop the familiar sadness and despair welling up inside her. 'How can I help being the odd one out? How can I help it if I can't think what to say when anyone speaks to me?'

She flopped down on her bed, saying to herself, as she usually did, 'Shopping on Saturday, then watching TV; Sunday lunch; more TV; then bed, ready for school on Monday. Hardly ever seems to be worth it.'

Then her mum called up the stairs. 'Jane! Can you come

down to the front room and stack all these boxes neat and tidy, somewhere? I want the bedroom cleared out before Dad gets home, and I can't do everything myself!'

'Coming.' Jane sighed wearily, thinking, as she went to the door, that at least having a room re-decorated might make the time pass a bit quicker. And it promised to provide some sort of change from the usual, boring routine.

She had carried three cartons of Mum's 'bits and pieces', as she called them, from the hallway into the lounge, and put them down behind the best sofa, before she noticed the folded piece of paper on the doormat.

At first, she was fairly certain it was something destined only for the wastepaper bin, or to be crammed into Mum's kitchen drawer and then forgotten. Then she saw a tiny bluebird painted in one gold-edged corner.

Slowly, she unfolded the paper, her eyes becoming very round and very wide, as she read the handwritten message.

'This is for the sweetest girl
With sunlight in her hair,
With eyes that shine, and cheeks so soft,
And skin so light and fair.
If you wear a dress of sweetheart blue
And watch out for me – I'll be waiting for you.'

It was a beautiful poem. So beautiful, that Jane had to keep reading it to make quite sure it really was for her. Yet – well, wasn't she the only girl in the house? And someone had put it through the letter-box – someone who hadn't wanted to sign his name.

She glanced out of the window, drawing in her breath sharply. A sudden thought had entered her mind, making her mood of almost unbearable happiness begin oozing away. Could it be one of the girls she knew, playing one of their jokes?

She read the poem again, and her heart lifted. Nobody in

her class had such neat, flowing handwriting, she was sure. Not only that, there was the way it was written; and the pretty notepaper.

'Mum!' she called excitedly, clutching the precious poem very tight. 'Mum, mind if I go out tonight, after all? There's that invitation dance on at the community centre.'

Whoever had written the poem was bound to be there, Jane decided, eagerly taking out a pale blue skirt with its own matching top from her warbrobe, and hanging it from the picture rail. Why else should he go to the trouble of delivering it by hand, that very evening?

She caught sight of her smiling face in the dressing-table mirror, and laughed out loud. Why, she was even looking a different sort of girl already. Who would have thought her cheeks could glow such a pretty pink? Or that her eyes seemed to have a sparkle of their very own?

As for her mousey-brown hair, she knew it would bounce and gleam after some of the perfumed shampoo which, Mum was forever assuring Jane, would bring out the highlights she had never guessed were even there.

Whoever her mysterious poet was, he should have no reason to be disappointed, Jane was determined. Nothing must happen to spoil things, not now.

So, she relished the time spent in preparing to meet him for the very first time. When she was ready, she began to make her way down the stairs, her head held high, and tried hard to be unaffected by the stunned astonishment which her mum and dad did not attempt to hide.

'Jane, you – you look lovely!' Mum couldn't help exclaiming at last. 'I always did say blue was your colour, didn't I, George?'

'That's right, love. I hadn't forgotten!' Dad nodded his approval and went to the front door, opening it proudly. 'Enjoy yourself at the ball, Cinderella. Sorry it won't last until midnight, but I'll see to it that your coach is waiting at around eleven.'

'Cinderella!' Jane repeated with a giggle. 'I haven't changed from being a servant into a fairytale princess yet, Dad!'

But a secret smile was playing around her lips by the time she was hurrying through the double doors leading into the community centre. Mum and Dad just couldn't have known she was about to meet her very own Prince Charming. Who could he be? She gazed around the hall with shining eyes, smiling expectantly, and aware that Tracey and Lisa had seen her come in, and were looking at each other in amazement.

'Thought you said it was Jane Grogan slamming that window when we were talking on the corner of Burton Road?' Tracey demanded. 'You must have made a mistake.'

'Well, she always seemed dead grumpy about almost everything we were doing, didn't she?' Lisa justified herself indignantly. 'Anyone could see she never wanted to join in, or enjoy herself. How often have you said that she's a real pain?'

'Ssssh. . . . I think she's coming over,' warned Julie.

'Er – hello, Jane. Thought you'd change your mind about coming to the dance.'

'Yes. Yes, that's right – I–I changed my mind.' Jane was too happily occupied with looking around for the first sign of her secret poemwriter to notice whether or not she stammered, or if she was going red – as she nearly always did when she had to answer anyone.

'Hoping to meet somebody special?' Tracey questioned craftily, noting Jane's carefully arranged hair, and the new bag matching the white sandals which she wore.

'Yes. Well. . . .' Jane faltered, blushing just a little. 'That is, not exactly.'

'Good!' someone broke in with a laugh, taking hold of Jane's

'Good!' a boy said with a laugh. 'That means I can have the first dance!'

hand. 'That means I can have the first dance!'

'Trust me to have a sister like Julie,' the boy continued, pretending to be highly offended, and raising his eyebrows until they almost reached a fringe of dark brown hair. 'Can't even come across and let me know your name. Mine's Adam!'

'And mine's Jane.' Surprisingly, it was quite easy to tell him.

'Friend of Julie's, are you? You don't live too far from us – Burton Road, isn't it?'

'Yes – the corner house, the one next door to the garden gnomes.'

'Mmmmm, thought so,' he grinned – seeming very cheerful about something, Jane told herself. What's more, he'd already known where she lived.

They danced quite easily and naturally together, Jane silently congratulating herself on avoiding Adam's feet, and quickly deciding to wait and see if he said anything about the poem before mentioning it herself. Firstly, because she never seemed to be able to choose a moment that was quiet enough, and private enough to ask if he'd actually written it. And then, by the time she'd worked out in her mind exactly what she was going to say, he was making her laugh again, and they were talking about something else.

Besides, she realized with a sudden pang, Adam might not even be the one who sent the poem. It could be Stuart, the boy who'd insisted on buying her a lemonade to celebrate winning a raffle prize. Or Tracey's cousin, Ian, introducing himself in the middle of one of those dances where everyone had to change partners.

The last record was being played, with people beginning to collect their coats ready to go home, when Adam ushered Jane towards one of the little tables set around the edge of the dance floor.

'We're all going to watch the charity football match tomorrow afternoon, Jane. How about. . . . I mean – like to come along with me?'

'Love to, Adam!' Surely, Cinderella could not expect so many wonderful things to happen in just one evening.

'Terrific!' he cried, and Jane could tell he was pleased. 'See you about two o'clock outside the park gates – right? Cheers, then!'

''Bye.' Jane was amazed she could answer so quietly, when she was bursting to shout for joy.

Jane's father beamed broadly. He could tell she was really happy, all the time he was leading her to the car park, then driving back to Burton Road. 'So, you had a good time, love,' he said.

'A fabulous time, Dad!' Jane corrected, with much enthusiasm.

'But I still don't really know if I met my poet,' she murmured, as soon as she could take out the piece of paper from under her pillow and read the words again. 'Still,' she went on thinking sleepily, nestling down into the bedclothes and reaching out to turn off the bedside lamp, 'I've already had a marvellous time, trying to find out who he is!'

Being with Adam made the search even more enjoyable, Jane soon discovered. Whether it was a pop concert, a garden party, roller-skating, or just a walk in the park, or a game of Scrabble, they always seemed to end up laughing together, with Jane deciding yet again to put off asking about the poem until the next time.

She always read the poem as soon as she came home from school, and before she went to sleep, slipping it under her pillow each night. She could barely remember the time when she hadn't known every single word by heart.

'Jane, you're a different girl,' Mum remarked one Saturday morning, watching her trying on some new hair slides, ready for a coach outing to the seaside.

'I – I know, Mum,' agreed Jane happily. 'And, it's only because, because . . .' she hesitated, thinking carefully for the right words to explain. 'Well, you see,' she began again, 'somebody wrote me a poem.'

'Not this one?' Mum held up the folded paper with the bluebird imprint for Jane to see. 'I found it under your bed.'

'Yes, that's it! Mind you, I still can't really say for sure who sent it, but . . .'

'Sit down a minute, dear.' Her mother's voice was unusually quiet and gentle. 'I don't want you to get too upset, or disappointed, but if you want to know who wrote it, it was your dad.'

'Dad?' Jane echoed blankly, staring hard at Mum.

'Yes. He wrote it for me when we first started courting. That's why I kept it all these years. It must have slipped out of one of those boxes, Jane,' Mum went on. 'Do you remember – when we were getting the bedroom ready for Dad to start decorating?'

'Yes,' Jane whispered, gulping hard. 'Yes, I remember. I – I should have known nobody would ever write something wonderful like that for me. And, all this time, I've been looking for the boy who sent it.'

She looked so downcast that her mother couldn't help smiling, leaning forward to pat her hand comfortingly. 'Does it matter, Jane? Dad's poem perked you up no end, and made you go out and find your secret admirer, didn't it?'

She turned her head slightly, still smiling. 'And – who's that ringing the door-bell, right this minute?'

Happiness spread across Jane's face, her eyes alight with a new truth. 'Adam!' she cried joyfully. 'It's Adam!'

He was outside, waiting. He smiled when he saw her, as he always did. It was then Jane knew for certain. Her own poem was just about to be written.

JOAN OF SOMEWHERE SURELY
Joyce Wilson

MY FATHER ALWAYS SWORE that University Scholarship or no
University Scholarship if he ever caught me hitch-hiking he
would throw me out of the house. He had a special horror of
what he called 'girl hitch-hikers abroad', and would read their
misadventures out loud from the Sunday papers with stylish
malice – pausing only to glare meaningfully at me, or to ease a
crumpet on to the bright brass toasting fork that was always
kept propped by the kitchen fire.

'If you haven't got the intelligence to pay your fare into
college every day from your grant and earn holiday money
doing odd jobs about the shop for me, then you'd better chuck
the whole thing in, and find yourself a nice young chap with a
nice little car to take you about – you and a couple of kids.'

Actually I already had a nice young chap, with a horrid
little car, but Dad was not yet ready to know we were serious.
After all, I was only at the end of my second year in college,
with a hundred years of medieval history between me and my
degree.

In fact it was Max, my temperamental, nice young man, to
whom I owed the whole idea of spending the long summer
vacation in France, exploring the scenes of so many moments
in history that had always fascinated me, and taking along two
other friends from college.

It was to his equally temperamental little sports car that we
owed the major quarrel that had ended with him sitting
sulking like Hercules in his tent outside Marseilles, and me

standing on the road going north out of Avignon without a sou to my name.

Luckily – if you can call it luck – we had quarrelled in the afternoon, and there had been just time for me to swing on to a country bus going vaguely north. I had had the whole summer evening to light me on my way, but had not got very far with only the small change tucked in the pocket of my jeans.

Still hurt and wildly angry, I could only think of getting to the coast as fast as I could. I would then throw myself on the mercy of a British Consul, or British Rail, in Dieppe or Le Havre, and borrow the price of a ticket for home.

With the new Autoroute du Sud cutting its fast line to my destination I reckoned I could get a lift at least to Lyon that night. But when the lorry stopped I nearly changed my mind. The burly young driver leaned over to his kerbside window and flashed a far too friendly smile in my direction. 'Eengleesh?'

Too late to refuse, I nodded, and he hauled me into the driver's cab with one hand as if I were a bag of sugar.

'Oh, Dad, watch over me, and please never find out.' I smiled carefully and prayed behind the smile, as the lorry pulled on to the crown of the road and gathered speed. Moments later a bare, muscle-bound arm reached down towards my feet, and I controlled the impulse to draw into the corner of the cab. But the driver merely fumbled for a rug that was folded under the seat, and left it to me to drape it round my legs.

I told myself to stop acting like an idiot, but I was grateful nonetheless for the sight of the lethal assortment of spanners on the seat between me and my knight of the road.

'Are you going to Lyon?' I asked. My French is simple but I usually manage.

'Further. I want to get home tomorrow. It means driving all night.'

I quailed at the thought of what 'further' might mean, and did not comment. 'It's very good of you,' I said. 'I have lost my money. I want to find a British Consul, and I think Lyon will have one.'

'That's all right. *Ne vous-inquietez pas*,' he said briefly, as he set his mind to manouevring the narrow streets of a town. Then when we were back on the main road again we really gathered speed, and he said with a grin, 'I like zee Eengleesh ve-ry much.'

We swept under a long avenue of poplar trees, and the stones from the roadside spat up against the wheels. A rat ran parallel to the lorry for a few seconds before it twisted into a crumbling stone gateway. Through the gates I glimpsed a small, turreted chateau. We were driving deep into my beloved France, and every inch of the way my heart ached for my friends, who must by now be wondering where I was.

We were approaching the next town when I sensed a sudden, slight movement in the lorry. It came from somewhere behind the partition that divides the driver's cab from the load. I froze. It had suddenly dawned on me that if this was to be an all-night drive then it would take more than one man at the wheel. If there was to be any of the trouble of the kind my father imagined, I was not likely to escape very easily if I had two lorry drivers to cope with.

The man at my side must have sensed my thoughts. He grinned. 'My co-driver,' he jerked his head to the back of the lory as the sliding grille in the partition began to move. 'He wants to learn English.'

Feigning a casual interest that was the last thing I felt, I turned, and looked straight into the sleepy eyes of a small boy.

'Papa, I'm hungry. Who is this? Are we there yet? He was six or seven years old, with a shock of black hair and staring blue eyes. His father laughed.

'Mademoiselle is Eengleesh. Speak what you know to her.'

I turned, and looked straight into the sleepy eyes of a small boy.

The boy yawned and clambered over into the cab, snuggling close to his father as he gave me a long appraising look. 'English is for school,' he said in French. 'I am too tired. I am hungry. What is your name?'

It was like reading aloud from my first French text book, and the simple questions and phrases formed a little pattern of comfort for me as outside the landscape grew-dark.

'My name is Joan.'

'*Jaune?* He gave an involuntary gurgle of a laugh.

'No. Not "*jaune*". I'm not yellow! Do I look Chinese?'

He wriggled delightedly and shook his head. I tried again. 'Joan. You would say "Jeanne", perhaps?'

'Ah! Jeanne! Jeanne d'Arc! And you look like her! Papa, does she not look like Jeanne d'Arc?'

His father smiled, but kept his eyes on the shadowy twilight road. 'No more questions, or you get no supper.'

His talkative son managed at least two minutes' silence before he returned to the attack. 'My name is Paul. We come from Rouen. Where do you come from?'

I was silent. I looked out on to the thinning ranks of the trees. We were approaching Lyon. To my horror, a tear started to run down my cheek, and I had to brush it surreptitiously away. Paul tugged at my sleeve.

'Jeanne d'Arc came from her village, and then from Orleans, and then to us at Rouen. She always knew where she came from and where she was going. You must come from somewhere, surely?'

'*Tu viens de quelque part, bien sur?*' The challenge in the young voice, his use of the familiar 'thou', as child speaking to child, were to stay with me all my life. But at the moment, dulled by the long drive, chilled by the stupid, quarrelsome scene with Max and my crazy desertion of my friends, I asked myself bitterly if there was anywhere – or ever had been anywhere – where I really belonged.

I lived at home, with Dad in London. Although my scholarship would have allowed me a place in a college hostel I had not been able to bring myself to leave since Mum had died. Yet I had grown away from my father years ago – perhaps even as long ago as my first day at the local High School, when I had come down to breakfast in the room behind the shop, in my stiff, new, navy blue uniform and he had given me a rare, awkward kiss. A kiss which I did not return.

Later, in spite of all the examination successes I had to boost me, I had started at the University with a sense of not belonging. I had not joined in, and I knew my work was not at its best from the very beginning.

Now I had rejected loud and clear the one place where perhaps I should have stayed, where perhaps I did belong – beside Max, and our tents, and the lurching little car on the road going south.

Paul gave an exhausted puff of impatience, and I answered him at last. 'Yes,' I said, 'of course I come from somewhere. But it's a secret!'

From then on the child and I were conspirators, silently watching the night as his father drove steadily on. We munched our way together through long slices of crisp French bread and sweet smoky ham, while Papa had a coffee in a roadside cafe. I heard about Maman, who was young and pretty and made pancakes at any time of day, for fun.

There were also, it seemed, three sisters. And though they made life bad enough for their young brother in term time, in the school holidays they were a special menace. Which was why Paul made these long trips with his father, smuggled to and fro across France in the back of the lorry like some precious contraband.

But the worst time of all was the Feast of St Joan, at the end of May. Then all the small girls of Rouen came into their own, with the new white frocks and the shining shoes and the ceaseless rehearsals for the processions. How could a boy feel at ease with all that going on? Could one imagine Paul carrying a bouquet or throwing flowers into the waters of the Seine? Paul confided that he could not see Jeanne d'Arc throwing flowers about the place either. She was a soldier. She was such a brave soldier that when the English burned her (and Paul hastened to assure me that he knew it was not my fault) her heart would not burn in the fire.

After supper, we all dozed, until at midnight the driver turned out again on to the road and began the long haul to the north. We avoided Paris, going through Orleans and Chartres, eating up the deserted roads and making fast for home. I envied the father and son their sure goal, and when Paul swayed in his sleep into the curve of my shoulder I held him tight. At dawn I woke from a light sleep to hear jazz on the radio. I pictured some pale limbo of a world where dancers never slept. I felt sick.

At the entrance to the narrow, ancient street where they lived in the north sector, Paul's father parked the lorry. While the boy ran down between the high houses calling his mother, the father shook my hand, directing me to the town centre. 'If you ever want to go back where you came from . . . there is always our return trip tomorrow, Mademoiselle.'

He smiled, as I had seen him smile at his son. And I knew that he meant what he said. Thanking him for all his kindness, and promising one day to return and repay, I walked quickly away.

'In Rouen Cathedral,' Paul had informed me at supper the night before, 'there is nothing at all but God.' Threading my way through the great yellow-grey pillars, my footsteps echoing on the cold flagstones, I was inclined to agree. My sense of history should have made this a marvellous moment, but something was missing. My nagging conscience prompting me to get help, check trains, borrow money, I wandered out again into the strong August sunshine.

I stood for a long time watching the waters of the river Seine flow under the bridge named after Jeanne d'Arc. Back in the Place du Vieux Marché where the scene of her death by fire is marked in the sidewalk, I seemed to hear her last cries, over five hundred years away. They were the cries of a girl, not of the brave soldier Paul thought her – of a girl whose faith and love of life were so strong that she could not believe until the very last moment that she was to die.*

Perhaps that is why I never think of Joan's death in terms of shadows. It was, after all, her bright optimism that made me decide to go back to the narrow street where I would find Paul and his three sisters playing in the cool of the evening.

As I turned my back on the old marketplace, I had a beautiful feeling that two days later I would find the friends I had abandoned, exactly where I had left them, and my stubborn-as-a-mule, nice young man sitting beside his tent in the heat of the day. I felt, too, that when we drove home together at the end of our holiday and walked, together still, into the room at the back of the shop, Dad would make us very welcome. And on both scores I was absolutely right.

*(St Joan of Arc was burnt alive at the stake, by the English, at Rouen, on 30 May, 1431. 'Oh Rouen,' she cried as she was brought into the streets to die, 'art thou then to be my last abode?')

TIME TO DECIDE

Toni Cornford

'RIGHT, GIRLS, THAT'S ALL FOR TODAY.' The Sister Tutor smiled around at us. 'You've got a long weekend coming up, and I know you all want to have a good time, but please don't neglect your studies. Your final exams are only a matter of months away, and I expect you all to do well.'

I gathered up my books and started to put them away. Final exams . . . it was a frightening thought. When I'd decided on a nursing career I was convinced it was what I really wanted. Now I wasn't so sure.

'Marie, could I see you before you go?' Sister Tutor said as I stood up.

I waited until the rest of the student nurses had left, then went up to her desk. I knew what she was going to ask me, but I didn't have the answer.

'Marie, you used to be one of my star pupils,' she began. 'But lately, your work seems to have deteriorated. Is anything bothering you? If there is I wish you'd talk to me about it.'

'No, there's nothing,' I said, shaking my head innocently. It wasn't easy to hide my feelings though.

Sister Tutor looked at me shrewdly. 'If I didn't know you better I'd think you were having second thoughts about being a nurse,' she said after a moment. 'If that's the case, Marie, please don't make any hasty decisions. If it's any consolation, a lot of girls go through the same doubts, and most of them eventually go on to become wonderful nurses.'

'But will I, Sister?' I asked quietly.

She smiled at me and patted me on the shoulder. 'Go and have a good weekend,' she said. 'Relax and enjoy yourself. We'll talk about it again next week.'

When I got back to the room I shared with Angela in the nurses' home, she was rushing around frantically. 'At last! I was going to send a search party out for you,' she cried as she tugged at the holdall in her wardrobe. 'Hurry up and get packed. We haven't got long.'

I gazed around the small room in horror. It looked as though a hurricane had just hurtled through. Angela's clothes were scattered over the chair and a pile of make-up, brushes and towels lay in a heap on the bed.

'Oh, Angela!' I cried in exasperation.

'Now don't nag,' she said, pulling a face, 'and get packed, for heaven's sake.'

'But where are we going?' I demanded.

Angela was a good friend, but she could be very frustrating to live with at times – like now!

She turned and looked at me in amazement. 'On Safari,' she said in a puzzled voice. 'You've forgotten, haven't you?'

'I thought that was just talk,' I wailed. 'No one told me it was a definite arrangement!'

'You just haven't been listening lately, Marie,' she said, stuffing clothes into the holdall. Then she grinned. 'But I bet your little ears will perk up when I tell you Sam's going with us.'

'Is he?' I asked casually.

'Ooh, listen to you.' Angela giggled. 'Don't play the innocent, Maria. You've been after him for weeks.'

'I think he's nice, that's all,' I told her, turning away so she wouldn't see my embarrassment.

'You'll get a chance to find out just *how* nice then, won't you? So will you get packed.'

Half an hour later we were on the steps of the nurses' home, waiting for Alan's worn out pick-up truck to collect us. A cloud of dust from the road told us they were coming, long before we heard the out-of-tune strains of Johnnie's guitar.

'Don't you ever tune that thing?' Angela asked as we climbed into the back.

'Sure, I do,' Johnnie replied with a wounded look. 'Every second Sunday in the month!'

When we'd picked up everyone, there were eight of us, three tents and all the camping equipment we could lay our hands on. Johnnie broke his golden rule and tuned his guitar – even though it was a Friday – and sang to us as we drove along the hot dusty roads to the bush.

Leaving the town behind, the landscape changed from concrete and stone to lush green. Along the way we saw herds of antelope drinking from one of the small lakes, while rhinos lay half-submerged in the water, watching them.

'Tomorrow I'm going to shoot me a few of them,' David said, eyeing the antelope earnestly.

'You wouldn't dare!' I exclaimed.

He turned to me and grinned cheekily. 'Only with this, Marie,' he said, waving his camera at me.

Sam was sitting opposite us on the wooden bench in the back of the truck. He smiled at me reassuringly. 'Don't worry,' he told me. 'We've got one rifle with us, but it'll only be used in an emergency. Wild animals are too beautiful to hurt needlessly.'

I'd deliberately not taken much notice of Sam on the journey, but I'd been very aware of him all the same. Now I smiled back, touched by the gentleness in his eyes as he talked about the animals. He really was a caring person, I thought, and I did want to get to know him better – even though I'd been too shy to admit it to Angela.

When we'd finally selected our camp site, we pitched the

tents and then started cooking. We'd brought plenty of food with us, and the long journey had given everyone a ravenous appetite. It was just starting to get dusk, and Angela lost no time in pointing out the advantages to me! 'Now, if he asks you to go for a walk in the moonlight – go!' she whispered, nudging me. 'Don't start getting all coy, you'll never get to know him that way.'

But Sam didn't ask me to go for a walk. In fact after we'd eaten, we were all so tired we decided to have an early night. Angela shrugged as we got ready for bed. 'Never mind, love. There's always tomorrow,' she said with a grin. 'Personally, I've got my eye on David – he's dishy, don't you think?'

So while Angela dreamed about David, I dreamed about Sam.

The following morning we spent most of the time swimming in the nearby lake and lazing around. Sam was never very far away and as the day wore on we seemed to drift closer together. When lunch was ready, we took ours over to the shade of a tree a little way from the others.

'Marie, have you got something on your mind?' he asked suddenly. 'Tell me to mind my own business if you like, but I couldn't help noticing you seemed a bit remote this weekend. Not your usual lively self.'

'I don't feel too lively,' I said with a sigh.

'Come on, tell me about it,' Sam invited. 'Maybe I can help.'

So slowly I told him all about the dilemma I was in over my chosen career. I poured out all my doubts and fears, and Sam listened patiently. 'I think what really worries me, is that I'm not good enough,' I said finally. 'When I'm qualified I'll be responsible for my own decisions all the time, and that scares me. What if I make a mistake? What if someone dies because of it?' My voice was hardly more than a whisper and I could feel the tears coming into my eyes.

'Hey, don't get upset,' Sam said softly. 'It's probably just nerves. You've been studying and working hard for a long time. Now you're coming up to your finals, and the thought of what happens after is a bit daunting.'

I felt the warmth of his hand as it touched mine and my heart missed a beat.

'Maybe that's not a bad thing either,' he went on. 'When you're dealing with sick people, it's better to be over-conscientious and double check everything you do, than to be over-confident and blasé. That's when the mistakes can happen.'

'I'd never thought of it like that before,' I told him. Whether it was what Sam had said, or the wonderful feeling of his hand holding mine, I don't know, but I felt much better.

'There you go!' Sam's face lit up in a smile. 'It's always a good idea to talk to someone, get another viewpoint. Hey!' he said as he glanced across at the others. 'I think they're ready to go.' He held his hand out to me as he jumped up. 'Come on, or they'll leave us behind.'

As we walked back, I was very pleased Sam was still holding my hand.

'Right, Johnnie, you take the gun,' Alan said, handing over the rifle. 'And no messing around. We don't want any accidents.'

'No problem,' Johnnie told him. 'I've been handling these things since I was a kid.'

David emerged from his tent, two cameras around his neck and his pockets bulging with filters, lenses and spare film.

'Okay, let's go,' Alan called. 'Now keep close together, and don't go wandering off. There are wild animals out there, and while we admire them for their beauty, some tend to look on us as tonight's dinner!'

As we walked through the low grass, we passed more herds

of antelope, giraffe, zebras and even elephants. David was ecstatic, pointing his camera at everything. 'This is fantastic,' he said, shaking his head with delight. 'All I need now is a really mean looking lion.'

'No thanks,' Angela said. 'I don't fancy being someone's dinner!'

'They won't bother you if you leave them alone,' David told her. 'I doubt very much if we'll see one anyway. We'll have to go much further into the bush.'

'D'you want a bet?' Sam asked quietly.

A hush fell over us as we all turned in the direction of Sam's gaze. Ambling through the grass, his golden coat gleaming in the sunshine, was an adult male lion.

'What a size,' David breathed. 'He's huge.' Quickly, he swopped his camera lens for a telephoto and pointed it in the direction of the lion. 'Come on, Leo,' he said softly. 'Smile for the folks back home.'

As though he'd heard him, the lion turned his head slowly in our direction. The huge mane framed his face, giving him a strangely kittenish look as he tilted his head to one side. It was an incredible sight, and one that David made the most of. Then suddenly the lion started to walk purposefully towards us, his amber eyes never wavering as he fixed us with a deliberate stare.

'Don't make any sudden movements,' Johnnie warned us. He lifted the rifle to his shoulder and released the safety catch. 'Now, start backing away – *slowly*,' he said.

Sam was holding my hand tightly and I was grateful he was there. I'd never been so scared in my life, and I'd never been so close to a wild lion before either!

We moved backwards one step at a time, but something must have distracted the lion. Without warning, his mouth opened and a deep, throaty roar shattered the stillness.

One of the girls screamed, and, at the same moment, the lion started to charge straight towards us. Johnnie dropped to one knee, the rifle ready to fire.

As the huge animal pounded nearer and nearer we all started to run in different directions. I clung to Sam, stumbling to keep up with him. Then suddenly a shot rang out. With a cry of pain, Sam fell to the ground clutching his leg, in agony. The lion veered off and ran into the bush, as birds seemed to fling themselves out of the trees and into the air, circling around in shrieking flocks.

'Sam!' I cried frantically as I ran to him.

Johnnie came up behind me, his face grey with fear. 'My God, I shot him,' he whispered, his voice shaking. 'Oh, Sam, dear God.'

Instinctively, my training took over. Forgetting that the boy on the ground was Sam, I knelt beside him and examined the wound in his leg. The bullet had only grazed his calf, but the flesh had been torn and needed urgent treatment.

'We must get him back to camp,' I told the others. 'I need the medical kit.'

The boys were marvellous. They took it in turns to carry Sam, but the long trek back to camp exhausted them. When we arrived, Angela took charge of sterilizing the things I needed, and I got on with looking after Sam.

'I'm afraid there isn't much I can do here,' I told him. 'I can patch you up for now, but we must get you to hospital as soon as possible.'

Angela went to see Alan about packing up the camp and getting back to town, but when she came back the news wasn't good. 'There are problems with the truck,' she said quietly. 'Alan's trying to fix it now, but he doesn't know how long it'll take. Stupid thing's falling apart anyway. How's Sam?'

'Not so good,' I told her. 'I've stopped the bleeding and cleaned the wound, but it's deeper than I thought and I'm worried about infection. He should really have it stitched, too.'

'Well, we'll just have to do the best we can in true nursing style,' Angela said with a sigh. 'You'd better get back to your patient – I'll organize some food.'

I didn't leave Sam's side that evening. As we talked quietly, I watched for signs of a temperature which would mean the wound was infected. Periodically, I changed the dressing and checked the wound carefully.

When it was dark, Alan came into Sam's tent, wiping his hands on an oily rag. 'Sorry, mate,' he said with a sigh. 'The light's gone, so I won't be able to finish the truck till morning. Don't worry though, it'll only take about an hour, so we'll have you at the hospital by lunchtime.'

Gradually, the camp became quiet as everyone settled down for the night. But I refused to leave Sam.

'You must get some sleep, Marie,' he urged.

'A good nurse never leaves her patient,' I told him with a smile. 'Anyway, I'm not tired.'

We went on talking long into the night. Sam told me about himself and his family, and in turn I found myself telling him about my hopes and dreams for the future. All my life, I'd been shy and reluctant to confide in people until I got to know them really well, but with Sam it was different somehow. It was as though I'd known him forever.

Eventually though, his eyes started to droop with tiredness, and I insisted he went to sleep.

'If you want anything, just let me know,' I said.

Gently Sam reached up and touched my hair. 'Thank you, Marie,' he said sincerely. 'I'm glad you were around today, and I'd like it very much if you were around every day. Not because you're a good nurse, but because you're a very nice lady to be with.'

I was sure Sam would hear my heart pounding as he kissed me tenderly, but then, perhaps his heart was beating just as hard.

'I'm afraid there isn't much I can do here,' I told him. 'We must
get you to hospital as soon as possible.'

During the few remaining hours of darkness, I watched anxiously as Sam slept. He was very restless and as I wiped away the beads of perspiration that kept gathering on his forehead, I knew his temperature was going up. Cautiously, I lifted the dressing on the wound and groaned when I saw the red, angry skin. My worst fears had materialized – Sam needed urgent medical help, and there was no time to lose.

The first rays of the sun were coming up over the horizon as I made my way to Alan's tent, but he was already up and working on the truck.

'How is he?' he asked with a frown.

'Not so good,' I replied. 'How long will you be?'

'Almost ready,' Alan told me. 'Give me half-an-hour.'

He was as good as his word, and without bothering with breakfast, we made Sam comfortable in the back of the truck. No one was annoyed at cutting our weekend short. They were too concerned about Sam – particularly Johnnie. Nothing any of us said would convince him that it had been an accident. He just kept watching worriedly over Sam and hating himself.

When we finally got to the hospital, Sam's temperature was soaring and the infection was spreading. Attendants came rushing out with a stretcher and Sam was wheeled quickly away. Then there was nothing left to do but wait.

It seemed like hours before the doctor came to see us. 'Which one of you young ladies is Marie?' he asked.

'I . . . I am . . .' I admitted hesitantly.

The doctor looked at me carefully for a minute before he smiled. 'Then I must congratulate you,' he said, taking my hand. 'Your excellent nursing under such poor conditions has made my job a lot easier. Your friend will be fine in a few days, but I want you all to know that if you hadn't looked after him so well, *and* got him here so quickly, he'd be a very sick boy by now. Well done.'

'Oh, please,' I said, breathless with relief, 'can I see him – just for a minute. I won't be any longer, I promise.'

'Most definitely,' the doctor said with a twinkle in his eye. 'In fact if I refused, I'd have a very angry patient on my hands! Just a minute though.'

As I walked to the side ward where Sam was, I felt as though a great weight had been lifted from me. When I had my talk with Sister Tutor next week I knew exactly what I'd be telling her. That I *did* want to be a nurse more than anything, and I was going to do my best to be a good one.

But that was next week. Right now all I could think of was Sam, and he was waiting for me.

WEDDING BELL BLUES

Jane Butterworth

I WAS WRAPPING UP AN ORCHID in a cellophane presentation box, when I glanced up and noticed him immediately, even though he was some distance away, in the middle of a crowd of people. It wasn't so much that he was good-looking, although there was no doubt that he was very handsome, with his cropped blond hair and his muscular arms. Nor was he particularly tall, although he towered over most of the shoppers he walked amongst. No, it was more that certain *something* he possessed, that turned girls' heads whenever he walked down the street and made me stop what I was doing and gape at him stupidly.

It had been a quiet afternoon and I was glad. It had given me a chance to get on with the orchids, which were needed for a rather posh ball at the Town Hall on Friday night. Jenny was off sick and Mrs Robins, the manageress, was out all afternoon visiting her husband in hospital, so I was all on my own.

I watched the stranger as he walked towards me down the High Street. I was impressed by the way he held his head high, unlike a lot of boys I knew who slouched along with their hands in their pockets. Then my heart started to thump because he was coming into the shop.

He was even more handsome close up. He had startling blue eyes which looked searchingly at you as though he could almost read your mind.

'Can I help you?' I asked nervously, feeling the colour flood into my cheeks.

'I hope so,' he said cheerfully. 'I want some flowers for my mum. Of course you know it's Mothers Day this weekend, but I'll be away then, so I thought I'd give her some today.'

Now, how thoughtful, I thought. How many boys did I know who'd buy their mum flowers on Mothers Day?

'My father died a couple of months ago, you see,' he confided, 'and she's been a bit down so I thought some flowers would cheer her up.'

'Oh yes,' I agreed. 'Well, we haven't got our weekend stock in yet but we've got some lovely spring flowers – daffodils, irises, tulips. Or how about some roses? We've some beautiful long-stemmed roses.'

'Red roses. What a good idea. I'll have two bunches.'

'I'm afraid they're rather expensive at this time of year,' I said shyly.

'It doesn't matter,' he replied.

So, I selected twenty-four of the finest roses we had, wrapped them in cellophane and tied them with a red ribbon.

'What are you doing with the orchids? Corsages?' he asked as he watched me.

I nodded shyly. 'There's a grand ball at the Town Hall on Friday and all the ladies get presentation orchids.'

'They're so beautiful,' he said. 'So delicate and so beautiful – just like you. You haven't got one to spare, have you?'

I hesitated. I hadn't really, but he was so very good-looking. 'Okay,' I said. I put one of the corsages I'd made up into a cellophane box and handed it to him with the roses.

He didn't take it for a moment. Instead, he reached across the counter and touched my hair. 'What lovely hair you've got,' he said. 'All thick and dark and curly. You're the prettiest girl I've seen all year.'

I looked at the floor, embarrassed.

'I'm sorry,' he said. 'Me and my big mouth. I always say what I think even though it can embarrass people.'

88

He smiled at me, a lovely warm smile, and it was impossible to be cross at him for long. He picked up the roses and the orchid and I wondered wistfully which lucky girl he was going to give the orchid to. If only it could have been me.

'That'll be seven pounds fifty, please,' I said.

He gave me the money and then picked up the orchid, carefully extracted it from its cellophane wrapping and handed it to me. 'Here. It's for you.'

'For me?' I echoed stupidly.

'Yes for you. You're like Cinderella, sitting here wrapping orchids for other people to wear to the ball. You're so pretty that an orchid can hardly make you prettier, but if you wear it, it can remind you of me.'

'Thank you,' I stammered.

He carefully pinned the fragile flower to my overall. 'There! It really should be on a ball gown, but that will have to do until I can take you to a ball. I'd take you to this ball but I won't be here. But come out with me tonight. Please,' he added persuasively.

'Well . . .' I said awkwardly. Things were happening so quickly I could scarcely draw breath. Then I smiled. 'I'd love to,' I said. 'But I don't know anything about you, not even your name.'

'Rod Miller.'

'I'm Louise Fletcher.'

'What a pretty name. I'll meet you outside this shop at, say seven o'clock? That should give you time to go home to change. Then maybe we can go and have a hamburger, and you can tell me all about yourself, and then when I go away I can think about you all the time until I come back. Then we can do it again.'

'Okay. Until then,' I said.

He picked up his roses and strode out of the shop, pausing at the door to blow me a kiss.

89

I wondered wistfully which lucky girl he was going to give the orchid to. If only it could have been me.

I don't know how I got through the rest of the afternoon, I was in such a fever of excitement. I could hardly wait until it was time to lock up and then, still with the wilting orchid pinned to my overall, I slipped on my coat and ran joyfully home.

I wallowed in a hot bath full of Mum's expensive bath oil, thinking of Rod. I'd never met a boy before who'd made me feel like this and I could hardly contain my excitement. I made myself up and dressed in my new bright green two-piece, and it was two minutes to seven when I arrived outside the shop to wait for him.

I could see the Jubilee Clock outside the Town Hall from where I stood. My heart pounded nervously and my mouth was dry with anticipation when seven o'clock struck. But then my nervousness turned to agitation as the hands moved round and the minutes ticked by. Seven fifteen . . . seven thirty . . . eventually eight o'clock. Then I knew he wasn't coming. Instead of the cold rage I tried to summon up, I felt nothing but a deep sadness. This boy had obviously just been larking about, having a joke at my expense, and he hadn't meant any of the things he'd said. Whatever the reason, I'd never know, because I'd never see him again.

The next day, I felt a deep ache inside, and although I tried hard, it was difficult to forget Rod's handsome, sun-tanned face and his blue, treacherous eyes. As I stood at the counter of the shop, I could see right down the High Street and I found myself searching through the crowds each day, even though I knew it was futile. When I made up the wedding bouquets my mind was faraway, thinking of Rod who'd come in here and swept me off my feet, and imagining what it would be like if I were making these bouquets for our wedding.

The orchid he'd given me I'd pressed in a book, and occasionally I'd take it out and look at it and wonder why he hadn't turned up for our date. I even wondered if he'd made up the story about buying the roses for his mother, and had really bought them for another girl.

The weeks had slipped by and the pain lessened, and I'd stopped dreaming about what I'd say to Rod if he ever came into the shop again. One day, I was cleaning the window outside the shop, when I saw him coming towards me in the reflection of the glass.

I rushed inside the shop in alarm. I knew it was him, even though he was some distance away. My heart started to thump wildly and I said to my workmate Jenny, 'Quick, for heaven's sake help me! Someone's coming towards the shop and I don't want to see him! Tell him I'm not here!'

I rushed into the back room and hid behind the door, my heart racing. I was trembling all over. What was I going to do if he saw me? But then, perhaps he didn't care whether he saw me or not. All I knew was I couldn't face him.

Cautiously, I peered through the crack in the door and strained my ears to hear what he was saying. He looked leaner and even more tanned than he was last time, and as good-looking as I'd remembered. All the time he was talking to Jenny, his eyes were searching around the shop – searching for me, perhaps.

Then I heard what he was saying.

'I'll have thirty carnation buttonholes and a selection of summer flowers to decorate the church. I'll leave that up to you. And here's what the bride wants for her bouquet and for the bridesmaids. I'm sorry she can't get in herself but she's in the navy, you see, and she can't get leave until next weekend. But she did give me strict instructions!'

My mouth went dry. Jenny said, 'It's very short notice for a wedding order.'

'I know,' he said in the same charming way he'd asked me to go out with him. 'But it was so difficult trying to find a weekend when everyone could make it. We're both in the Services, you see. I'm off to Gibraltar next week.'

I closed my eyes and blotted out the rest of what he said. So, he was getting married. He was ordering his wedding flowers, and all these weeks I'd been dreaming about a faithless and two-faced man. Why, he must have been engaged when he'd asked me out!

I opened my eyes to see Jenny standing in front of me.

'Louise,' she whispered worriedly. 'He wants to speak to you. I told him you weren't here but he said he saw you come into the shop.'

'Tell him I've gone out the back,' I hissed. What a nerve he had, expecting me to speak to him!

When he'd gone, Jenny said, 'He's coming to pick the flowers up on Friday afternoon and says he'll see you then.'

Will he? I thought truculently. We'd soon see about that!

The following day I started making up the bouquet for Rod's bride – sweet-smelling freesias and roses. I don't think I'd ever made such a beautiful bouquet. Even Jenny commented on it.

Everything was ready on the day he was due to collect them, and even though I hated the thought of seeing him, I still came to work with my hair newly washed and my make-up perfectly done and a pretty blouse underneath my overall.

The day went by and still he didn't come. Mrs Robins was upstairs making wreaths and Jenny went off for her tea at four when, would you believe it, in he walked.

'I was watching the shop to see when you were alone,' he said candidly. 'I expect you're mad at me, aren't you?'

'Why should I be?' I said, trying to sound unconcerned.

'Because I let you down.'

'Oh that,' I said. 'I never expected you to turn up.' I felt tears welling up and angrily brushed them aside.

He caught hold of my hand and said, 'Louise. Please let me explain.'

'Why?' I said. 'I'm not interested in what you do. I suppose you've come for your wedding flowers.' I marched out and got the bouquets and laid them on the table.

'They're beautiful,' he said. 'Did you make them?'

'Yes,' I said shortly. 'I hope your future wife will like them.'

'What?' Then he laughed. 'You silly girl! It's not me who's getting married!'

I looked at him suspiciously. 'Who is it, then?'

'You thought . . .' He looked incredulous. 'You thought they were for me? They're for my sister, Sue. She's marrying my best friend, Doug. Doug and I are in the navy and Sue's a Wren, and we just managed to get leave on the same weekend. So we had to arrange the wedding in a hurry. Sue doesn't arrive until tonight so I've arranged everything for her. I'm giving her away, you see.'

A huge weight seemed to roll away from my heart – and then I remembered how he'd let me down. 'You stood me up,' I said accusingly.

'I know, and I haven't stopped thinking about you ever since. The afternoon I met you I got home and had an urgent recall to my ship a day early. It was a top-secret mission in the Atlantic. It was too late for me to come back to the shop, and I didn't know your address. So I asked my kid brother, Tim, to go along to the shop and explain. He reckons he went along and you weren't there. But then I discovered the daft so-and-so went to the wrong florist! He went to the one on the other side of the Town Hall. I nearly murdered him!' He looked at me ruefully. 'Will you forgive me? I never stopped thinking about you all through those long days and nights on the ship. We weren't allowed to send any letters, even to our parents.'

I looked at him and my heart melted. 'I forgive you.'

'I've got a few days before I go to Gibraltar. Long enough for us to get to know each other.' Then he grinned impishly. 'How about coming to the wedding tomorrow?'

LANTERN OF LOVE

Toni Cornford

SU LING SAT BY HER BEDROOM WINDOW staring unseeing into the street below. Today was the last day of the Chinese New Year, the Feast of the Lanterns. It was the day Lao Tien had talked about in such a romantic way, when every house in every street would display bright, colourfully-patterned lanterns, and the children would dance through the streets, their lanterns held high as they followed the age-old tradition of their people.

In readiness for the magical day, Lao Tien had given Su Ling a white silk lantern, with a beautiful design of orange and blue flowers to express his love for her. It hung in her bedroom all ready for the big night, but Su Ling had no use for it now. Not since the argument with Lao Tien when she had refused to see him again.

Dusk was beginning to fall as Su Ling sat on alone. Her heart was heavy with regret, but her pride wouldn't let her make the first move to apologize. Yet the argument had been her fault, blown up over something so trivial it brought tears to her eyes whenever she thought about it.

Lao Tien worked in his father's bakery shop, and with the New Year festivities almost upon them, everyone in the family had had to lend a hand to make sure the orders were ready on time. It meant working late into the night with precious few hours left to relax.

So when Lao Tien's father insisted on his having an evening off, Lao Tien only wanted to do one thing. There was a film he particularly wanted to see, and the thought of sitting in the dark without having to think about cakes and pastries seemed like heaven to him.

Unfortunately his evening off coincided with a birthday party Su Ling's cousin was having, and when Lao Tien suggested their going to see the film, Su Ling had seen it as a personal snub to her family.

'But we *must* go to the party,' she'd insisted. 'All my family will be there, and they're expecting us.'

'Oh, Su Ling, I'd completely forgotten about the party,' Lao Tien had sighed. 'I've been so busy lately, everything just went out of my head.'

Su Ling had been annoyed, but tried not to show it. But when Lao Tien had smiled, pleased with the solution he'd just thought of, Su Ling couldn't hold back any longer.

'Why don't we do both?' Lao Tien had suggested. 'We could go to see the film early and go on to the party afterwards. We'll be a bit late, I know, but I'm sure no one will mind.'

'Maybe they won't, but I will!' Su Ling had told him crossly.

The angry words had gone on for quite a while, but no amount of persuasion would make Su Ling change her mind, and she stubbornly refused to see Lao Tien's point of view.

In the end Su Ling had issued her ultimatum. 'If you want to see your silly film, you go, if it's that important to you,' she'd told Lao Tien. 'But I'm going to the party. I think you're being very selfish, and if you won't come with me, well . . . I don't think we ought to see each other again.'

Lao Tien had been surprised. Su Ling was a quiet, shy girl, and he'd never heard her talk like this before. But he'd been angry, too, and her ultimatum had brought out his own stubborn streak. 'All right, Su Ling,' he'd said quietly. 'If that's the way you want it.'

He hadn't even said goodbye when he'd left, just turned and walked quickly away. Su Ling had gone straight up to her bedroom, still smarting from their argument.

What right did he have to be so high-handed, she kept asking herself. He'd known about the party for ages, and she couldn't accept that he'd forgotten so easily. No, Lao Tien had just wanted his own way. Well, if he couldn't sacrifice seeing a stupid film for her family's sake, it just showed the sort of person he was.

Su Ling tried hard to convince herself that she was better off without him, yet as she lay in bed thinking over their bitter quarrel, her anger gradually turned to regret.

Maybe she had been a little hasty. She knew the long hours Lao Tien had worked lately, and he deserved some relaxation. It wouldn't have caused any hard feelings with her family to have arrived at the party a little late either. They liked Lao Tien a lot, and they'd have understood.

Facing up to the fact that it was herself who'd behaved unreasonably wasn't easy for Su Ling, and along with the realization, came heartbreaking tears that almost tore her apart.

They'd known each other a long time before Lao Tien had shyly asked Su Ling to go out with him, and as they'd got to know each other better their warm friendship had turned to love.

Su Ling had been so happy the night Lao Tien had told her he loved her, there'd been tears that night, too, but they'd been tears of happiness.

It wasn't long after, that everyone began to make their plans for the New Year celebrations, and Lao Tien was no exception. 'The Feast of the Lanterns I love best,' he'd said with an excitement Su Ling found infectious. 'The last of the New Year holidays. Every house will be alight with lanterns, the children will sing and dance through the streets, and not one person will be unhappy, Su Ling.' His eyes had shown his love for her as he'd taken her hand and kissed it gently. 'Especially not us. It will be a happy day for us. I promise you that.'

A happy day . . . Then why had Su Ling been sitting by her window for most of the time, her heart heavy and tears never very far away? The answer was simple. Deep down she'd had a feeling that on the Feast of the Lanterns Lao Tien would ask her to marry him.

Their parents had been hinting for a long time that a marriage between them would be welcomed with great joy. Su Ling's mother had even said she thought they were destined for each other, and only a future of love and happiness could possibly lie in front of them.

Not now though, Su Ling told herself with a sigh. If only she'd been able to swallow her pride and go to Lao Tien and apologize. If only she didn't feel so embarrassed and ashamed about the way she'd treated Lao Tien that night.

'Su Ling, your brothers and sister are waiting,' her mother called up the stairs. 'Come. Hurry up, and don't forget your lantern. The procession is starting.'

By then, Su Ling's bedroom was dark, yet the lights from the swinging lanterns in the street gave her enough light to see by. She looked at the beautiful silk lantern Lao Tien had given her and reluctantly reached up to take it down. It had been given with love, to be used with love, but she had rejected that love.

'Su Ling!' Her mother called again. 'Quickly now, we're waiting for you.'

With hesitant steps, Su Ling went down the stairs to join her family. Her younger brothers and little sister were starting to get restless, and looked at her accusingly for keeping them waiting.

'Come on, Su Ling,' her sister said. 'We want to go. We're missing all the fun because of you!'

'You haven't even lit your lantern yet!' one of the boys said impatiently.

His mother's hand shooed him out of the door. 'Let's go,' she said firmly. 'Su Ling can catch us up.'

'Here, let me light it for you,' Su Ling's father offered with a smile. 'It's certainly very beautiful. You'll be the envy of all your friends.'

Carefully he lit the lantern and patted his daughter's hand. Both her parents knew how badly Su Ling had felt after the argument with Lao Tien, but they hadn't interfered. Instead, they'd shown her in small ways that whatever she chose to do, she would have their love and support.

One by one, the family left the house and joined the throng of people in the street. For the sake of the rest of the family, Su Ling tried hard to enter into the gaiety of the evening. Like herself, the younger children had been eagerly looking forward to displaying their lanterns and discussing with their friends who had the prettiest and the best.

As they walked through the town, the crowds grew until every street was ablaze with lights and filled with happy, laughing people. Su Ling saw a lot of her friends, most of them walking with their boyfriends, their faces reflecting the magic of the occasion. Yet there was no sign of Lao Tien.

It came as a shock to Su Ling when she realized how much she was hoping to see him. Maybe if she did, the happy atmosphere might give her the courage to say she was sorry, and to ask his forgiveness.

The idea grew in her mind as she nodded hello to neighbours and friends, and with the idea, came a feeling of quiet confidence. It was pride which had held her back, and now she began to wonder if her pride had been misplaced. Surely if you really loved someone then pride should not exist. And it was pride which had caused her so much pain and kept her from the only boy she'd ever loved.

The more she thought about it, the more it seemed to make sense to her. If only she could find Lao Tien, she knew exactly what she'd do. It would take courage, but not nearly as much as she'd need to live without him.

Suddenly Su Ling realized she hadn't heard her young brothers laughing and teasing each other for a while, but then she'd been locked in a world of her own thoughts and hadn't been aware of what was happening around her.

Quickly she turned to where her family had been following her, and was surprised when they weren't there. All the people behind her were strangers. She wasn't unduly worried, she had nothing to fear on such a happy night, yet she would have liked to have been with her family right then. They'd been patient with her sadness for so long and now she wanted them to see it was over. Su Ling wanted them to know, too, that she'd grown up a little on the Feast of the Lanterns.

Looking out for them, Su Ling continued to walk towards the main square of the town, certain she'd catch up with her family soon. As a crowd of people turned off into a side street, the road ahead of her emptied and Su Ling could see the square in the distance.

Then she stopped, her feet refusing to move another step as her heart began to pound. She could hardly believe her eyes. It was as though her prayers had been answered, for, coming towards her through the gap in the crowd, was Lao Tien.

His lantern, an exact copy of her own, was held high, casting a light across his handsome face. As he came nearer, Su Ling could see he was unsure of what her reaction to him would be, and she knew it was up to her. Drawing on the happiness around her to give her strength, she smiled at Lao Tien.

It was enough. His steps didn't falter as he ran to her, the sound of his footsteps matching her rapidly beating heart. There would be time enough for words later, but now it was enough that they were together on their special night.

Their hands reached out and touched, and as Su Ling and Lao Tien walked together through the streets, it was every bit as magical as Lao Tien had promised.

Su Ling stopped, her feet refusing to move another step, as her heart began to pound.

THE VICTORY

Maureen Spurgeon

DONNA HAD ALWAYS KNOWN that the only one Jason Miller really cared about was *Abigail*. Who could blame him? Everyone was always saying how beautiful *Abigail* was, the way she moved, her perfect body. No wonder she never failed to attract attention, wherever he took her.

'It's *Abigail* this, and *Abigail* that, almost every time Jason opens his mouth!' Donna grumbled, pulling out a stool at the breakfast bar. 'That's when anyone manages to speak to him. When he isn't spending all his time with *her*!'

'Hardly surprising,' Dad remarked mildly, pouring himself some coffee. '*Abigail* is by far the best little boat in Toria Marina!'

'Sailing dinghy,' corrected Donna.

'And don't forget, his uncle built her himself!' Nick put in, grinning across at Donna's disgruntled expression. 'With a bit of help from Jason, of course!'

'Yes, I know all that!' Donna snapped back. How dense big brothers could be sometimes! 'Only, I'm just sick and tired of him thinking how wonderful *Abigail* is!'

'Then don't spend so much time pretending to do sailing practice,' Nick teased her.

But Donna's shoes were squeaking determinedly across the tiled floor, followed by the back gate being slammed shut.

Donna debated whether to take Nick's advice and stay away – just for one morning. Perhaps then, Jason would miss her being there, and start wondering why she hadn't come along to take her boat out.

Her boat. Not much more than an old tub, compared with
Abigail. Just big enough to fit on the roof rack of the dormobile,
when they'd lived in town, and any sailing was done at
weekends.

'But,' Dad had said, as he'd helped Donna carry it over the
shingle, first week they moved to Toria, 'You've kept her
weatherproof and waterproof, and the rigging's still good – I
checked it over.'

'Thanks, Dad,' Donna had beamed, tying the tags of the
new life jacket Mum had bought as an early birthday present.
'Can't wait to see if I can sail around the cove!'

Not just the cove, Donna discovered. A little further out was
a cluster of tiny islands, where thick bushes and trees huddled
together, and seabirds wheeled overhead, lazily diving for fish,
now and again.

'This is the best practice you'll get,' Dad had told her,
watching the sail. 'With the wind blowing through these little
channels between the islands, you've got to keep on your toes.'

'You can say that again,' Donna groaned, seeing the sail
beginning to flap hard. 'Oh, why didn't I see I was sailing too
close into the wind?'

'You'll be all right, just as long as you keep your distance
outside the largest island. There's quite a wide reef there –
enough to make you capsize, or run aground. Can you see the
warning marker-buoys?'

She had looked – and that's when she'd first seen Jason. Or
rather *Abigail*, lifted by the frothy waves and her bow gleaming
satin smooth, like a fine horse raising its proud head.

'Heck!' Dad exclaimed. 'See the way he cuts through the
water so fine?'

Donna had said nothing. She had just moved the tiller until
the sail billowed out again, although this didn't stop her

studying the way in which the boy threw back his dark head as he pulled on the rigging. Then, she'd given a secret smile, feeling a warm kind of fluttering inside. Perhaps she would soon be enjoying her sailing for a new reason!

'Just shows how wrong you can be,' Donna complained, stamping down the path leading to the marina. 'There's Dad always chatting to Jason's uncle about how he always wanted to live near the sea, and the uncle going on about his fishing and the boat-yard. Yet, Jason and I, we hardly talk. Only when he goes on about himself and *Abigail*, and how they're going to win the Chew-zee Spearmint Challenge Race on Saturday!'

He had won the race twice before in *Abigail*, she knew. Only one more victory, then he'd get a silver trophy for keeps, same as the one displayed in his uncle's workshop window.

There were going to be newspaper men, photographers – even a visit from the boss of Chew-Zee Spearmint, the firm who put up the prize money each year – all coming to see if he could do it again. She pictured him now, adjusting each sail at exactly the right moment, weaving *Abigail* so neatly through the water, and making each turn far tighter than she knew she ever could.

'Hey!' came a mad shriek behind her. 'What the blue blazes do you think you're playing at?'

She glanced around, amazed and then annoyed at finding herself pulling in front of the magnificent *Abigail*.

'W–what? But, I–I just didn't see you, Jason.'

'That's because you didn't keep your eyes open.' He was yelling even louder, even though he was dodging under the boom to the other side of the dinghy. 'I was getting a record practice time, till you go and mess things up.'

'I was only sailing my boat, same as you!' Donna retorted,

equally loudly. 'You could have run into me.'

Jason sailed *Abigail* past, pretending to ignore Donna, but growling so that she could hear him quite plainly. 'The whole channel, and she can't even steer a straight course! And she still says she's going in for Saturday's race, with a potty little boat that doesn't stand a chance against *Abigail*!'

Donna let out the rigging, trying to get more wind into her sail and chase after him. 'It was your uncle who told me about Saturday's race first off, seeing as I know my way around Toria Islands almost as well as you do, now. You thought it was a great joke, but I'll make you change your mind! And, what's more – Aaaagh!'

A sudden gust of wind had blown into the sail so swiftly that Donna could not stop it lurching heavily, tossing her into the sea with a noisy splash. She managed to scramble back on the starboard side, feeling not so much cold and wet, as furious to see Jason's shoulders shaking with uncontrollable laughter. 'Just like a girl! I've got plenty to worry about, with you on my tail – I don't think!'

'Before next Saturday's out,' Donna snarled between her teeth, 'I'll make that great big show-off eat his rotten words!' She wished she could feel pleased about it.

Saturday morning came, bringing a good deal of cloud and showers.

'Doesn't look too promising for the race,' Mum commented, twitching a lace curtain. 'Think they'll call it off, Ed?'

'Be the first time if they do,' Dad informed her. 'And everyone knows how the weather can change around here, this time of year.'

'Besides,' Donna cut in tartly, 'don't forget all the press people and the boss of Chew-zee Spearmint are coming to see the star of the show. And we all know who that is, don't we?'

Mum threw down a scouring pad, at the same time as Nick

Donna was feeling not so much cold and wet, as furious to see
Jason's shoulders shaking with uncontrollable laughter.

rolled his eyes towards the ceiling, and Dad slapped his hand on the top of the freezer, making them all jump. 'That's enough, Donna! You ought to have enough sense to see that today's race must mean a lot to Jason, and we're all sick of hearing you talking against him!'

'I–I'm not talking against him.'

'You could have fooled us!' Nick rapped out. 'If you must go in for the race, then be a bit more sporting about it.'

'And think how pleased his uncle Ben would be,' Mum began wheedling. 'He needs cheering up, in that old boat yard of his.'

Donna's response was to pull on her old woollen hat, so that she wouldn't hear what else they said, before she stormed out of the house.

'Oh, well,' sighed Mum. 'At least this can't go on for much longer.'

'What do you mean, Ma?' Nick demanded with a grin. 'The weather or Donna?'

The rain stopped, although the clouds still hung low, Donna noticed, despite her anger. A few creamy patches blotted the sky where the sun might have struggled through to warm her up, if it weren't for the cold wind, already whipping her hair around her face.

'See what big-mouth Jason Miller makes of this!' she couldn't help snapping out, pulling on her life jacket with a jerk of impatience. 'Him and his wonderful *Abigail*!'

Jason certainly seemed very pleased with himself, posing for photographers with a large, prosperous-looking man who introduced himself as Raymond J Mann, President of Chew-Zee Spearmint Gum.

'Smile, son,' directed one of the photographers, and Jason obliged with a wave of disregard for the overcast skies.

But, the scowl which replaced the smile as soon as the press men turned away, told Donna that he knew she was there, trailing out to the starting line with competitors from further afield. She was half inclined to call out, 'Good luck, Jason!' seeing how unusually tense and strained he suddenly looked. But, she sighed to herself, he'd probably think she was trying to be funny. And, she wasn't.

'I wouldn't say this weather was ideal,' she heard her dad telling another spectator – Mum, probably. 'Still, the wind's holding, and that should help.'

There was a general buzz of excitement, as Raymond J Mann let off the flare for the race to begin.

'Our Donna's made a good start!' Dad cried, holding on to his wife's shoulder, and pointing. 'Right on the track of *Abigail*, I'd say!'

Nick took up the commentary. 'The others are holding well, but mostly thanks to the wind. They don't really know the course, not like Donna and Jason!'

'Hope the wind helps them to make a good time,' croaked Jason's uncle, turning away to light his pipe. 'We're due for more than a few showers before the day's out.

The rain had already begun to sting Donna's face before the first of the Marina Islands came in view, and she soon wished she'd brought some gloves to stop her hands being chafed by the fierce breezes. Instinctively, she clenched her teeth, squinting through the misty veil which the weather cast in front of her, hardly able to feel the tiller with her numbed fingers.

'I–I'll be glad when this is over,' she said, more for the comfort of hearing her own voice than anything else. 'Once I turn away from the wind, it should get easier, even if I do lose my chances of a fast time.'

Jason was taking that chance, she noticed, seeing the unmistakably sleek shape of *Abigail* rising and falling some distance ahead. Of course he knew these waters like the back of his head. In this rain, she could have sworn those stormy shadows on the sea were really the marker-buoys over the reef.

'Th–they *are* the marker-buoys!' Donna screamed, the coldness seeming to become a mass of icy fingers that clung and crept over her. 'Jason! Jason!' The wind snatched at every word. Her boat was thrown forward as one surge of water followed another, and the black marker-buoys loomed ominously nearer.

'I've got to go with him,' Donna told herself as firmly as she could with the rain trickling down her aching back, and her hands rough and sore. Rain had made the sails and rigging doubly heavy, and she was almost relieved to see *Abigail* flung helplessly into the channel ahead.

She could see Jason leaning as far back as he dared to. He pulled the sail tighter and turned around again, his eyes glittering like pin-pricks of light as he caught sight of Donna's boat. 'Get back, you little idiot! Don't you know, you're heading for the reef?'

'Y–yes!' Donna prayed he could hear above the high-pitched whine of the wind. 'I thought you'd made a mistake, Jason. You've got to turn back!'

He made a wild grab for the tiller, trying to hang on to the sail at the same time.

'Turn back, Jason!' Donna yelled again, steering her boat as near as she could. 'You'll never do it!'

The two dinghies were almost level now, Jason glaring in fury as he reached for the rigging once more.

'This is the only chance I've got, and that's why I'm ready to take the risk. Satisfied? Now turn back, before you lose your dratted boat!'

'No! Jason, I won't let you do it!'

Donna let the rigging rope slither through her hands, so that her sail flopped back like a dead bird. She leaned across her dinghy for one desperate grab at *Abigail*.

'Didn't I tell you, this is my only big chance?' He was panting hard, his voice wild and choking. 'You – you get into my dinghy, and I'll be disqualified. And, I've promised the prize money to Uncle Ben, to help sort out the boat yard!'

They stared at each other for only a moment, seeming to be sheltered in a pocket of silence, out of the wind and rain which raged all around them.

Then Donna said calmly, 'We'll never do it on our own now, Jason. Not in this weather.'

'Y–your boat, Donna.' She had never heard him speak her name before. 'You can't just leave it.'

'It's almost aground, anyway,' she gabbled quickly, scrambling down beside him. 'Drifted on to the reef, just like you said.' She sighed.

'Maybe, we'll be able to salvage something of her, with the trees fairly near to give cover.'

Donna smiled, hoping he couldn't notice her bottom lip trembling, just a little. 'We're coming into the home stretch now, Jason,' was all she said.

The people watching on the narrow shore had gathered in a tight knot, each one peering anxiously into the rain.

'Don't fret yourself, Mary!' Donna's father was saying. 'They've been gone less than an hour, and the coastguard's been sent out.'

'B-but, the other boats turned back!' Mum quavered. 'All except Jason's *Abigail*, and-and our Donna.'

'Wait a sec – this looks like *Abigail*, now!' Nick bellowed, shading his eyes. 'And, yes – Donna's with Jason! Wonder what happened to our boat?'

It seemed a long time until *Abigail* was sailing around to face the wind, and the sails slackened for an almost perfect stop. Raymond J Mann was holding up a monster-size stopwatch, and proclaiming, 'A record time for this race so you would have been a third-time winner. However, I understand that it doesn't count since two of you have sailed the boat.'

'But only because I sailed too close to the wind, and Jason had to help me off the reef,' Donna said quickly. 'That's right, isn't it?'

Jason opened his mouth in protest. Then, he noticed what Donna had already seen – his uncle looking at him with a smile, arms folded in front of his chest, now puffed out like a young soldier preparing to do battle. 'Maybe we'll be able to bring the boat back and patch it up, Donna' he said, 'now that I can afford the spare parts for my boat yard tools. Mr Mann here wants a boat for his daughter, specially made. He's given me an advance towards it,'

'That's right,' added Mr Mann. 'I could see what a fantastic boat *Abigail* was, the moment she came back into sight after battling through that weather. I want one just like her.'

Everybody started crowding around to congratulate Uncle Ben, and take photographs of him, and Jason and Donna.

Donna suddenly noticed that Jason was squeezing her hand, very tight. 'Wait till next year's race!' he was murmuring into her ear. 'Maybe we'll have your boat back then, all spruced up!'

'My boat?' Donna asked, puzzled. 'Why are you interested in my boat?'

'Well, one of us has to win next year. We can practise racing against each other, and then no one else will stand a chance!'

Donna laughed. 'As long as I don't get stuck on the reef again,' she said happily, giving Jason a hug.

SWEET SOUND OF SUCCESS

Joyce Wilson

THE NEW LOCAL RADIO STATION opened in Mapleton on a Saturday morning in early summer. First the mayor delivered his message of goodwill, then the station manager explained what an experienced broadcaster he was, before the members of the radio programmes' staff were introduced one by one.

Jane Baxter was listening on her battered transistor. There was one voice that she liked at once. That of Phil Maxwell, the young producer of what was to be a Saturday morning programme for school leavers. There was something in it that really drew her to him. Janie made a note of his name. In three or four months' time she herself would be leaving Mapleton Grammar. She would have two or three O levels, but did not know yet what sort of work she could do. Jobs were very hard to find in the town.

If her mother would agree, Janie thought of leaving Mapleton when the time came. But to do so without any qualifications or job experience seemed ill-advised. From what she heard, most places were the same when it came to work for school leavers. And in any case, there was the inevitable opposition from her stepfather to think of.

Josh Collins was a hard man. He had become so in a hard school. After the Second World War, he had received a small disability pension, and had taken what work he could to augment his income. But he had never made anything of himself, and now ran a one-man taxi service in a half-hearted fashion, working when the mood took him. He had met Janie's mother when she booked his taxi one day on their return from a holiday with her sister. He had driven them to the small flat she owned, and made himself very useful with the luggage. After that, Janie had some vague recollection of his courtship of her mother, a widow. They had married quietly.

The worst thing was the way in which Josh chose to sneer at everything Janie tried to do to better herself. It was as if he was afraid her mother's approval would be lavished on her, and there would be nothing left for him.

Three months after leaving school Janie was still unemployed. And when she announced that she was going to write to Phil Maxwell and ask to help with his Saturday morning programme, Josh went beserk.

Though none of them had ever seen Phil in person, Josh claimed he was a long-haired idler. Anyone who earned a living just talking must be no good. And how would a man like that find Janie, who had nothing to recommend her, anything to do? Let alone pay her for the privilege.

Janie was used to this sort of abuse, and let him run on for a while. Then she quietly let herself out of the flat, and walked to the headquarters of the radio station. It was Saturday, and Phil's programme was on the air. She carried her transistor as she walked, holding it close to her ear. A passer-by smiled at her air of total concentration. When Phil was talking, she found that every word meant something to her.

She had often seen the radio building, but never dared to go inside, although she knew that members of the public were welcome, and the link between the town and the broadcasters was a lively reality. Now, as she pushed through the gleaming revolving doors and crossed the deep carpet to the reception desk, she almost lost her nerve.

Then on the tannoy in the reception area, she heard the last moments of Phil's programme, and his signature tune. It made her feel very much part of the scene, and with a deep breath she asked the receptionist if she could see Mr Maxwell after the broadcast.

'Got an appointment, have you?' The girl seemed more interested in doing her nails than listening to Janie.

Janie shook her head, thinking fast. 'But I've got a very good idea for the programme. I – I'm out of work, you see, and so are a lot of us. If – '

At that moment the green baize doors marked 'No Admittance' that led to the recording studios opened, and a young girl with a very efficient air about her came through, followed by an older man.

'Is that Mr Maxwell now?' Janie whispered to the receptionist.

'Better hurry if you want to catch him – ' but Janie knew that, and was at the revolving doors before Phil Maxwell himself. She found herself looking into grey eyes that only just controlled an impish sense of humour. Phil looked much younger than she had expected. She was glad she was wearing her best jeans and had taken special care over her eye make-up that morning.

The words spilling out in her eagerness, Janie told him that she was an out of work school leaver and would do anything on the programme, if he would only give her a chance.

'You can leave your name and address,' his companion, who was apparently his assistant, said crossly. 'The next lot of auditions are not for a month. We'll contact you if there's a cancellation.'

Janie's face fell.

'Wait a minute,' Phil Maxwell said. 'I do have a spare slot for next week – and a talk from someone who has really not been able to find work after leaving school in this town would be good. Can you write, Janie?'

At that moment Janie felt she could produce a best-selling

novel in seven days if he asked her. 'I'll be able to write a good talk on that subject, anyway,' she said.

'Well, bring it in by Thursday. And leave your phone number. Vera – ' he indicated the girl at his side, 'will ring you.'

'There's just one thing – how long should the talk be?'

'Good girl,' Phil said. 'Very professional. About a thousand words – that's six or seven minutes, and four or five pages of typing. Can you type?'

She nodded. She would borrow a machine for Thursday if she could. And anyone could type.

With a superior backward glance from Vera, the producer then left, and Janie walked home on air.

The next few days were hectic. Janie really went into the various ways of finding work in Mapleton, with much more care than she had done when it was work for herself that she wanted. She went to see Youth Officers, talked to people at the Job Centre, and went round the private employment agencies. From her notes she wrote a detailed, practical piece of information exactly a thousand words long. And on Wednesday night she drove both Josh and her mother mad by reading it out again and again, as if she were already at the microphone.

On the Thursday, she delivered the piece by hand to the studios, keeping a copy of it safely at home. The receptionist was just about to put it into a tray marked 'IN' when Vera herself appeared through the baize doors and held out her hand for it, deliberately ignoring Janie. 'Anything for Phil has to go through me,' she said to the receptionist. 'He's a very busy man.'

There was not much more Janie could do. She had left the phone number of the flat at the top of the script, and Phil had said Vera would ring her. Now began the long, nerve-racking

On the Thursday, Janie delivered the piece by hand to the studios.

wait for the call.

But by Friday night nothing had happened, and Josh, answering the phone for his taxi service, had begun to sneer in advance every time it rang, saying it was not going to be for Janie.

By Saturday morning, with only an hour to go to Phil's programme, she knew with a sinking heart that Josh was right. After all, she had caught the radio producer at an awkward time. He could hardly ignore her when she confronted him in the studio foyer. He was just being kind when he asked her to try to write the piece. Worse still – perhaps what she had written was of no use to him. And she had not the nerve to contact him again and find out.

It was Saturday morning a week later, when the phone rang and someone asked for Janie. Josh handed her the receiver with a shrug. 'Didn't know you had a boyfriend,' he said.

It was Phil himself. 'Janie? Remember me? Phil Maxwell speaking.' Her heart beat so fast and loud she was afraid he would hear it over the phone. 'I have only just found the talk you wrote, Janie. And I know from the front office that you delivered it on time. I can't explain now, but something pretty unfortunate happened, and it got lost. I was too busy to ask for it. But in half an hour's time I've got a man from the Department of Employment coming in to speak on the programme. How about coming round yourself, and joining in? Do you think you could do that?'

It was a chastened Josh Baxter who drove his taxi round to the studios twenty minutes later, just in time for Janie to be rushed through the 'No Admission' sign and into a silent, carpeted room. Above the door a red light flashed. Through a thick glass panel a man with a set of headphones put a warning finger to his lips. Janie was almost pushed into a chair at a large, round table which had a microphone built into its centre. On one side of her sat a middle-aged stranger who looked like the man from the Ministry, in pin-striped suit and formal tie. On the far side of the table sat Phil, whose face lit up when he saw her. Beside Phil sat Vera, notebook in hand, and when he gave Janie a stunning smile and the thumbs-up sign Vera froze in annoyance.

A year or two later, when Janie herself was an experienced broadcaster and working full-time for Radio Mapleton, she always advised a newcomer to her programme to arrive just before they were going on the air, have a quick chat and a coffee, and then get into the recording studio and start talking before there was time to be nervous.

'I had my baptism just that way,' she would explain. 'I was put in a chair, my script was on the table in front of me, and the producer introduced me. I don't remember anything else about it – I just had to get on with it. And nobody complained about the results!'

What she did not add was that she had been very good indeed. That her love of radio, her knowledge of the style of Phil's programme, and her very natural speaking voice had made her an instance success – much to Vera's annoyance.

But she was not given a job straight away. The thousand words were the first of many more she had to write before she had anything else accepted. By that time she had also learnt to type at a commercial school.

She was about to leave Mapleton and stay with her aunt in London to look for work there, when one morning her mother called her down to breakfast early, with the news that there was a letter for her.

Her fingers trembled as she opened the envelope marked Radio Mapleton. Inside she found a letter signed by Phil.

'Owing to an unexpected vacancy in my office,' he wrote, 'we are interviewing candidates for the post of assistant secretary on Monday and Tuesday of next week. If you can now offer secretarial qualifications and are prepared to lend a hand in the everyday running of the office, then we would be pleased to make an appointment for you on one of those days.'

'They only want someone to make the tea,' Josh growled. But her mother smiled quietly. She had watched her disappointment over the last months with growing concern. She could not believe that someone with all her enthusiasm should end up with no niche in life.

'I'll make the tea any day,' Janie told him. 'At least I'll be earning a living.'

To her relief she discovered when she phoned to arrange the interview that it was Vera who had left Phil's office. She never did find out if the way she had tried to suppress Janie's first contribution was behind it. Janie was not important enough for that. But she did find, when she began to work for Phil Maxwell herself, that the one thing he hated was jealousy.

'You'll have no need for jealousy, ever, Janie,' he told her one day, when he had signed off the programme and the green light had come on again above the studio door. 'You're going to the top. You'll leave us all behind. And I shouldn't be surprised if you're rushing out to lunch from Broadcasting House itself in a few years from now, when a poor unknown disc jockey called Phil Maxwell stops you in the hall and asks you for a job!'

'I've got a much better idea than that, Phil,' she laughed. 'Why don't we just both go out to lunch now, in Mapleton, and I'll tell you a super idea I've had for next week's programme.'

Phil took her hand, and they stepped into the sunshine together, smiling.

TRIP TO TERROR

Jane Butterworth

'BYE SALLY. SEE YOU TOMORROW.' Kate gave a brief wave to
her best friend as they parted company at the crossroads, and
she set off to pedal the rest of the way home. She was feeling so
happy, she could have shouted with joy. For tonight she had a
date with the super boy who worked in the coffee bar at the
disco. She didn't know anything about him other than that his
name was Steve and she'd fancied him for *weeks*. When he'd
finally plucked up courage to ask her out, she was in heaven for
the rest of the week.

She was going to get home as quickly as possible to give
herself plenty of time to get ready. She wanted to look her
absolute best when she met him outside the cinema in town.
She was absolutely convinced she was in love.

She was so wrapped up in her thoughts, that she wasn't
noticing where she was going. And then she suddenly realized
that she didn't recognize the quiet country road she was
cycling along. She stopped her bike and stood in the middle of
the road, looking around. How could she possibly have taken
the wrong road? She'd lived in Millfield for three years and
every afternoon she cycled home from school. Yet here she was,
in a quiet country lane with high hedges and grass verges, and
not a soul in sight – and she had no idea where she was.

Puzzled, she started to cycle back the way she'd come, but
after ten minutes she still didn't recognize the road. Worse,
there didn't seem to be any houses or telephone boxes or even
signposts. Eventually, almost crying with anger and frust-

ration, she got off her bike and sat on the grass verge. Where on earth had she got to?

Suddenly, she became aware that all around her was totally still and quiet, and even though she was a practical and down to earth sort of girl, a sudden fear gripped her. Then she shook it off – there had to be an explanation. She'd been so busy thinking about Steve, she simply hadn't noticed where she was going and she must have cycled up a disused road or a farmtrack.

Then with relief, she saw a cyclist approaching. As he drew nearer she saw that it was an old man on a very new, gleaming bicycle, quite unlike any she'd ever seen before. He cycled up to her and she waved him down frantically.

He looked at her curiously and stopped, rather unsteadily.

'Excuse me,' she said. 'Could you tell me where I am?'

The old man gazed at her. 'By heck,' he said looking at her bike approvingly, 'that's a grand machine you have there. I haven't seen one of those for years.'

Silly old man! It was new last birthday!

'Yes, I had one just like it when I was younger. I had a car then too,' he added. Then he looked straight into her face and he seemed to pale as though he'd seen a ghost, and he clutched at his chest, pulling out a large red handkerchief and mopping his brow.

'By God, you're her, aren't you?' he said. 'I never thought I'd see the day when something like this would happen. And yet your mother came here and cursed this village, and swore you'd never rest, and she was right! You've come back to haunt us!'

Prickles started to rise on the back of Kate's neck. This old loony was beginning to give her the creeps. Trust her to stop the village idiot!

'I'm sorry, I don't understand,' she said helplessly. Then he muttered something she didn't hear properly, jumped on his bike and pedalled off as fast as he could, leaving her staring after him, open-mouthed with amazement.

'Well, for heaven's sake!' she said out loud. She started cycling along the road in the direction he'd disappeared off to, and was relieved to see, at last, a village. It was strangely quiet and she realized it was quiet because there wasn't a single car. Not even a parked car. Then she saw a phone box. At least she could ring her mum.

Well, it looked like a phone box even though it was painted white. But inside, there was some sort of push-button newfangled computer thing, and you needed a card to make it work, not money. She sighed in frustration. There must be someone to help. Across the road was a row of pretty terraced cottages and she went up to one and knocked cautiously on the front door.

After a couple of minutes an old woman answered the door. She wore a shapeless dress and an old scarf, and she regarded Kate with hostility. 'Yes?' she asked abruptly. Then she stared at Kate hard, gave a loud shriek, and promptly banged the door shut in her face.

Kate was so shocked by this, that she almost burst into tears. What was wrong with everyone? She wheeled her bike through the village, feeling that unseen eyes were watching her every move. She wanted to scream. Surely she was in the grip of some terrible nightmare. How could she get away from this terrifying place?

Tears started to slide down her face and she brushed them aside angrily. In the distance she could see the old man she'd spoken to, talking to a group of people. They were obviously talking about her, because he kept pointing at her. She felt afraid and very, very alone.

'Don't cry.' She felt a light touch on her arm, and when she looked round, a tall, very good-looking boy was smiling down at her.

He had deep brown eyes and a shock of thick dark brown hair. She'd never seen a boy with such weird clothes before. He was wearing a sort of smock top and baggy trousers. But at least he was friendly.

She pulled herself together and smiled wanly. 'I'm sorry,' she said. 'It's just that I'm lost, and everyone I talk to here, takes one look at me and runs off. The woman in that house over there banged the door in my face.'

'Ah, that'll be Mrs Fleming,' he said. 'She's a bit, well, funny in the head, you know? She has been ever since her son died 'bout fifteen years ago. Only my age he was, too. But he'd fallen in love with a girl who moved here with her husband. They'd only been married a short time. It was the talk of the village, although I was too young to remember it.'

'What happened to them?' Kate asked curiously.

'Well now. Somebody in the village told the young girl's husband that she was seeing Johnny Fleming. He went after him with a gun, and caught them together. Nobody believes he meant to harm them, only to frighten them, you know? But there was a struggle and the gun went off, and the girl was so upset – her husband had shot Johnny Fleming by mistake. So she grabs the gun off him and shoots herself as well. The husband went to jail – came out five years ago and died the following spring. They say he never got over the tragedy.'

'How sad,' Kate murmured.

'Well, it was sad. Because when the girl moved here folks weren't very nice to her – they don't take kindly to outsiders – and they say that's why she took up with Johnny Fleming. They say, at the funeral, her mother stood up and cursed the town and blamed them for killing her Kathy. Kathy Lambert, her name was. That's why old Mrs Fleming went funny when she saw you. I heard old Jack up the hill telling folks that he'd seen you and how you were a dead ringer for Kathy Lambert.'

Kate jumped. 'Why, my name's Kathryn!' she said. 'But

nobody calls me Kathy – I'm Kate. And my surname's
O'Brian. But still, it gives you a really spooky feeling, and it is a
coincidence, isn't it?'

He nodded. 'And you're lost, are you?'

'Yes, and what's worse, there are no signposts. I can't
understand. I know every bit of Millfield and Rye Cross.'

'Rye Cross?' The boy was looking at her oddly.

'Why yes. that's where I live. I was cycling home from
school and it's only a short distance.'

'I've never heard of those places,' he said, bewildered. 'This
is only a little village – Soar Green.'

'I've never heard of that,' she said in despair. 'Aren't there
any buses?'

'Buses?' He laughed. 'Don't be daft. You know there have
been no motor vehicles since the oil crisis of 1990. There's the
monorail but that only runs from Dorchester.'

She was staring at him in horror. 'Is this some sort of joke?'
she asked. 'I thought you wanted to help me.'

'But Kate,' he said in amazement, 'You must know there are
no buses. There haven't been for years.'

'Years? What year is it now?' she asked frantically.

'Why, 2001,' he replied.

'And where are we?' she asked fearfully.

'Soar Green, near Dorchester in Dorset,' he said cheerfully.

'My God, what's happened to me? My school, my home are
in Surrey,' she whispered in anguish. '2001 . . . oh, why doesn't
this nightmare stop?'

Then Kate had a terrible premonition. 'This Kathy girl, the
one I remind everyone of, when did she die, what year?'

The boy frowned. 'Let me see now . . . it would have been
1986. She was only twenty.'

'Oh no,' Kate whispered. 'I'll be twenty in 1986. What are
you all trying to do to me?'

But the boy just smiled at her, a wide relaxed sort of smile that seemed to cover his whole face. Terrified now, Kate looked around her, and everywhere, she seemed to see spying eyes staring at her disapprovingly. With a sort of sob she jumped on her bicycle and rode off as fast as she could, hardly noticing where she was going, just wanting to put as much distance between her and these terrible people. They were still standing, staring at her, like frozen statues. It was a joke, a joke.

Then her wheel hit a sharp piece of stone in the road, and she was catapulted over the handlebars and everything went black.

Are you all right?'

She opened her eyes. She was lying on the grass verge beside her bicycle and a woman was standing over her, looking concerned.

'You came off your bike with such a bang I thought you must have hurt yourself badly,' said the woman.

'I only banged my head,' said Kate, blinking, a little bewildered for the moment. 'Where am I?'

'You poor thing, you must be suffering from concussion,' said the woman. 'You're on the road from Millfield to Rye Cross.'

Kate breathed a sigh of relief. 'Thank goodness for that,' she said. She stood up shakily and looked about her. She knew exactly where she was now, little more than a few hundred metres away from her home.

'I think I'd better call an ambulance,' said the woman.

'No,' Kate said quickly, 'No, I'm fine. I'll walk home, it's not far.' She wheeled her bike away, leaving the woman staring after her. It had been a dream – nothing more. She must have fallen off her bike, knocked herself out for a few minutes and dreamt it all!

But now she felt fine and she started to sing to herself as she

Kate jumped on her bicycle and rode off as fast as she could.

walked home. She didn't think she'd tell her mum, as she'd only worry. But even more important, her mother might not let her go out with Steve that night.

By the time Kate had soaked herself in a hot bath and put on her new fuschia-coloured dress she felt happy and relaxed and had almost forgotten about her nightmare. She set off to meet Steve, and the ten-minute bus journey had never seemed so long. When she saw his tall figure pacing up and down outside the cinema, her heart leapt for joy.

They saw a film and then went to a club. She'd been a little shy when they first met, but her shyness disappeared when he put his arms around her and held her close so that they were hardly dancing at all, just moving gently in unison, conscious of each other's nearness.

It was a wonderful, magical night. She felt it and she knew he did, too. All she was conscious of was that she was in love, she was convinced of that, and that she wanted to be with this boy forever.

He walked home with her, his arm protectively around her waist. 'I've never believed in love at first sight,' he said wonderingly, 'but even after such a short time, I think I've fallen in love with you.'

'I love you, too,' she said softly.

'I think I want to marry you, Kate,' he said. 'Kate . . . I think I prefer your real name, Kathryn. Or Kathy. Yes, I think I'm going to call you Kathy from now on. It's softer, more like you.'

She stiffened slightly – nobody had ever called her that before.

'Marry me? I'm still at school,' she laughed. 'Besides, I don't know anything about you. I don't even know your surname.'

'I don't care if you're still at school,' he said, stroking the top of her head. 'I'll wait for you forever if necessary. And what do you want to know about me? My name's Steve Lambert, I'm twenty-one, and when I'm not working in the coffee bar I'm studying agriculture at college. When I leave at the end of the year I'm going to go back and help run my father's farm.'

But all she heard was the name, *Lambert*, and a cold feeling of horror was seeping through her every fibre. Kathy Lambert – that had been *her* name.

'What did you say your name was?' she asked.

'Lambert.'

'You – don't have any connection with Dorset, do you?' she asked, hardly able to breathe for the tightness in her chest.

'Well, that's funny you should ask. My dad's farm is in Dorset, in a little village called Soar Green. I'm going back to it in the summer. You'll love it there, Kathy. It's a beautiful part of the world. Say you'll marry me and then you can help me run the farm.

'Kathy? Kathy, what on earth's the matter? Why have you turned that terrible colour?'

RIDING TO SUCCESS

C. J. White

'I'M SORRY, KAREN, but if you want to have riding lessons you'll have to pay for them yourself. Your dad and I just can't afford to give you any pocket money, let alone money to waste on learning to ride.'

'But it wouldn't be wasted, Mum.' said Karen.

'You know how it is, with your father unemployed and six of us to feed. Every penny counts, and it's difficult enough finding money for necessary items. We haven't any left for luxuries.'

Karen ran out of the kitchen quickly, so her mother couldn't see how disappointed she was. She went to her favourite hiding place behind the shed at the bottom of the garden and threw herself on the grass to think. It was so unfair. Why did times have to be so hard? Her father never seemed to be able to get a job for long – he'd been working for a firm that installed swimming pools in people's gardens, but nobody seemed to want swimming pools any more. So he'd got another job doing construction work on the new motorway that was being built round their town. Now the motorway was finished, he'd been laid off and there seemed to be no prospects for the future.

Her father had promised her that as soon as they could afford it, she could have riding lessons, but there seemed little chance of this happening soon.

Every morning on her way to school, Karen passed the Park Riding Stables, and she longed to go riding. Her friends thought she was mad. After school, they'd all go down to the local cafe and listen to records on the juke-box, but she preferred to hang round the stables, dreaming of the day when she'd be a famous rider.

'Karen, Karen, come and help with the supper.' She heard her mother calling from the house. She suddenly felt guilty, because her worries were nothing compared to those of her parents.

'Come on, pull yourself together,' she told herself, and resolved to try to find some way of earning enough money for riding lessons herself.

'WANTED. Schoolgirl or boy for early morning paper round. Must be responsible and hard-working. Apply Roberts Newsagents.'

'Perfect,' thought Karen to herself as she skimmed the advertisements in the local paper. And then she saw another one:

'Kind person wanted to look after 4-year-old boy for two hours, three evenings a week. Please apply Cathy Willis, 63 The Avenue.'

A couple of hours later, Karen had found herself two jobs. The newsagent had asked whether she liked getting up early and when she could start work, then Cathy Willis had introduced her to her son Ben. For once, Karen was thankful that she had three younger brothers and sisters which made her an expert at dealing with young children. Ben seemed to like her, and so did his mother, so Karen agreed to start the next Monday.

She rushed home to tell her parents, who were as pleased as she was. 'I wish I had as much luck finding jobs as you do,' said her father, half joking, half serious.

'Come on Dad,' said Karen, trying to cheer him up. 'When I'm a famous showjumper, we'll all live a life of luxury, sitting back and enjoying my winnings!'

'That'll be the day,' scoffed her brother, Paul.

'Haven't you got a proper riding hat or jodhpurs? What do you mean by coming to ride dressed like that? And you can't possibly go on a horse if you don't have a riding hat.'

Jane Templeton, immaculately dressed in perfect riding clothes, turned up her nose and stormed out of the tack room. Karen wanted the floor to open up and swallow her. It was her first Saturday lesson at the stables.

Suddenly she heard a soft voice beside her. 'The school has lots of hats that people can borrow if they don't have one of their own. Come over here and try one of these for size. And jodhpurs aren't essential.'

Karen looked up and recognized the boy she'd often seen working at the stables on her way home from school.

'By the way, my name's Tom. I work here. I'm the groom, assistant instructor and general dogsbody. If you need anything or have any problems, just yell.'

'Thank you, thank you so much . . .' Karen started to stammer.

'When you've found a hat that fits, come outside and I'll show you how to mount.'

Karen told herself to ignore Jane Templeton's rude remarks, found a hat, took a deep breath and stepped outside. Much to her relief, she saw a string of riders heading off into the local fields, including Jane Templeton, while Tom was leading a docile-looking grey mare out of a loosebox.

'This is your ride. Her name's Beauty. The owner of the stables, Mrs Brown, is taking the ride out today while I give you your first lesson in the home paddock. Now, this is how you mount . . .'

An hour later, Karen felt slightly confused, but overwhelmingly happy. Although she realized she had a lot to learn, she knew she was going to love every minute of it. And especially when she had a good teacher like Tom.

'By the way,' he called out as she was hanging the hat back up in the tack room, 'if you want to buy one of those hats we sell them very cheaply. And here, catch . . .' A strange bundle came flying through the air at her. 'We used to have another groom working here who was about your size. She left behind this pair of jodhpurs, and we were going to send them on to her. But you may as well have them if they're any good to you.'

Karen couldn't believe her luck.

Two lessons per week meant that Karen's riding improved rapdly. She got to know all the horses by name, and was soon off the leading rein and able to ride on her own.

Once or twice when she was out with the other riders, she felt Tom's eyes on her. This made her even more determined to do well, to show that she could be as good as any Jane Templeton.

One Sunday morning, as she was helping him to unsaddle the horses after the 11 o'clock ride, he suddenly said, 'You know, Karen, you're a natural with horses. Have you ever thought of taking riding up seriously?'

She was so astonished that she could hardly answer. And then she didn't know what to say. She knew that to be good you needed to spend hours practising, and every hour cost money. She was already getting up at six in the morning, doing her paper round, going to school, looking after baby Ben, trying to fit in her homework, and she had important exams coming up this year at school.

She didn't like to admit that she couldn't afford any more lessons, or that she didn't have any more time to spare. 'Come on, don't pull my leg,' she replied. 'I bet you say that to all the learners.'

'No, I'm not joking,' he replied, looking her straight in the eye, so she felt a shiver go down her spine. 'It's rare that someone picks it up as quickly as you do.'

With that he turned and went into the office. She felt sorry that she'd sounded so flippant, but underneath she was thrilled to bits.

'I think you're about ready to join the special jumping class now, Karen,' said Mrs Brown, the owner of the stables, a few days later. Take Silver Birch – he'll be a good horse for you to start on, and I know you like riding him.'

'Are you sure this new girl is capable of coming with us experienced riders. After all, we don't want beginners holding us back,' complained Jane Templeton.

'If Karen finds it too difficult I'm sure she'll say so,' retorted Mrs Brown. Karen felt grateful for Mrs Brown's kind words, and told herself that on no account would she hold anyone up.

Once the string of riders reached the jumping paddock, they were given basic instructions. 'I know some of you will have heard this before, but it will do you no harm to hear it again,' said Tom, glaring at Jane and her cronies. 'And those of you who think you know what you're doing can ride without stirrups. That will be good training for keeping your seat.'

Tom asked Karen to help him set up some bars on the ground and some cavalletti. Then, one by one, the riders took their horses over. Karen felt as though Jane was willing her to fall off, but she soon forgot all about the other riders, so hard was she concentrating on learning how to jump.

'Yes, that's very good, Karen. Just keep your hands down a bit as you go over the bars,' shouted Tom.

Suddenly there was a commotion at the far end of the paddock.

'No, don't, Jane, it's too high!'

'Stop, you'll get into trouble!'

'Come back, don't be so silly!'

Karen stared, horrified, taking in what was happening immediately. Jane had obviously got bored with what Tom

133

had been making them do, and had spotted a high double fence at the other end of the paddock. She'd decided that she was good enough to try it, and was whipping her horse as they cantered towards the fence. But it was far too difficult a jump, anyone could see that.

The chestnut, Royal Mail, bravely leapt at the first part of the jump, though his ears were firmly back and he obviously was unhappy. Miraculously he cleared it, but as they approached the second part of the jump, he mistimed his stride, half-heartedly tried to leap high enough, but failed, crashing into the poles which fell all around him.

He went down, and Jane came hurtling off him, turning a double somersault and hitting her head on one of the side pieces of the jump. She lay motionless on the ground. All the other riders rushed over to her.

Meanwhile, Royal Mail pulled himself to his feet, took a frightened glance around him and decided to escape as quickly as possible. He galloped over to the boundary fence, took a wild jump and cleared it, clattering off down the road as if he were running in the Grand National.

Everyone else seemed to be more concerned about Jane than Royal Mail, but Karen suddenly had an awful thought – 'The new motorway! He was heading straight for it!' She kicked on Silver Birch, quickly opened the paddock gate, and set off after Royal Mail. If she acted fast she might catch him – there was no time to spare.

Suddenly, as she rounded a bend in the road, she pulled her horse to a halt. There was Royal Mail, calmly grazing on the verge in front of them, nibbling a succulent patch of grass. She grabbed his reins, dismounted, and checked that he was all right. Running her hand down his legs and over his body, everything seemed fine, so thankfully she began to lead him back to the paddock.

Halfway along the lane, she met Tom who was cantering to

Royal Mail mistimed his stride, half-heartedly tried to leap high enough, but failed, crashing into the poles which fell all around him.

meet her. 'Thank goodness you're all right,' he said. 'But that was a stupid thing to do – you might have hurt yourself and your horse as well.'

'I'm sorry, Tom, but I couldn't bear to think of Royal Mail on the motorway and I had to try to save him.'

'Next time, leave it to an experienced rider. But thanks anyway.'

Underneath Tom's rough manner, Karen knew that he was pleased with her. 'How's Jane?' she asked.

'She's suffering from slight concussion and her ankle's hurting her, so two of the girls have carried her to Mrs Brown. She'll probably take Jane to the hospital for an X-ray. At any rate, Jane won't be riding again for a while.'

Karen and Tom had their work cut out taking all the horses back to the stables, removing the tack, rubbing them down, and getting the other ponies ready for the next ride. However, it was enjoyable work, and the time passed quickly.

'Would you like to help me take out the next ride?' Tom asked. 'Just a way of saying thanks for acting so promptly earlier on, and for helping me.'

'Oh yes please,' Karen said, hardly believing her luck.

The end of the summer term soon came, and Karen longed for the holidays when she'd be able to spend even more time at the stables. However, there was one major hurdle to be overcome first – her school report.

Her parents called her into the dining room one evening when she'd come home from looking after Ben. 'This report is the worst one you've ever had. Your exam results were atrocious. What has happened to you? I think it's spending so much time at those riding stables that does it,' said her father, looking very stern.

'They say you've been falling asleep in lessons and take no interest in any school activities. I know you don't much like school, but even so . . .' her mother's despairing voice tailed off.

'You'll never get a job if you don't do well at school,' said her father.

'But Dad, even if I do well at school, job prospects are awful. And you know I've never been much good at lessons. I can't do anything well, except riding. In fact,' she took a deep breath, 'I want to leave school this summer. I'm old enough now, and there doesn't seem much point in me staying on any longer. And if I leave I can at least try to find a job. You never know, there might be something suitable around.'

From the shocked looks on her parents' faces, Karen knew she'd dropped a bombshell. Even though her results hadn't been good, she knew her parents hoped she would stay on, improve, and perhaps even go to college eventually.

'Well, this is a bit of a shock. We'd better think about it for a few days, and maybe you'll have changed your mind by then,' said her father, looking crestfallen.

After her next Saturday afternoon riding lesson, Karen stood rubbing down Silver Birch, who she'd been riding that day. She stared into space, lost in thought, wondering what on earth she was really going to do with her life. Although she wanted nothing more than to become a champion rider, it wasn't that easy to achieve.

'You've been standing there dreaming for the past fifteen minutes. Haven't you got anything else to do? You can come and help me clean some tack if you've finished Silver Birch.' Tom's voice interrupted her thoughts, as she came down to earth suddenly.

As they sat together soaping down the bridles, Tom asked Karen what she'd been thinking about. 'But you needn't tell me if you don't want to,' he said.

She looked at his kind face, his soft brown eyes, and suddenly she knew that she could trust him absolutely. All her troubles came flooding out: her parents; the last term at school when she'd been falling asleep because of her early morning paper round; how she wanted to leave school and get a job but also wanted nothing better than to be with horses all day; how her parents needed the money and she knew they'd be glad of a bit of extra cash each week once she was working.

At the end of it all, she felt relieved that she'd unburdened all her problems. Tom looked thoughtful, then said, 'What you need is a complete change of thought. How about coming out with me tonight? There's a good film on at the cinema in town, or we could just have something to eat somewhere.'

She was astonished. 'You needn't ask me just to cheer me up,' she said. 'I'll be perfectly all right tomorrow.'

'No, it's not just because of that,' he replied, looking a bit embarrassed. 'I've wanted to ask you for ages, but I've never dared. You always seemed so busy, though now I can see why. I would really like to go out with you tonight.'

They met at seven o'clock, had a quick hamburger then went to see the film. Halfway through, Tom took Karen's hand, and when he was seeing her home afterwards he put his arm round her shoulders. The last words he said as she opened the door of her house were, 'Don't worry, Karen. I know something will turn up.'

I only hope he's right, she said to herself, never believing for one moment that he would be.

When Karen arrived at the stables the next day, there was no sign of Tom, but Mrs Brown was waiting for her. 'Will you come into my office, Karen, I'd like a quick word with you,' she asked.

Oh no, thought Karen, what have I done wrong now?

'Sit down there. Now I understand from Tom – ' Karen quickly cursed him, wishing she'd sworn him to secrecy – 'that you're looking for a job. Is that right?'

'Why yes, I am, but . . .'

'No buts, my dear. Just listen to what I've got to say, then you can ask whatever you like. Now, as you probably know, we used to employ another groom here as well as Tom, but Susan left to go and work for a racing stable. I haven't been able to find anyone to replace her, and she was marvellous, a very hard worker and terribly keen. However, I've been watching you and I've realized that you've got a way with horses and have learnt very quickly. I had no idea that you were looking for a job, but if you'd be interested in working here we'd be very pleased to have you. The wages are fair, and we'd give you as much training as you wanted.'

Karen couldn't believe what Mrs Brown was saying.

'No need to tell me your answer immediately,' she continued. 'Think it over and talk to your parents, but I do hope you'll accept.'

Karen went rushing to find Tom. She looked everywhere, finally tracking him down in one of the stables, putting a bridle on a pony. She rushed in and threw her arms round Tom's neck, giving him a giant hug.

'Thank you, thank you so much,' she said.

'Steady on, you'll frighten the pony,' Tom gasped, laughing. 'And anyway, I didn't do anything.'

'Well you must have told Mrs Brown that I was looking for a job, because she's just offered me one here.'

'Congratulations,' said Tom, trying to look surprised. 'It's hard work here, but it's enjoyable, and I get the feeling we're going to make a great team.'

FOR LOVE OF ELIZABETH

Maureen Spurgeon

'ALAS MY POOR, DEAR BET, I cannot see how I may help you.'

A cool, white hand, half covered in a lace mitten, and with rings on every finger patted Elizabeth's fiery cheek.

'I own, I may have commanded a navy, stood firm against foreign kings, brought honours and victories to England, such as those before me would fain have said were theirs!'

'Indeed, Your Majesty.' Elizabeth bowed her head to the Queen whose name she bore.

'But, to change the mind of my friend, and Lord Mayor, Sir John Spencer,' the Queen continued. Her fine auburn head tilted back in a flow of tinkling laughter, showing how gracefully the deep ruff fitted her neck. 'Bet, you must know that is plainly impossible! Your father is a good man, loyal and kind – but there's naught can say he does not possess a will of iron!'

'But Your Majesty . . .' Elizabeth began.

'Yes, I know well!' the Queen nodded, her slippers gliding so silently across the floor that her fur-trimmed skirts hardly swayed at all. 'You love Lord Compton, and he loves you. And you wish to be wed!'

'Yes!' Elizabeth almost shouted. 'Yes, Your Majesty, we do! Whatever my father says!'

'So!' The Queen sat in a high-backed chair, drumming her fingernails on the wooden arm-rests. 'I can see that you have inherited Sir John's determination! Yet, 'tis not a good thing to turn away from a father's love,' she advised, more gently.

'Think on it, Bet.'

'If I could but know why he dislikes Lord Compton,' Elizabeth persisted. 'He is comely, and handsome, and you yourself know how pleasing he is!'

'Yes.' Her Majesty sighed. 'A fine, young nobleman, to be sure. But, there is naught else I can say.' The rich voice began sounding sharp and impatient, a sign that the meeting was nearing its end. 'And, now, Bet, if you please.'

'Y – yes, Your Majesty. I shall ride back to Father's country estate at Canonbury, and – and think on all you have said.'

The lady-in-waiting dutifully opened the oaken door. Her Majesty made quite certain that Elizabeth's footsteps had tapped their way along the landing and down the main staircase, before tossing her head back in great amusement, pressing her hands together. 'Oh, such noises there shall be at Canonbury Tower, anon! Such tempers fly, and tongues sting like lashes of a whip! To think on an obstinate man about to be beaten – how it does my heart good!'

'Kit.' She beckoned to her lady, 'Send for a goblet of best wine and ale-cake. Elizabeth Spencer gives us good reason for celebration!'

The boots that stamped up the staircase from the main hall at Canonbury, were enough to make the kitchen walls shudder, setting the servants' bells clinking faintly.

The servants looked upwards, and then at each other, with Nance, the youngest maid, first to speak. 'I only hope Lady Elizabeth don't throw the silver creamer at the door again. Rolled right beneath the oak settle last time, it had!'

'There'll be no peace till she weds Lord Compton!' Cook predicted wearily. 'My heart fair bleeds for poor Sir John, wanting only the best for his daughter!'

'What's best for her is the man she loves!' Nance responded sharply. 'For all that she's pretty.'

'And young, and clever,' nodded the gardener, clasping his gnarled hands against his apron.

'And,' chimed in the smooth tones of the cellar-keeper, 'daughter of one of the richest men in England!'

Nobody said anything more, each one aware that the cellar-keeper was nearest the truth of Lord Spencer's anger. Their belief grew stronger with each word that thundered through the house.

'You dare to seek audience with the Queen? To go behind my back? By my life . . .'

'Your life!' countered Elizabeth, working herself into a rage. 'Does not my life matter, Father? My life – and my lasting happiness!'

Sir John tugged at his silvery beard, breathing hard, and glaring at Elizabeth, marvelling that such a good-hearted and loving girl could screech like a barn owl.

'John Compton wishes us to be wed, and I have accepted him! Mayhap, he is not so rich as you wish, yet . . .'

'Yet, you deserve so much more, Elizabeth!' Lord Spencer spoke quietly, taking his daughter's hand. 'You are so precious to me. I do not want you to act hastily.'

'I love Lord Compton,' Elizabeth screamed, snatching her hand away, 'and he loves me! And,' she went on, stamping her foot at every word, 'I am to be his wife!'

'Wife, indeed?' Sir John challenged, striding to the door. 'Then see what a fine wife you will make, kept under lock and key.'

'No! Father!' exclaimed Elizabeth, running after him. 'Father, please! Please, listen.'

But the door was being firmly shut, the lock grinding with the turn of a heavy key.

'Nance will bring you food and water!' her father shouted above a torrent of violent sobs. 'Being alone with naught but your thoughts will perchance make you see the folly of all this.'

"Tis not folly!' Elizabeth hammered at the door with her fists. 'I love him, Father! Can you not hear? I love him!'

And, in reply, there was nothing but his heavy tread on the stairs, and the sputtering of candles.

Elizabeth gave a loud wail, more in anger than distress, and marched to the window, her fists clenched at her slim waist. John would be waiting at the grove by Hopping Lane, expecting to hear good news. Had she not said she was to see the Queen, seeking royal help in persuading her father to consent to their marriage? His objections would soon be no more, she had almost promised.

A draught blew in under the casement, and she felt her temper beginning to cool. 'I – I do love my father,' she said firmly, linking her fingers together, and pacing to and fro. 'But, I love John – so dearly.' She pressed a hand to her mouth, determined not to let anyone hear that she was crying.

In the servants' quarters, Nance was receiving strict orders from Lord Spencer, himself.

'And, after you have unlocked the door, serve Lady Elizabeth's food on a platter, and sit outside her room till she has done! Then, lock the door and bring the key back to me!'

'Yes, My Lord.' Nance curtsied low. 'Will there be aught else?'

'Nay.' Lord Spencer was beginning to feel very tired. 'You may go.'

'Yes, My Lord.' Nance curtsied again, and laid the key on a napkin, secretly deciding to pick some late strawberries from the kitchen garden.

'Lady Elizabeth so enjoys strawberries. And, by heaven, she needs some little cheer,' Nance thought as she crept into the kitchen garden later that day.

'Nance!'

She turned her head sharply. Could it be that someone was calling her name? Someone near at hand.

'Nance!'

It was hardly more than a whisper, and a rustling behind the mulberry tree. But enough for her to guess who it was. 'L – Lord Compton!' she gasped, looking all around for any sign that they might be overheard. 'Oh, Lady Elizabeth – she – she can't see you, this eve. Sir John would not give his consent, and th – they quarrelled. We all heard it.'

'And, now?' Lord Compton questioned, his eyes resting on the key.

'If – if you please, I am to take her supper up to her.'

'Then, tell Elizabeth, I already have a priest waiting at the church on my family estate.' He broke off suddenly, a shrill whistling making the hens squawk and fluff their feathers.

'No cause for fear, Sir!' Nance assured him, seeing a cap and crumpled jerkin pass above the hedgerow. ''Tis but one of the wash-house boys, come with the laundry basket. Fair breaks my back to lift, it do.'

The church bell chiming over the fields from Islington reminded Nance of her duties, and she tossed a handful of strawberries into a pap-dish, her heart beating fast as John Compton leaned further forward from behind the mulberry tree.

'Tell her we shall leave the morrow, Nance! As soon as the wash-house lad comes! She will know well my meaning!'

Elizabeth was facing the door as Nance entered, watching carefully to see the key being taken from the lock.

'My – my father's instruction?'

'Yes, My Lady.'

'Then, take the food away, for I'll have none of it!'

'Pardon me, Madam,' Nance insisted boldly, 'but you must refresh yourself! Lord Compton's in the gardens,' she added in a low murmur. 'You've a priest waiting and, he says, prepare to leave by morning, soon as the wash-house boy comes. That's what he said, My Lady,' Nance confirmed, watching Elizabeth turn aside, with only the slightest movement of one slender hand giving any sign that she had heard.

Suddenly, Elizabeth whirled around, setting her skirts billowing against her ankles. 'And, how long can my father keep me here, imprisoned in such a dull chamber?' she shouted, in a rage that belied the glow of triumph in her eyes. 'There shall be flowers from the garden, rose-water on the table, and clean linen in every corner!'

Already, she was beginning to tug at the heavy drapes around her bed, sending a cloud of dust rising to the wooden beams overhead. 'Nance!' she called softly. 'How would you like to attend me at my wedding, anon?'

Below, Sir John Spencer sucked at the stem of his new pipe and chuckled to himself. As long as Elizabeth's spirit thrived, it was all to the good. Her tempers fell as quickly as they flamed. When she had wearied of it all, she would turn again into her sweet ways. Then he would dry her young tears, and she would understand that he wanted nothing more than to be sure of her happiness.

Next morning dawned bright, but a mite chilly, Nance noted, glad of an excuse for hands that trembled just a little as they pulled a big wicker basket across the flagstones.

''Tis glad I am that you will be carrying that up to Lady Elizabeth's chamber, after all her loud commands on wanting clean linen,' Cook remarked, threading meat on a spit. 'Lor, as if we cannot find enough to do!'

A loud, tuneless whistling shrilled from the top of the kitchen steps, outside.

'N – no matter.' Nance answered hastily. 'I – I shall seek the help of the wash-house boy.'

Cook raised her eyes to see a cap, that might have been any colour, flopping down over the lad's face, his bare feet crunching on the cinder path.

'Hasten, then, else he will shirk the duty. And then, Lady Elizabeth will have still more complaint!' Then, shaking her white head, she closed the door, and shuffled back to the warmth and peace of her kitchen.

'My Lady Elizabeth, pray – do be quick!' Nance was saying at the same moment, upstairs. 'Oh, how often have I wished these linen baskets to be smaller, until this day.'

'Hush, good Nance.' Elizabeth ordered quietly, her voice becoming muffled by the satins and brocades crumpled around her, inside the great basket. ''Tis comfortable enough to be taken but a short journey, I vow.'

'And how glad I am that you were never heavy and plump, my lovely Elizabeth,' said Lord Compton, feeling his unshaven chin. 'But, oh what pain it is to become a beardless youth once more! Come, my dearest.'

Nance took care to make the key grate loudly in the lock, before lifting one handle of the basket. As they crept past Sir John's chambers, she fleetingly pitied him. There had always been such love between this father and daughter. If only they had not been so alike.

But, the time had come when Elizabeth could think only of freeing herself from him. Gladly she leapt on to the horse which Lord Compton held in the quiet copse nearby, ready to take her and Nance to his coaching house. And from there, to a country church – and her wedding.

A year passed so swiftly, Nance would often imagine herself still at Canonbury Tower but delighting in the cool, country air, away from the city she had always known. 'But, then, one year past, and you were yet to be born,' she smiled at the sleeping baby in her arms. 'Oh, what a dear poppet you are, and how My Lord and Lady adore you!'

For an instant, the baby pouted in his sleep, showing the lines of his firm chin.

'That be the chin of a Spencer,' Nance pronounced. 'Of Lady Elizabeth and good Sir John.'

Her voice trailed away, and she gazed into the distance, half expecting to see Sir John come striding across the lawns, his satin doublet gleaming in the sun as he reached out his arms to take his first grandson. Yet, from all that she knew, it could never be.

She began rocking the child, looking around at the great, stone staircase, leading up to the magnificent archway and the fine windows that stretched above. Who would have thought that some day she would be so near to a queen?

'Young Nance seems to make a fine nurse-maid,' Her Majesty observed with a regal smile. 'And, he is a comely child, to be sure. A most noble heir to you, my Lord Compton!'

'You – you are most kind, Your Majesty.' He bowed slightly, holding his wife's hand. 'We – Elizabeth and I – could not be happier.'

'Yes.' The auburn head nodded. 'That I do know, from everyone at Court who tells me how well you love each other.' She tapped her fan against her chin, eyeing Elizabeth wisely. 'Sir John Spencer has remarked upon it, so I have heard.'

'Yet, he will not visit us!' Elizabeth cried passionately. 'Nor know me as John's wife, by allowing us to call at Canonbury, my favourite home!'

'You won a battle over him,' the Queen reminded her. 'Men cannot bear to be wronged, nor yet by a woman, nor yet if she is proven right!'

She clasped a jewelled thumb around the rows of pearls hanging from her neck, her head lifted high. 'Yet, must he be beaten again. Oh, foolish man.'

'Come, Bet,' she beamed, tilting the Spencer chin towards

her. 'We must plan a christening, anon! I trow, your son shall make me a proud godmother!'

Sir John was still a fine gentleman, the Queen considered, as he took her arm to accompany her to the royal chapel. But, these days, his head sagged on his shoulders, his eyes no longer bright and alert, even though he spoke merrily.

'So gracious of Your Majesty to ask that I be godfather at this christening. I am indeed pleased to accept your invitation!'

'Marry, 'tis my pleasure, Sir John! If I should be godmother, who could be godfather, when my young friends have no family to bring blessings upon their only child!'

'Tragic, tragic.' Sir John mumbled into his beard, but whether from disinterest or thought for Elizabeth, the Queen could not tell.

'They await in the antechamber, just here,' she announced, pulling aside a velvet curtain. 'Perchance you know them.'

'Father!' exclaimed Elizabeth, tears springing to her eyes at the sight of Sir John standing quite still in the doorway. 'Oh, my dear, dear Father. I – I am so sorry.' She flung her arms around his neck, planting delighted kisses on both cheeks.

'Elizabeth. You – you cannot know how you distressed me. Nor yet, how I have missed you.'

'We wished to see you, Father, many times! Yet, you would not receive us, nor send word. Mayhap then you would have known the glad news on the birth of your grandchild! Does he not look like you?' She lifted the baby from his crib, cradling him carefully into her father's waiting arms.

'Come, Sir John. 'Tis no time for silent weeping,' the Queen instructed kindly. 'Are you not a grandfather? Aye, and a godfather, too? And, you have a fine son who has made Bet the happiest wife in my kingdom.'

'A son.' Sir John turned his gaze to the young man who

stood beside his daughter. 'As Lord Mayor, I could have sent you from all merchants' houses, even from Court. You may have lost everything. Yet, all that you risked – for love of Elizabeth.'

Tenderly, he handed the cooing baby back to Elizabeth, and raised a hand towards her husband. 'Come,' he invited, all sadness forgotten. 'We have much to talk about.'

Elizabeth, holding her son closely, watched them walk together out into the corridor, quite forgetting that the Queen was with her, until a gurgle of laughter bubbled into a roar.

'So, my dear Bet, we have won through, between us!'

'Y – yes, indeed, Your Majesty.' Elizabeth smiled, a quiet contentment stirring within her. 'All thanks, from the very bottom of my heart.'

'Yet, was it not you who went into battle, Bet? You, with all the wisdom, all the courage, all the sweet justice of Diana, daughter of the mighty god, Jupiter. How many times did her womanly skills succeed where men failed?'

She began laughing again, clapping her hands lightly, and making the sounds of happiness fill the little chamber.

Elizabeth, holding her son closely, watched her father and husband walk together out into the corridor, quite forgetting that the Queen was with her.

SOMETHING MORE THAN A SPRARSI

Joyce Wilson

FROM SHAMMY'S GROYNE TO TIN KETTLE BAY, Alan was the youngest blacksander working the Brighton beach. It had been a long hot summer, bringing crowds from London and its suburbs to the coast. And, at the end of each day, the trippers had left, and lost, many small treasures which were covered by the tides. Now in the early light of the November mornings the blacksanders reaped their harvest. Poised at the water's edge they watched as the sea pulled back from the grey stones. Then, at the glint of metal – a ring or a coin – they would jump, snatch, and turn, before the returning surge of the sea could snatch at them.

Beneath the shifting pebbles was treasure – for those with the patience to wait for the signs. Treasure that since the great storms of '66, had included long-lost gold sovereigns, making this a valuable hunting ground. Alan worked barefoot, venturing close to the waves while the others scrambled in heavy wellingtons. He laughed if a wave caught him, while the others would have cursed.

'That shoeless idiot,' they called him. And with his shock of black hair, his great vague blue eyes and his quiet, infuriating smile he had perhaps the look of a wise fool. It was as if he was laughing in the world's face, defying the sea as he did – defying it to yield its stolen ware to someone who knew best how to value it.

But Alan did not need to do this for profit. He made what money was necessary from the window-cleaning round he had bought from the old man. The others, there for the living such as it was, hugged their finds to themselves. Alan had no reason to be so close. They watched him sometimes, narrow-eyed, as if he would lead them to something better, some once and for all legendary treasure. A find that would put them in the papers, or on TV, and make their fortune.

'You'll come up with trouble on that beach one day,' the old man warned him. 'You'll come up with something more than a sprarsi one morning. And they'll be watching for you, boy.'

A 'sprarsi' was the old man's slang word for the now rare silver sixpence. Alan had found one once, yellowed by the sea water and blurred by the constant friction of the stones. He had sold it to a coin specialist in the town's antique market one Saturday morning.

'I don't want trouble,' he assured the old man. 'I'm a nice person.'

But the old man's words were not so far from the truth. And the day Alan came up with something more – something much more – than a 'sprarsi' was the day he found Josie.

He was out even earlier than usual. It was a bright winter morning, with a full gale blowing up from the South East and a promising sea. He leapt free from a large wave that would have dragged a slower man down, and, dripping with water, examined a small Victorian ring, set with amethysts in soft gold. He leaned for a moment against a large rowing boat. It was one of the several boats left by summer sailors on that stretch of the beach – a thirty-footer, clinker-built, and ready for any sea. From somewhere up in the bows, Alan heard a cough. It was cut short, as if hastily suppressed. Unmistakeably a girl's cough, yet deep – an unwell sound.

'You all right in there?' Alan called.

There was a short silence, then a very young voice with an accent he thought he knew. Pure Brum, from the heart of

England – and belligerent with it. 'What's it to you?'

Alan waited, shrugging mentally at the rebuff. Whoever she was, he was not going to drag her from her hiding place. She would have to make up her own mind. But that was a bad cough, and he waited, just in case.

From the marauding bands of females that hit the town in the summer from all parts of the country, Alan had expected something very different from the voice. The girl, who at last crawled over the side of the boat, was not more than sixteen, with soft frightened eyes to belie the strong set of the chin. Long fair hair, darkened by spray, clung round her thin neck and shoulders. She fell rather than jumped to Alan's feet, still clutching a large cardboard folder to her long, dark green velvet coat.

'Well, what a lovely bit of seaweed!' Alan said.

The girl coughed.

'You're not well, girl,' he tried again. 'Not run away from the hospital, have you?'

'Do you mind? I ran away from me ma, that's all.'

'Oh, a missing person.'

'Yes. I went missing. What's it to you?'

'What's your name?' He gave her question for question.

'Same as me mam's, and me gran's, and you can work that out and come up with some more of me story.'

'I mean your first name.' It seemed best to ignore the little undertone of bitterness in her replies.

'Josie.'

He looked round the beach. Now that he had given up the treasure hunt for the day, the other blacksanders had no interest in him. 'Well, Josie,' he put out a hand to help her to her feet. 'Either I get the police to you, or you're coming back with me. No – nothing to be scared of. The old man and Duchess are there.'

'You're a beachcomber.' The green eyes were suspicious.

The girl was clutching a large cardboard folder to her long dark green velvet coat.

'No. A blacksander. The sea washes up any old rubbish for them. We have to use our eyes. The stuff we're after is hidden more often than not.'

He tucked the amethyst ring into a pocket. Josie seemed not to notice. She was devouring the boats with her eyes, reluctant to move. She touched the wooden boat lovingly. 'Who is this Duchess when she's at home?'

'She *is* home, she and the old man. It's his place. I live there. Have done for years. Duchess is his dog.' With that he turned and began to walk up the beach. Josie trudged after him, the cardboard folder hugged close.

'I'll take that,' he offered as they reached the seawall.

'I came to draw the boats,' she shook her head. 'It's all I have.'

'Aren't there any boats in Brum? That's where you're from, I take it.' She nodded. 'You've got the canal, then.'

'It's not the sea,' she said. As if that closed the subject.

Alan and the old man lived in a rambling basement in a high terraced house on the corner of a side street. Alan and Josie went through a side gate, skirted the long blank brick wall of the house itself, down a stone step or two, and into a small, wintery garden. The back door was open, a glimpse of a kitchen beyond.

And Duchess, a white bull terrier, all thumping tail and rolling pink eyes, was there to greet them. While she jumped up at Josie, an old man stood in contrasting silence in the kitchen, teapot in hand. Alan turned to him, and found the small bright blue eyes in the weather-beaten face staring hard at the newcomer. He sensed an objection.

'She's only come for a cup of tea and to get warm before we ring her mum,' he said.

Maintaining the disapproving silence, the old man set out a neat tray and carried it into the room beyond the kitchen.

There, Josie sat at a big old-fashioned round table, a rug round her shoulders, a fierce oil stove pulled up beside her. The old man poured the tea. Alan, changing into his working jeans in the kitchen, called through to them that he had the windows in two arcades to clean before nine, or he'd lose his weekly contracts with the shops involved.

'You're not leaving me here, are you?' Josie called back.

'He'll have to go out anyway, to phone your people, so what's the difference?' It was the old man's first words, and his voice was gruff but gentle.

Alan came through into the living room. 'Duchess will look after you. I'll come back the moment I've got through to your place.'

'Mum won't go to work with me missing. We had a bad scene. And there's no phone at home.'

'What's the betting then that she'll go to work, where she knows you can reach her? I wouldn't be surprised if you know the number by heart?'

Josie ignored this, and he knew his guess was right.

'She doesn't care,' Josie said.

'Do you know who it is who gets all the kids back who go missing? Who tells the papers? Gets the police? Waits up all night till they're home again? All those mums who don't care, that's who,' the old man told her.

She glared at him across the teacups. 'I'm not going back. I came for the sea. I want to be an art student.'

'And why not,' Alan patted her on the head. 'Got all your O levels, have you? We'll go straight round to the College for Knowledge in the morning.'

When Alan had gone, the telephone number tucked in a top pocket of his jacket, the old man pulled a deep armchair into the centre of the room close to the fire. Josie crept into it, thanking him, and closed her eyes, opening them again in surprise as he returned from the kitchen later with a hot-water bottle, and a rug. For an hour she slept fitfully, aware of his quiet, deft movements as he cleared the table and went about his kitchen routine. Duchess lay heavily at her feet, breathing with a gentle, reassuring snore of a sigh every few minutes. After an hour, perhaps longer, the old man came in with a bowl of soup. She drank it at once, and slept again. This time she did not stir until he began to sort the ashes in the open grate.

She opened her eyes as he struck a match, and the twirls of old newspaper he had laid with the wood and coal began to burn. She watched him bellow the small flames into large tongues of fire with his own breath.

'Has Alan always lived with you?' she asked him at last, and was surprised at his willingness to answer.

He told her that when his parents were alive Alan had been at the grammar school and helped with the window-cleaning round in the school holidays. Then came the accident. Both mother and father killed in a car crash. Alan had inherited a little money, and when he heard that the old man was giving up his round, he bought it from him. And moved in.

'Who looks after you both?'

'I do. Better than a woman round our necks.'

'And why is Duchess called Duchess?'

'You're all questions, aren't you. Ask Alan. He named her. He's a clever boy, could have gone to University. The white Duchess, he calls her. From a play he saw once at school.'

She dozed off then, and woke again to find the old man standing at the table, staring closely at the contents of her folder – which he had obviously opened thinking she would sleep on. The fire burned steadily, and the room was warm. All her belligerence lulled away, she asked him what time it was.

'Time for Alan to be home in an hour. He came back, but you were sleeping so deep we didn't have the heart to wake you. He says he's phoned your mum, and told her we've found you. How did you know all this about the sea, and boats?'

'I'm glad Mum knows I'm here. What did she say?'

'She's glad, of course. And Alan is fixing you up with a hostel – only for a night. There's not much room here.'

She nodded. 'I've never been to the sea before. But I've seen films. Moby Dick. And I go to the museum at home.'

'Then you ought to go back, and go there again. Back to school too.'

She got up and asked if she could wash. The little outside loo was a bright, clean blue and white, and Duchess made her giggle, trying to prise open the door before she came out. A light rain had begun to fall, and she skipped back into the kitchen from the garden, to find the old man putting the kettle on again.

'Keep those muddy boots off my clean deck,' he told her, but his tone was kindly enough. 'So you were at sea, before you cleaned windows?' she asked. 'I was many places in my time. But come with me. I'll show you whether I was at sea, girl.'

Past the living room was a long dark corridor that led to the front section of the basement flat. She guessed that the rooms in that part looked on to the street. Duchess ran ahead, sensing new territory for the long stretch of the evening that lay before them. Stopping first to collect her folder of drawings and paper, Josie followed, and was in time to watch the old man light two enormous hanging lamps that must once have swayed and creaked in the bowels of some ancient ship. The brass corners of a solid, sea-chest glinted as the lights reached the far corners of the room.

Josie hesitated in the doorway, and Duchess came back to her, tail wagging. She stepped into the room then, and in her memories of the day many years later she described the moment 'as if she had stepped into her own dreams.'

The old man's room was a memorial to the past, and to the

sea. It was hung with oil paintings of frigates in everything from a storm to a sunset. There were smaller pictures embroidered in wools of many, faded colours, showing life on board ship, and sewn by the sailors themselves, the old man told her. The shelves each side of the fireplace were stacked with ships in bottles, model ships fashioned by masters, rough little boats hewn for children's toys. Priceless models and worthless toys were all dusted and polished, dancing on their shelves as if breasting the waves.

Sinking into one of the large easy chairs that stood like sentinels each side of the grate, the old man began to talk of his life as a boy at sea. And as he talked the girl began to draw. They had not moved when Alan found them an hour later on his return.

'Your mum said she knew you'd be back because you've left a lot of your drawings. And I begin to see what she means,' Alan said as Josie went on working, raising her head only to smile briefly in his direction. He waved a piece of paper. 'And here's the number where you can ring her tonight, at her friend's place she said. She wants you home, tomorrow, Josie. And I said you'd be there.'

'Is she all right?' Josie put down her drawing.

'She was crying a bit at first, I could tell. Then she got a bit nasty, till I told her we'd find a hostel for you for the night. Then she said to say she's sorry for the row.'

'Me too,' Josie said. She got up and stretched, then closed the folder of her drawings. 'Thank you,' she turned to the old man.

'There's fish and chips in the next room,' Alan said. 'And something more.'

By her plate was a small black box. While the others watched, she opened it slowly, and gasped. Nestling in a small slit of white velvet, for all the world as if it had come straight from a jeweller's shop, was the amethyst ring.

'I found you both on the same morning. I reckon you belong together,' Alan said.

'How can I thank you?' Josie's eyes sparkled as she tried the ring. 'It's perfect.'

'Just be a good girl, and go home tomorrow – and come back here to art school when you can.'

That night they walked, holding hands, along the seafront until they came to the hostel where Josie was to stay. Next day, early, Alan drove up to the door in a small van slung with ladders and buckets, and Josie ran down the hostel steps smiling. She ducked into the passenger seat, still clutching her cardboard folder.

'You'll need to bring that back with you when you come for your college interviews,' Alan said.

'Pigs may fly.'

'And before that there's the summer. The boats are all painted fresh new colours. You'll have to come back for that too.'

They reached the railway station in minutes. Alan thrust some money into Josie's hand. 'You can pay me back out of your student grant,' he grinned. 'See you next summer?'

She nodded. 'Don't get out, Alan. You're busy. And I hate goodbyes. Thank you for everything. I'll write to you.'

'You're a nice girl, Josie. I'm glad you hid in that boat.'

'So am I,' Josie said.

ON WINGS OF LOVE

Toni Cornford

'DOMINIC, I'M SCARED,' I WHISPERED. 'I didn't know I'd feel like this.'

The dark ribbon of road stretched endlessly ahead of us.

'Do you want to go back?' Dominic asked evenly. 'If you do, I'll take you.'

I smiled at him in the dim light as the familiar rush of love filled me. And I did love Dominic – loved him with all my heart. I knew he loved me, too. When we'd made our plans he'd kept asking me if I was sure.

Yes, I was sure. Sure that I loved him, sure that I wanted to be with him, and sure that running away was our only answer.

'No, I don't want to go back,' I told him softly.

He reached out and squeezed my hand. 'Then don't worry, my darling,' he said. 'I'll look after you from now on. I love you, Elsa.'

His words reassured me, calmed me. Nothing could go wrong, not while I had Dominic to protect me. I leaned back and closed my eyes. In a few hours time my mother would go into my bedroom to wake me, a cup of coffee in her hand and a smile on her face. She'd announce what a lovely day it was, and then she'd see my bed hadn't been slept in and she'd find the note I'd left.

Then I pictured her running to the dining room where my father'd be having an early breakfast, and stifling her tears while he read my note. As he controlled the shock I knew he'd feel, he'd put his arm around my mother's shoulders and tell her everything would be all right.

Part of me rejoiced at the scene – it served them right! But another part of me shared their despair.

'When will we get to Bonn?' I asked Dominic.

'In about two hours,' he replied. 'Are you tired?'

'No,' I shook my head. 'Where are we going to stay?'

Suddenly the uncertainty of our future posed problems I hadn't considered before. I'd only thought of the next few days, a week at the most. Now the time ahead became months, even years.

'We'll find a small boarding house,' Dominic told me. 'Somewhere cheap, until we can get an apartment of our own.'

An apartment of our own. It sounded so permanent, and a little frightening. I'd only known life with my parents, safe in the house I'd grown up in. Now I felt as though I'd been snatched from that security and plummetted into an alien world.

Once again the scene between my parents came into my mind. When the initial shock had worn off what would they do? My mother would cry softly to herself, leaving all the decision making to my father, and he'd probably call the police.

'They'll never find us where we're going,' Dominic said in answer to my frantic question. 'Remember why we chose Bonn – it's the last place they'll look.'

Yes, I thought, they'd never think of searching for us in Bonn, because Bonn was where the university was – the university my parents had chosen for me. The stupid thing was, I wanted to go there, but on my terms, not my parents. And that had been the start of the argument.

'You'll have to work hard, Elsa,' my father had said firmly. 'There'll be no wasting your opportunities with parties and enjoying yourself now. There'll be time enough for that when your degree is hanging on the wall.'

'I know all that,' I told him. 'But I don't intend giving up *every*thing to study.'

My mother had looked at me carefully then sighed heavily. 'I suppose you mean that boy,' she said with a disdainful sniff. 'Really, Elsa. After all your father and I have done for you, surely you don't mean to throw it all away on some *boy*.'

'No, I don't,' I retorted sharply. 'And his name's Dominic!'

'Elsa. Elsa,' my father coaxed. 'You're on the brink of your future, my child. You haven't time for boyfriends now. In a few years . . .'

'What's wrong with now?' I flared. 'And what's wrong with Dominic?'

My parents glanced at each other. 'Nothing at all,' my father said with a shrug. 'We only want the best for you, Elsa.'

'And you don't think he *is* the best.' I said bitterly. 'Just because he's not a doctor or a lawyer, and just because his parents aren't rich and live in a big house. Well that's not everything. Dominic's a wonderful person, only you can't be bothered to get to know him, can you?'

The argument had raged until I'd rushed up to my bedroom in tears and locked myself in.

If only my parents could have climbed down from their pedestal of pride, but they'd worked hard to make our lives good and they wanted the best for me. As I glanced sideways at Dominic's handsome profile, I wished they'd understand that I'd already got the best.

We reached the outskirts of Bonn just as daylight was breaking. Dominic stopped the car at a small restaurant that was just opening.

'Good morning,' the proprietor called to us. 'You look exhausted. Have you travelled far?'

'Quite a way,' Dominic replied. 'Are we too early for breakfast?'

163

'Not at all,' the man said with a smile.

We followed him into the warm restaurant and enjoyed the hot coffee he put in front of us while he cooked our breakfast. After we'd eaten, he joined us for another coffee and we began to talk. Dominic told him we'd just got married and were moving to Bonn for me to go to the university.

The proprietor showed great interest in our story and when Dominic asked if he knew of anywhere we could stay for a few days he gave us an address right in the town centre. 'My sister,' he explained. 'She has a rooming house. Nothing fancy, but clean.'

When we arrived at the address, Frau Engler was waiting for us. She ushered us in and up to a first-floor room. 'Settle in, then come down to the kitchen for coffee,' she told us.

There were six other boarders, most of them students, and all of them friendly. But we had to be careful. We couldn't risk anyone finding out we were runaways, and that the police might possibly be looking for us.

During the afternoon we went on a tour of Bonn. Dominic bought all the papers he could get and we started our search for an apartment. We scoured the vacancies section, but everywhere seemed far too expensive for us. We didn't even go to look at any of them.

When I woke up next morning, it took a few seconds for me to remember where I was. Then I quietly got out of bed and went to the window.

Outside, the sun cast a golden-brown glow on the old buildings, making the windows sparkle and the streets look warm. Bonn was certainly a beautiful city. And then I remembered why Dominic and I were there.

My heart sank a little as I turned back into the room. Oh, why did it have to be this way? Why couldn't my parents understand the way I felt about Dominic?

Once again we spent the day getting to know the city. We even went to see a few apartments, but they were all far too expensive for us. Deep down I began to wonder if we'd rushed into this too quickly. Maybe if we'd waited a little longer, and saved a little more money . . .

I kept my anxious thoughts from Dominic. He was trying so hard, and I knew how worried he was. Yet my doubts and fears grew, and later that night, as I was getting ready for bed, I couldn't hide them any longer.

As I pulled my nightdress over my head, I kept wishing that when I opened my eyes I'd be looking around at my bedroom at home. But it was Frau Engler's bedroom I saw, Frau Engler's furniture, Frau Engler's everything!

Suddenly I burst into heartbreaking tears, and that was how Dominic found me. 'Darling, what is it?' he asked as he cradled me in his arms.

'I'd dreamed about it being so different for us, Dominic,' I sobbed. 'If only my parents weren't so stubborn. They've pushed us into this!'

'Elsa,' he whispered. 'I know how you feel, but I'll look after you, I promise. We'll manage somehow.' He held me close as my tears subsided, then he stroked my hair.

'Dominic,' I ventured carefully. 'Would you be cross if I rang them tomorrow?'

He looked down at me and smiled. 'Of course not.'

'I just want them to know I'm all right,' I said. 'They worry, and . . .'

'You ring them,' Dominic said firmly.

Next morning I was up early and went for a long walk before breakfast. What was I going to say to my father? How could I even start the conversation. He'd be angry, furious. He'd shout, maybe even call me names. One thing I knew for sure – he wouldn't understand.

Suddenly, I burst into heartbreaking tears and that was how Dominic found me.

As soon as breakfast was over, Dominic took me out to the phone box. He pressed some coins into my hand and stood with his arm around me as I dialled the number. I was so scared, I was sure I wouldn't be able to say a word.

'Hello, Daddy,' I stammered when I heard his voice. 'It's me – Elsa.'

There was a brief pause, then my father's voice came back, slightly breathless and jerky. 'Oh, my Elsa, where are you?' he asked. 'Are you all right?'

'I'm fine,' I assured him, forcing myself to sound normal and not to betray my sudden pang of homesickness. 'There's no need to worry. I just phoned to let you know we're safe . . .'

'Elsa, come home.' My father's voice cut off the rest of my sentence, and his words had a desperate note to them. 'Darling, don't leave your mother and me like this – we love you so much. We've talked, Elsa, we were wrong.'

'Daddy, please . . .'

'No! Don't ring off – listen to me first.'

I could hardly believe this was my stern, upright father speaking. All of a sudden he wasn't the strong person I knew any more. He was vulnerable, and he sounded as frightened as me. 'Elsa, I was too hard on you – expected too much. You've always been my little girl, but I couldn't understand you'd grown up.'

The tears were running freely down my cheeks and I leaned against Dominic for support.

'Elsa, are you there?'

'Yes, Daddy, I'm here,' I whispered.

'Elsa, we'll talk things over,' he went on. 'And we'll get to know Dominic, too. We've never given him a chance, and if you love him enough to run away with him, he must be very special to you.'

'He is, Daddy.' I said quickly. Then I looked at Dominic. He kissed me gently on the lips then he nodded. 'Daddy, I miss you very much, so . . . so we'll be home by tonight, and . . . and I'm so sorry.'

On the way back to the boarding house I didn't know if I was happy or sad. 'Dominic, do you hate me?' I asked him.

'No, of course I don't,' he said. 'I love you, and whatever you want to do is all right by me.' He stopped and turned me to face him. 'In fact I'm glad in a way, Elsa. I don't think either of us are really ready for this yet, do you?'

As our lips met, I knew Dominic was right. We'd run away more as a protest than a serious bid for freedom, and now we were going back, back to carry on our lives as we'd originally planned. Only this time my parents would be on our side, and that is all I'd ever wanted.

STRANGER FROM THE PAST

Maureen Spurgeon

LORI STOOD WATCHING BLAKE DEACON tinkering with his new racing bike, and wondered, not for the first time, how someone could change so much.

It wasn't just that he seemed so bad-tempered these days, she argued. Nobody had ever described Blake as mild-mannered, from the first day his family came to live on Borne Island. Lori still had a tiny scar on her thumb where he'd bitten into her for grabbing the last yellow crayon in the kindergarten at Queenstown School. They'd both been teased about it for years afterwards.

And, how about the time he'd pushed those two bullies from Port Della into the bay, after they'd threatened to wreck their beach party? She could almost see the enormous splashes again, with everyone cheering and clapping, and Blake trying hard not to look smug as he put the first disc on the portable turntable borrowed from her dad.

Lori hadn't realized what a perfect time it had been – not until she'd been left with only the photographs pasted in her album. Photographs of picnics, parties, threading fairy lights around the trees on Christmas Eve – always with Blake. Always smiling. Always happy.

She didn't notice the tinkering noises had stopped, until Blake gave a muffled groan, and kicked the ground with annoyance.

'Need some help, Blake?' Lori thought she might as well offer, even though she guessed what he'd say.

'No! I don't! But I sure wouldn't mind if you went somewhere else and left me in peace.'

'Somewhere else?' Lori repeated with spirit. 'I live here, next door to you, remember?'

'Some chance I've got to forget it.'

Lori changed her tactics. 'Look, Blake,' she began, more gently. 'I don't ever mean to upset you.'

Blake's response was to scowl bitterly, which Lori considered to be a bit better than ignoring her completely, so she carried on. 'We – you know, the usual gang – we think you've been overdoing things since you started law school at Jedson City. And, seeing as there's a festival and barbecue come Saturday. . . .'

'Aw, knock it off!' He threw down a fierce-looking lever with such force that it bounced on the path with a loud clang. 'How many times do I have to tell you? I'm not interested in discos, barbecues, or anything else you and your stupid school-chums have got lined up.'

Lori opened her mouth to protest, but Blake's shouting would have drowned the twice-weekly aircraft coming in to land.

'I'm past all that kids' stuff – understand? What would the other guys in my grade think if they ever got to hear I'd been fooling around in a – a comic hat, eating coconut slices on sticks? Besides,' he continued, his voice dropping a little, 'the whole thing's a waste of time. And time's something I can't afford to waste.'

'Pity you don't look happier about it, then,' Lori retorted sharply, and had the satisfaction of seeing Blake's wide mouth gaping open as she marched towards the patio door.

It was only when she was inside the cool kitchen, pressing an icepack against her burning forehead, that she recalled how wise and sort of grown-up he'd sounded.

Perhaps that was the trouble. Her dad had warned him he'd

have to take life a bit more seriously once he started studying for a position in his father's business agency.

Lori sighed heavily, and started to go upstairs, thinking she might get the photo album down from the top shelf of her bookcase, just to remind herself of Blake's once-smiling face, and the way his eyes lit up with fun. That was in the days before his black hair was neatly parted and combed flat. Trouble was, Lori admitted, yesterday's memories only made you feel worse about today.

She began wishing she could say something like that to really impress Blake, when the shrill call of the telephone broke into her thoughts.

'Hi – Lori? It was her friend, Carla. 'Listen – okay if we start off for the festival a bit earlier tomorrow? There's going to be a whole lot happening.'

'I – I don't know . . .' Lori hesitated. 'Don't reckon I'm too keen on going. . . .'

'Okay, so Blake's still giving you the cold shoulder. But why worry about him when there'll be plenty of guys coming over from the big towns, like St Rosa and Martinas? Better not be late, now.'

'So,' Lori muttered brokenly, putting down the receiver, 'here's where I carry on pretending I don't mind being on my own.' Her throat began feeling very dry and tight. Nobody guessed how tough it was, always thinking about someone who just didn't care.

Carla seemed determined to see Lori enjoying everything, from the pageant parades, to the folk dancing and the steel band competition – even the model boat racing in the lagoon, where girls threw lotus flowers to float into the sea.

'To think, girls used to do this hundreds of years ago, as love tokens for their fisher-boy sweethearts,' Carla said, giving a long, dreamy sigh. 'The further the flower floated, the stronger

'Girls used to throw flowers into the lagoon hundreds of years ago, as love tokens for their fisher-boy sweethearts,' Carla said, giving a long, dreamy sigh.

172

their love would grow. Don't you think it's romantic, Lori?'

She gave Lori an impatient nudge. 'Throw your flower into the water, and make a wish. Why else do you think we came up here?'

'A – a wish?' Lori echoed, blinking hard so that she wouldn't see Blake's face looking up at her through the ripples on the water. 'Guess I – I don't really know what to wish for.'

Carla watched her tossing away the lotus flower without looking to see whether it did float, or even where it landed. 'See here, Lori,' she said firmly. 'Reckon I know how you're still carrying a torch for Blake. But, he's a different person, now. So all you can do is put him right out of your mind. Then maybe he'll come round.'

And Carla was right, Lori told herself fiercely. Hadn't she said the same thing – to her own reflection in the wardrobe mirror – hundreds of times?'

Carla was leading her towards a cluster of little stalls and booths set in a leafy hollow of the wide bay, where the thick giant ferns bent to give shelter from the sea breezes. 'Look – the Condi women have travelled here from the north of the island,' she whooped excitedly. 'Remember those gorgeous bangles we bought last year, when they gave us some good luck charms?'

'Haven't had much luck so far,' Lori protested. But Carla was already hurrying up to one of the women who was coming forward to greet them, the long, wispy fringe of her silk skirt lifting just enough to show her tiny, bare feet.

'I tell your fortunes?' she invited. The pearl beads woven around her black hair glimmered softly in the sunshine, matched only by the whiteness of her teeth as she smiled. 'You,' she said to Lori, reaching out a dusky hand, 'are much unhappy. You lose a friend, yes?'

Her fingers traced the lines on Lori's palm, and her bone bracelets clattered quietly. 'But, soon – very soon – a tall, dark stranger will appear. Then, happiness will come once more.'

'Hey, how about that?' breathed Carla, giving Lori a friendly push. 'I wouldn't mind a tall, dark stranger, myself!'

'Perhaps. But you share your friend's happiness, first,' the woman explained, quietly smiling at the disbelief shown in Lori's face. 'Women of the Condi tribe are never wrong. Never.'

'I just don't believe it.' Lori kept saying, all the time she and Carla were strolling around, buying things like herb-tea sachets and fancy hair combs from an assortment of wicker baskets and bamboo trays.

'Besides,' she went on, almost under her breath. 'I don't even want a tall, dark stranger. I only want to be friends with Blake, again.'

'Seems like the Condi woman was right, anyhow.' Carla persisted. 'Seen who's coming this way – and looking straight at you?'

'Hi, there,' grinned the boy – tall, dark and handsome, sure enough. 'Your name Lori Mason? I've been looking all over for you.'

'No kidding?' Lori didn't know what else she could say.

'Sure. Fact is, we're having a disco party on the beach later on, to raise funds for the island hospital. Mr Prescott here said you could get some records from a guy called Blake Deacon.'

'Don't mind, do you, Lori?' Mr Prescott asked anxiously. 'See, I recollected, awhile back you and Blake putting on a family type of show.'

That's in the past, she wanted to scream. But, how can I forget, when folks keep reminding me of everything Blake and I did together? So much for the Condi woman's tall, dark stranger, too. She never did believe in fortune-tellers, anyway.

'Okay, Mr Prescott,' Lori said, sounding quite calm. 'I – I'll go and see Blake. Even if he does bite my head off!' she added, when she was sure nobody would hear.

He was outside the front porch when she got back, wiping

his hands on a rag, and eyeing the racing bike propped up against the fence with morose satisfaction.

'Blake,' she said timidly, 'mind if I borrow some records for a disco party tonight? It's for hospital funds.'

'Okay, okay! Skip the long explanations! Just take what you want out of the woodshed, and put them back when you've finished.'

A few months ago, Lori couldn't help thinking, Blake would have helped to sort out the whole collection, given a hand to carry them back to the beach. This time, she was having to struggle along in the hot sun, wondering whether she could borrow a shopping trolley from the drug store, and trying to juggle the pile of records so that she could see who was coming towards her.

'Hey! Hey, that you, Lori? It's me, Sam Huggett, you know? Jim Prescott's buddy. One of the men from Mr Logan's plantation.'

'Sure, I know you, Mr Huggett.' Lori put the records down on a handy stone slab by the roadway. 'Something wrong?'

Sam tugged at Lori's arm, pulling her across the long grass growing wild along the bank. 'It – it's Boxer, my old dog. After a rabbit, he were, when – dang me if he don't run straight into the swampy patch, over yonder. And I just can't get near him.'

Lori followed Sam's shaking finger, pointing to where a shaggy head and two front paws thrashed pathetically against a pool of slimy green, while barks and yelps shattered the air like gunfire.

'That bit of broken fencing, Lori. Maybe we can lift it atween us, so's it'll reach him. D – don't reckon he can last out much longer.'

But, one look at the fencing, and Lori knew it would be too heavy to move that easily. 'We'll need someone to help us, Sam!' Already she was sprinting away as fast as she could. 'You stay here, while I go and grab the very first person I see.'

'Gee, thank goodness,' she panted, her heart thumping wildly as she heard the unmistakeable hiss of wheels on the road, gradually becoming louder.

'Hey! Hey, stop!'

The shine on the racing bike seemed even brighter, the wheels whizzing around in a blur, before sending up a spray of grit from the road.

Lori had to take a deep breath, closing her eyes tight. It definitely wasn't her lucky day.

'Not you again!' Blake snapped angrily. 'D'you want to get knocked down?'

She grabbed the gleaming handlebars. 'Blake, listen. Sam Huggett's dog. It's stuck fast in that bit of marshy land by the river. You know, the stretch my dad says never drains properly.

'And what do you want me to do? Miss my first bike practice for the law school team? You're crazy.'

He lifted his foot on to the top pedal, giving Lori just enough time to step in front of him, her eyes blazing. 'Crazy? You say, crazy? That dog's like a child to Sam, and it's near drowning! Yet, that's not half so important as what Blake Deacon wants to do, right now!'

'Here – just you listen a minute –'

'No! You listen to me for once! I'm sick of you acting Mr Big the whole time, see? And when poor old Sam mourns his dog, I hope you'll remember that you could have tried to save it!'

Blindly she rushed away, not seeing that Blake was pedalling hard, sounding a bit long-suffering as he called out, 'All right. Guess I'll be along.'

If Sam Huggett was surprised to see Blake, he didn't show it. Together, with a lot of puffing from the old man, and the occasional painful grunt from Blake, they managed to heave the fencing strip across the ground, towards Boxer, now, to

Lori's horror, with just the tips of his paws showing, and his eyes rolling hideously behind a fringe of matted fur.

'Oh, hurry! P – please hurry,' was all she could say, until, at last, Sam stood up very straight, clutching his head weakly.

'Th – think you can help, now Lori? Quick as you like – only, take care.'

Lori didn't have to be warned. As soon as she started pulling herself along the slats of the fencing, the muddy ground squelched underneath, and Sam called out, 'Steady, Lori! Steady!' Then he called to his dog. 'Take it easy, Boxer. Not long, now.'

Blake didn't say anything. Not even when Lori had finally made her way across and grabbed desperately at Boxer's collar, hauling him towards her so clumsily that he whined.

'You – you're fine, now, Boxer, old boy,' she crooned, burying her face thankfully into his wet coat. 'Need a bath, though. We both do, I reckon.'

It sounded a funny way to talk to a frightened dog, but Boxer seemed glad to hear Lori's voice. He kept very still under her arm while she crawled back to where Blake and Sam were holding the fencing strip steady.

'Thanks a million, Lori,' Sam croaked, cradling Boxer in his big, hairy arms like a baby. 'I'm that grateful to you. And to you, Blake,' he added hastily, turning around.

'Blake's already gone,' Lori almost whispered, adding silently, 'And he didn't even trouble to ask if I was all right. I – I never thought he'd changed that much.'

'Now, don't you fret none.' Sam ordered. 'Soon as we've gotten Boxer back to the boss and sent for the vet, I'll run you home, so's you can clean up. Then I'll take you wherever you want to go. That'll be back to the festival, I'm thinking!'

The journey back, Sam's delighted explanations, being ushered into the shower-room by Mum, then changing into a clean, beach outfit – all of it seemed so far-off and unreal.

Same as being friendly with Blake Deacon, she supposed vaguely, the familiar hurt stabbing at her again. He might just as well be in another country, along with that Condi woman's tall, dark stranger.

It was Carla who seemed to be the lucky one, introducing the boy who'd asked Lori about Blake's record collection as Brian.

'Nice, isn't he?' she smiled at Lori. 'No sign of your tall, dark stranger, yet?'

'Absolutely not!' Lori was beginning to wish she'd stayed at home, right from the start.

Carla was still smiling. 'Well,' she drawled. 'Someone's been waiting for you to get back here. See who I mean?'

The black hair was still neatly parted and combed flat. But, the wide mouth was set in its long-remembered grin, making Lori marvel that a whole year had passed since they were last on the beach together.

'Blake! Oh, Blake, it's good to see you!'

'Lori. Guess I don't know how to put this. But, y'know, when you stood up to me, I thought maybe you've grown up a whole lot more than me. And I never bothered to notice.'

Lori laughed happily. 'Let's forget it, shall we? Look – Carla and Brian are waiting for us on the boat.'

'Carla,' he echoed thoughtfully. 'What was she saying just now about some tall, dark stranger?

'Only something one of the Condi women said earlier on. The whole thing was a mistake, anyway.'

Blake squeezed her hand, and they started strolling through the little groups of people beginning to crowd towards the shore. It was only when Lori caught sight of the Condi woman waving happily to her from across the bay that she realized.

Blake was tall, and dark, and, she'd always thought, not bad-looking. And, hadn't he seemed like a stranger, someone she'd never known?

COUNTRY BOY

Jane Butterworth

I WAS JUST WALKING OVER LETTS HILL with our sheepdog, Mist, when I saw the car pull up outside the farmhouse, far below. One of those real flash cars it was, too, all shiny chrome, and sheepskin seats. I haven't got a lot of time for these people who spend all their lives cleaning and polishing their cars. There always seems to be far more important things to do, as anyone who's worked on a farm will know.

Still, I reflected with a grim smile of satisfaction, a few days staying on our farm would soon muck that car up! Mist stood and looked at me enquiringly, wondering why I'd stopped when every afternoon at the same time, I go inside for tea. But I thought I'd give Mum time to install the guests first.

I just couldn't believe it when Mum told me she was thinking of taking in holiday guests. 'After all Colin,' she said worriedly, 'This is a big house to keep up, and since your father died, things have been more and more difficult.'

'I do my fair share,' I said, hurt.

'You work yourself into the ground,' she said soothingly. 'And you really need another pair of hands to help you. If we start doing farm holidays we can afford to take on someone to help you with the sheep.'

I thought we'd managed pretty well since Dad died: Mum ran the house; my sister, Lindy, looked after the chickens and bred a few horses; Gary, a local lad came in and milked the cows; I looked after the sheep and drove the tractor.

'Anyway, my mind's made up Colin,' Mum said firmly, in the tone of voice which I knew meant she wouldn't put up with any further argument on the matter. 'Look, Molly Franklyn was telling me only the other day that she's made a tiny bit of money since they started doing farm holidays last year. We only need to let two rooms. City people like farm holidays.'

'Yes, and they like leaving gates open and starting fires and frightening the animals,' I retorted. 'Well, it's up to you, but I don't want anything to do with them.'

Mum looked upset then and I felt guilty because I'd spoken so roughly. But honestly, I knew all about city people. I'd caught a car load of them once, parked in a field of ours during haymaking, and they'd actually stacked up a wall of bales for shelter so they could light a fire!

'Well, I think it's a good idea,' Lindy said, looking up from the book she was reading. 'You really ought to be more adventurous, Colin. We could meet some really interesting people. You only ever see the same old people down the Young Farmers Club and that's just because the girls down there fall all over you. Why,' she added sneakily, 'we might even get some pretty girls staying here. And who knows? They might not fall about whenever you walked into the room, and you might have to put yourself out to chat them up – who knows?'

I threw a cushion at her – she really was getting out of hand. She had a great desire to have what she called 'fun', which usually meant getting dressed up in daft trendy clothes and taking herself off to the nearest city and dancing half the night away. But to be fair, she was good with horses and she rode like a dream.

So the first lot of visitors arrived last month, and even I grudgingly admitted that they weren't too bad. They were quite interested in how a farm is run, but they did get on my nerves a bit, and they let their kid climb all over the tractor.

I gave Mist a pat, and then my eyes nearly popped out of my head. For out of the shiny new car, parked down below, stepped the most astonishing girl I'd ever seen.

She was tall and slim, and had fair hair so long she could have sat on it. She was wearing a short skirt, and she tottered into the house on spiky high-heeled shoes. I couldn't see her face from that distance, but I imagined it was plastered with make-up. I'd never seen anyone on a farm so inappropriately dressed.

'Good heavens,' I muttered, out loud, and started striding down the hill, the dog at my heels. What on earth was a girl like that doing on holiday in the country? She'd be better off holidaying in a town like Blackpool, with its crowds and noise and lights. I guessed her mum and dad had dragged her down here.

When I reached the house Mum said, 'Ah, Colin – put the kettle on, there's a good lad, while I show Mr and Mrs Randell and Tina their rooms. This is my son, Colin.'

They all nodded and smiled at me as I said hello, and then they followed my mother upstairs. I had to admit that Tina was devastatingly pretty – well, she would be if she hadn't got great black lines drawn round her eyes, which were large and a deep cornflower blue.

Cross with myself for even thinking about her, I put the kettle on the range to boil.

'It's beautiful around here, isn't it?'

I hadn't heard Tina come back into the room and she made me jump. 'I would have thought you'd have found the country boring,' I said shortly.

'Now, why would you think that?' she asked.

'Well, coming from the city, you must be used to going to night clubs and discos and things. There's not a lot of that sort of thing around here.'

'I haven't had any time to do that sort of thing,' she

She was tall and slim and had fair hair so long she could have sat on it.

exclaimed with a laugh. 'I've just finished taking my A levels and I've been working so hard I've hardly been out at all. That's why Mum and Dad decided to come here, to give me a break.'

I was almost glad when Mum came back with Tina's parents because she wasn't at all like I'd imagined her to be. She was quieter, more thoughtful. But nevertheless, I decided that I didn't like her. I suppose knowing she wasn't stupid, made me feel even more resentful towards her, because she must think me a right country bumpkin. Well, she wasn't my cup of tea at all. I preferred more homely sort of girls. But she still troubled me, with her fine silky hair, her tight fashionable sawn off jeans and her skimpy tee-shirts.

Often, I saw her walking on her own, or on her knees examining some plant or other, or just sitting on a tree stump gazing into space. One day I came across her when I was off to check the sheep and she came running towards me.

'Look Colin, isn't it beautiful?'

'My God.' I dashed the deadly-poisonous Death Cap toadstool from her outstretched hand. 'You haven't eaten any, have you?'

'Of course not,' she said, upset. 'I'm not that stupid. I just thought it was nice to look at.'

'And deadly to swallow. I should keep away from fungi if I were you.'

Upset, she turned and walked away, and I felt remorseful as I watched her, her shoulders hunched with misery.

'That Tina's ever so nice,' Lindy told me that evening. 'I've been trying to teach her to ride this afternoon, and d'you know, she's not doing at all badly! I think she'll have quite a good seat on her, and she's promised to show me how to do my make-up like hers and cut my hair.'

'What on earth do you want to make up like her for?' I growled. 'You'll look like a painted doll.'

183

'You're so boring sometimes,' she said, 'and so horrid to her.'

'Look,' I said, exasperated, 'I bet she thinks we're real country bumpkins, and when she gets home she'll tell all her friends in Birmingham and have a good laugh about us. So I wouldn't get too friendly with her if I were you.'

'She's not a *bit* like that,' Lindy said indignantly. 'I don't know why you're so funny about her. Anyone would think you fancied her. I believe you do. And you're put out because she doesn't run round you, and you can't order her about like you do all the silly girls around here.'

'Shut up!' I said savagely. 'I wouldn't fancy her – all done up in her stupid clothes and make-up!'

But Lindy just raised her eyebrows disbelievingly and stalked out, head in the air! What a nuisance girls were.

The following day I was leaning on a gate checking the sheep when Tina came up behind me. 'Isn't your dog clever, the way he rounds the sheep up?' she said.

'It's only training,' I said briefly. I looked at her high-heeled shoes. 'I'm surprised you don't ruin your feet wearing those,' I said.

'It takes more than that to ruin my feet,' she said lightly. 'Why don't you like me, Colin?'

I felt myself blush at the directness of her approach. 'Who says I don't?' I asked.

'I can tell. Are all country boys as unfriendly as you?'

I looked at her, and she was so pretty that all of a sudden I realized what a pig I'd been. Yet I still couldn't bring myself to say so.

'Anyway,' she added, 'not everyone thinks the country is the best place to live, which is just as well as there'd be no industry if nobody lived in cities.'

'It's the best place to live as far as I'm concerned,' I

muttered, turning and walking away.

Why was I behaving like this? Bad-temperedly I kicked a rock and cursed as it stubbed my toe. That wretched girl had wriggled into my thoughts so much that I could hardly concentrate for thinking about her – and everywhere I looked, she was there. I started to wonder what it would be like to hold her in my arms, to kiss her.

At tea, Lindy said, 'I think there's going to be a really bad storm tonight. It's so still out, and the horses are nervy and twitchy, as though they're expecting one too.'

'Can the horses really tell what the weather's going to be like?' asked Tina. She seemed to be ignoring me.

'Oh yes,' said Lindy.

'Well, I don't think it'll storm,' I remarked sourly. 'The sky's too clear over May Hill.'

But I was wrong. I was woken at two o'clock that morning by a tremendous crash of thunder, which seemed to shake the house to its very foundations. I jumped out of bed and ran to the window. A few seconds later, the yard was illuminated by the biggest shaft of lightning I'd ever seen, and I could hear the horses stamping and whinnying in fright. The rain had started to fall in enormous droplets and I felt a sudden feeling of unease. Then I saw that my worst fears were confirmed. The red glow told me that the haybarn had been struck by lightning, and as I struggled to get my clothes on, I could smell the smoke and see the sparks shooting skyward.

I ran through the house and opened Lindy's door. 'Barn's on fire,' I panted. 'Ring the fire brigade and then come and help me get the horses out. The fire might spread to the stables.'

I ran out into the yard, and then I noticed the slight figure wearing a white nightie tucked into her jeans. She was leading Steamheat, Lindy's favourite horse, out of the stables, and he stood beside her as quiet as a lamb.

'Where shall I put him?' Tina asked.

'In the paddock over there,' I shouted. By the time Lindy and Mum and Tina's parents had arrived, we'd got all the horses out and were unravelling the hose so we could try to douse the flames.

Alas, our efforts were in vain, for the fire had started in the roof of the barn and by the time the fire-engines arrived it was well alight.

We watched helplessly as the firemen fought the fire, and it wasn't until the first light of dawn that it was finally quenched. I gloomily surveyed the blackened shell of the haybarn, and the smoking remains of the hay inside.

Suddenly I felt very weary and I sat down on the fence and put my head in my hands. Then I felt a light touch on my arm and I looked up to see Tina, holding a steaming mug of tea.

'Thought you could do with this,' she said shyly. Her face was creased with tiredness and blackened with smoke. Her hair hung over her face, but she was quite unconscious of how she looked – and to me she looked beautiful.

'Thanks.' Gratefully, I took the mug from her, and she sat on the fence next to me. I could feel the warmth of her body.

'Poor Colin,' she murmured.

'I'm grateful for what you did,' I muttered shamefacedly. She'd been so brave the way she'd got those horses out. It was then I realized what I'd known all along really, but hadn't liked to admit because I'd been afraid of rejection: that I was very, very attracted to her. 'I'm sorry I've been so unfriendly,' I said.

Her small hand stole into mine as I carried on talking. 'I don't suppose – well, that is, I don't suppose you'd like to go out with me one night? I mean, I know there's not much to do, not like you're used to, but if you didn't mind . . .'

She laughed delightedly, and snuggled closer to me. 'I thought you'd never ask,' she said.

DANGER IN THE SAND

Toni Cornford

THE EARLY AFTERNOON SUN was beating down on my bare shoulders as I sat on the rocks above the beach near our new house in San Diego. But I was cold. Cold, miserable and brooding. I didn't want to be here, I wanted to be back in damp, drizzly old England where all my friends were.

California was so different to the life I'd always known. Even the time was different. Right now my friends would be just about getting up and having breakfast, while I'd just had lunch.

The truth was, I'd hated California from the moment our plane had landed, and I couldn't forgive my father for taking the job which had meant moving so far away from everything I loved.

Yet when I'd told the kids at school I was going to live in San Diego, they'd been really envious. And my form teacher had been so impressed, she'd devoted a whole lesson to telling us all about California and the sort of place I'd be living in.

'Oh, Gayle, you're so lucky,' Penny had sighed on the way home that night. 'Not just because the sun shines all the time, or the beach'll be only a few minutes walk away,' she'd grinned at me and winked, 'but because of all those beautiful bronzed American boys with blond hair and blue eyes, surfing all day and looking fantastic!'

'That's all you ever think about,' I'd retorted.

I remember smiling to myself though, because at first it had sounded good to me, too, and I'd thought much the same as

Penny. Yet as our moving date got nearer I began to panic.

Another reason I'd been so reluctant to leave England was Ben.

I sighed as I put my shirt over my burning shoulders. There'd been a crowd of us who always went around together, and during the few weeks before I'd left, Ben and I had somehow drifted together. There was no chance of a romance then though. All we could do was promise to write to each other.

Slowly I got up and started to walk back to the house. We'd been here almost four weeks now and Mum was still fussing around getting the house as she wanted it. It was so much bigger than the one we'd had in England. That had been small and cosy, cluttered Mum had always said, but looking back we'd been so happy there.

As I turned into our street and stared down it, I didn't think I'd ever get used to California. It was so very different to what I'd known all my life. Low storey houses, wide roads, and wherever you went – palm trees!

'Hi, Gayle!' A voice called from a car window. 'How's it going?'

I groaned as I recognized Davey's voice. I didn't answer him, just gave him a small wave and a tight smile. He lived next door to us, and he'd been hounding me from the day we'd moved in.

'Oh, give him a chance,' Mum had scolded. 'He's trying to be friendly, that's all, Gayle. In fact all our neighbours seem really nice, they can't do enough to help.'

Mum had been in her element as she bustled around getting the house to look like home, but I couldn't get enthusiastic at all. The last straw came when my little sister's accent started to show distinct signs of becoming American. That was one thing that wouldn't happen to me. I was determined *never* to adopt any American ways.

'You're going to end up very lonely if you go on like this, Gayle,' Dad had warned one night. 'Look, love, we all miss things about home, and we all feel homesick, but this job is a good one, and it'll mean a step up for all of us. We'd never have been able to afford a swimming pool in England, would we? But we've got one here.'

He'd looked at me carefully, but neither his teasing nor his logic could talk me round. 'Give it a try, Gayle,' he'd finished. 'And you could start by being a bit more friendly towards Davey. He's a nice kid.'

Maybe he was, I thought miserably, but he wasn't Ben.

Davey kept up his campaign of being friendly and I did try to go along with him. The trouble was he kept asking me questions about England; the customs, traditions, if I'd seen the Queen, and so on, until one day I got really upset and burst into tears.

'Gayle, what did I say?' he asked, his voice filled with concern.

'I'm fed up with you going on about England,' I cried. 'If you're so interested, go and see for yourself!'

Davey looked shocked by my outburst, then suddenly he started to smile. 'You're homesick!' he exclaimed as though he'd just made a world-shattering discovery. 'Oh, I'm sorry. Hey, don't get upset.'

He went to put his arm around me, but I pushed him roughly away. Wasn't it bad enough that he'd brought memories flooding back, without having to paw all over me.

'Just leave me alone!' I screamed at him. 'And get your hands off me!' I jumped up and ran into the house and straight up to my bedroom. Slamming the door hard, I flung myself on to the bed and sobbed my heart out. 'Oh, Ben, I miss you so much,' I cried. 'If only I could come home to you.'

After that, things between me and Davey cooled quite a lot.

He was still nice and always said hello, but he kept his distance.

I was glad. I'd much rather he left me on my own to cope in my own way. Ben's letters helped a lot. He gave me detailed accounts of things that were happening, who was going out with who, and all the gossip and scandal he could lay his hands on.

When his letters came, I'd take them down to the secluded cover I'd discovered and read them over and over. I'd sit for hours amongst the rocks, remembering the good times I'd had with the crowd: the practical jokes we'd played on kids at school, and the long weekends of swimming and ice-skating.

More often than not, these moments of nostalgia would end in tears, but I didn't care. I missed my friends, I missed our old cluttered house, and I wanted desperately to go back.

Strangely enough, sitting there and watching the ocean always made me feel better. At least living on the coast was some consolation. Then Dad started coming the heavy father and out came all the dire warnings. 'You shouldn't be down there on your own,' he told me. 'You heard what Davey said. A lot of boys prowl those beaches, and make it a dangerous place for a girl alone.

'Oh, Dad, it was the middle of the afternoon. What's going to happen to me in broad daylight with loads of people around?' I protested with a sigh.

'That's just the point,' he went on. 'You never know. This is a strange country to us, Gayle, and we've got to get to know it. There are enough horror stories around to scare me silly. So, please stay away from that beach unless there's someone with you. Better safe than sorry, don't you think?'

I sighed and went up to my room. The one thing I enjoyed doing, I wasn't allowed to do any more. As far as I was concerned it was yet another black mark against America. Ever since we'd arrived all I'd heard were the bad points. Like: if you break down on the freeway, stay in your car until the police arrive to help you; never walk alone at night; if you have to go anywhere – drive. The whole thing was alien to me. When was I going to discover something good – something I could do, without having a whole list of restrictions attached to it?

Well, they weren't going to put any restrictions on me going to the beach. So, contrary to all the warnings, *I didn't* stay away. Nothing had ever happened to me, and the chances were nothing ever would. Mind you, I didn't tell Mum when I was going down there. Parents had a nasty habit of worrying and mine were no exception.

It was the day of the barbecue that my longing for home became almost unbearable. The house looked like something out of a glossy magazine, and Mum and Dad had invited loads of people to our house-warming party. To me it emphasized the fact that we were staying. Any secret hope I'd nurtured of our going back to England was gone. This party was to signal our desire to share in the neighbourhood, and become a part of the community.

During the morning of the party I helped Mum with the food and getting everything ready in the garden, but after lunch, I announced I was going for a walk.

'Be back early then, love,' Mum called after me. 'Our guests are arriving at seven, and we want you here to greet them.'

Up in my bedroom, a new dress hung in its cellophane bag, all ready for me to look the pretty teenage daughter of the house. New shoes lay in their box, and the delicate gold chain Dad had given me was around my neck. All presents for the big night, but I knew it was my parents way of trying to help me overcome my unhappiness.

Down on the beach I thought of the evening ahead. Oh, if only by some miracle Ben and Penny could be there. I'd be the happiest person in the world then. That was only a daydream, though, one of many I'd had recently that I wished with all my heart would come true.

Instead, I'd have to stand around being polite to people I didn't know, who'd introduce me to their sons and daughters with the idea that we'd make friends.

Tears started to run slowly down my cheeks but I didn't brush them away. My heart was breaking too much.

I sat there on the rocks for a long time, gazing out across the ocean and not taking much notice of what was happening on the beach below me. Then I heard voices shouting.

'She's real cute, isn't she?'

'Young and pretty – just how I like 'em!'

'Isn't she the English girl who's just moved into the Crescent?'

'Yeh! Hey, I wonder if she's as friendly as she looks. Let's find out.'

Quickly I brushed the tears from my eyes and stared down at the gang of boys looking up at me. There were five of them, all dressed in denims and tee-shirts and bronzed by the sun. I hadn't seen any of them before, and the way they were looking me over scared me.

One of the boys took a step closer, and my father's words came rushing back to me.

'Don't go to the beach on your own, Gayle. Better safe than sorry.'

But I hadn't listened to him or anyone else. I'd looked on the beach as my refuge from the misery I felt inside. Now that refuge had taken on a nightmare quality, and instead of the peace and tranquility I always felt there, all I had now was a terrifying fear.

'What's your name?' one of the boys called out. 'It's Gayle, isn't it?'

My heart was thudding as I glanced around the beach for someone I could run to for help, but my parents' warnings had become stark reality. There was no one around – only one family so far away they'd never have heard me shout or even scream.

'Hey! She's afraid,' another boy called out. 'We're not going to hurt her, are we? We just want to be friendly.'

The three boys standing behind him started to laugh and throw themselves around stupidly. Then they jostled one another laughing and whooping as they pushed each other over in the sand.

I stood up and started to turn away.

'Hey, she's going without even saying hello!' The first one yelled.

I glanced over my shoulder and to my horror he'd begun running up the sandy embankment towards me. Behind him, the others had stopped fooling around and were joining in the chase.

What was I going to do? Oh, why had I stubbornly refused to listen?

Quickly I stumbled up the rocky sand-dune. Behind me, the boys were gaining ground, their voices getting louder as they got nearer. If only there were someone around. I was too far away from the road or the car park, and the whole beach seemed deserted.

Then, like an answer to a prayer, I saw someone sunbathing at the top of the dune. It was a boy lying face down on a green and blue striped towel, a radio playing quietly close to him.

'Hey!' I called out, starting to run forward. 'Oh, please . . .'

My voice sounded panic-stricken. I didn't know who the boy was, but right then I didn't care. There were five boys behind me, and it didn't take a genius to work out that their intentions weren't strictly honourable!

'Come on! Don't let her get away!' The voices behind me were a babble. 'She's prize of the day, guys. Come on!'

Sheer terror pushed me on. I reached the top of the sand-dune and then stopped dead as I recognized the boy lying on the towel. It was Davey.

Oh, God, what was I going to do? After all the nasty things I'd said to him, and the cruel way I'd treated him, how could I possibly turn to him for help? But I had no choice. The gang behind me were getting very close, and it was time to stop hesitating and swallow my pride. 'Davey!' I yelled at the top of my voice. 'Oh, Davey, please help me!'

At the sound of my voice, Davey looked up. Then he was on his feet and running towards me. I'd never been so relieved in my life. When he got to me, he put his arm around me and pushed me behind him as he faced the boys scrambling up the dune towards us.

'Sorry, guys, you've picked the wrong girl,' Davey said forcefully. 'This one's mine – hands off!'

The boys stopped at the top of the dune and looked at each other, then at me and Davey. They were obviously wondering whether to take their 'prize' or not. Eventually, after what seemed like ages, the leader made the decision. 'Sure, sure,' he said. 'Okay, guys.' He turned and motioned the rest of them back down to the beach. 'Better luck next time,' he added, looking at me.

I watched in amazement as they slid back down the sand and jumped on to the flat, hard beach. With their hands in their pockets they sauntered off. I literally felt my heartbeat return to normal, as I shakily sat down.

'Oh, Davey, thank you so much,' I breathed. 'I . . . I . . . well, they scared me.' I was embarrassed and didn't know what to say to him. I'd behaved like a spoilt brat, but now I felt very different. Not just about Davey, but about a lot of things.

'Try to relax now,' Davey said. 'You don't want to be flustered for your parents' party tonight.'

'Are you coming?' I asked, surprised.

Davey laughed. 'Of course,' he said with a shrug. 'Your sister's told me about your dress, and I want to see you in it.'

Now I felt very different, not just about Davey, but about a lot of things.

195

I blushed furiously. Trust her to spout out everything. She could never keep a secret.

'Davey, I owe you an apology,' I said. 'I've been really nasty to you, and you didn't deserve it.'

'Oh, now forget it, Gayle,' he said, looking slightly embarrassed himself. 'I know it must have been hard for you settling into a new country. No doubt, I'd feel the same if I had to go and live in England and leave my friends behind.'

'That's no excuse,' I said with a shy smile. 'I was unforgivably horrible.'

Davey smiled at me and touched my cheek. 'You're forgiven,' he said softly. 'On one condition.'

I looked at him expectantly.

'You let me have the first dance with you tonight, and you come to the drive-in with me tomorrow.'

'The first dance,' I echoed. 'That's a bit old-fashioned, isn't it?'

'Maybe it is,' he said. 'But so what. I'd like to be the first to dance with you tonight.'

Suddenly I felt all my animosity and hostility towards America begin to lift. And then I realized the truth of what I'd done. I just hadn't given it a chance. Even before I'd left England I'd set my mind against moving, and had been determined not to like anything on principle. Now all that had changed. When, through my own stubbornness and stupidity, I'd been in trouble and needed help, who'd come to my rescue? Davey. What a fool I'd been. I certainly didn't deserve to be sitting here with him now.

'You know, I'm really looking forward to the party now,' I said. 'What time are you coming over?'

Davey's eyes lit up and my heart skipped a beat. 'On the dot of seven,' he said. Then he laughed. 'Your mother warned me not to arrive any earlier or she'd throw me out!'

I stared at him, then I saw the twinkle in his eye.

'Oh, Davey!' I exclaimed.

With that we both burst out laughing and I felt as though I suddenly belonged.

It hadn't been America that was wrong at all. It had been me. But now things would be different. I gazed around at all the palm trees, and I just knew I'd get to like them a lot. I knew, too, that I'd learn to love my new life and the people I'd meet.

Next time I wrote to Penny I'd be telling her all about the blond-haired, blue-eyed American boy who lived next door, and I had a feeling Davey's name would be cropping up in my letters quite a lot in the future.

RIVER RESCUE

C. J. White

IN A MAN-MADE CLEARING among the densely-forested slopes of Kiunga, in Papua New Guinea, lies the airstrip, the town's main link with the rest of the island since there are very few roads in the Western Province, where Kiunga is situated.

Here, one day early in September, Sarah and her parents were waiting patiently for the plane from Port Moresby, the capital of the island. This weekly plane brought post, supplies, visitors – and today it would be bringing a young man from England called Michael Brown. He was a VSO volunteer who would be spending two years as a teacher at the local high school which Sarah's parents ran. They were very excited because he was the first volunteer they had had, though they desperately needed help in the school, which was extremely short-staffed.

'Isn't that it? I'm sure I can see something coming now,' cried Sarah.

'About time, too. Why this plane is never on time I can't imagine,' said her mother, 'because after all, Port Moresby isn't that far away.'

Soon the small plane was taxiing to a halt, and Sarah and Mr and Mrs Kerema watched eagerly as the passengers began to disembark.

'I bet that's him,' said Mr Kerema, as a pale, handsome blond-haired man, looking very hot in a suit and tie, clambered down the aircraft steps. He looked thoroughly disgruntled, but then the journey from England was enough to try even the most patient of people. Still, he'd arrived at last!

'You must be Michael Brown – welcome to Kiunga,' greeted Sarah's father, introducing his wife and daughter. 'I hope the journey wasn't too exhausting.'

'Yes, I'm Michael. The journey has been rather tiring. Is this Kiunga? What a dump! I'd expected somewhere much bigger and grander. What a disappointment!'

Sarah and her parents were rather taken aback, but her father managed to reply: 'No, it's not a very grand place, but we hope you'll soon feel at home here, and will enjoy your stay.'

'Quite frankly, I doubt if I will be staying long,' retorted Michael, storming off towards the back of the plane to retrieve his luggage.

During the walk back to the house nobody said much. Mr Kerema pushed a handcart with Michael's bags on it, and Michael trailed behind the others. Sarah was filled with dread – perhaps their English visitor was going to prove more than they bargained for.

When they reached the house, Sarah showed Michael his room.

'The bathroom's over here, and we'll be having supper in about an hour. Just yell if you want anything – we won't be far away, and meanwhile I'll get you a cool drink.'

Supper turned out to be a further ordeal. Mrs Kerema had tried to cook an English-style meal to make Michael feel at home, but he took three mouthfuls, grimaced, put down his knife and fork and pushed away his plate.

'Do you eat food like this every night?' he asked, scornfully.

'Well, no, we usually eat more traditional food,' Mrs Kerema replied, trying to be polite. 'But since we have to rely on either what's grown locally or expensive imported food, there's not a great deal of choice, and menus are usually determined by the seasons. There's only two stores in Kiunga, though we do have a good bakery which was set up by the Mission.'

The look on Michael's face showed he was not impressed.

Sarah thought that he was probably homesick, and that perhaps talking about home would make him feel better. She began asking him about where he came from, his teacher-training college, what life was like in England. However, she had an uphill struggle as he answered in monosyllables and was obviously reluctant to talk at all, so she soon gave up.

They finished their meal in silence. Afterwards, Mr Kerema said,

'If you'd like to see round the school I'll show you it now, then we can discuss your duties tomorrow. Term starts in three days, so our days of rest are numbered!'

When they'd gone, Sarah grinned ruefully at her mother. The school was her parents' pride and joy – they'd set it up twenty years ago after training as teachers themselves, and now it had reached its present size of about 120 pupils. Her parents had two helpers, Emmioni and Joe, but it was hard work for them all and they'd been thrilled that a VSO volunteer was being allocated to them.

After breakfast the next day, Sarah suggested that she show Michael round the small town of Kiunga. It was a place full of contrasts, from the large house and garden of the police commissioner to the 'corners' – clusters of houses built of traditional materials in clearings around the town. Hills towered above Kiunga, which lay next to the Fly river. Apart from the airstrip, the river was their only link with nearby towns and villages except for dangerous trails which led through the hills and mountains.

The weather was hot, and Michael was obviously suffering from the humidity. After they'd walked for about half an hour, he suddenly asked, 'Can we go back now? I feel exhausted.'

'Yes, of course,' replied Sarah immediately. 'You must find

it all very strange, and it'll take you a little while to get used to the heat. But later on this afternoon, if you like, I'll introduce you to some of my friends. Once a week a film is shown at the Mission, and they're usually not too old. There's one on tonight at six o'clock.'

'But your friends will be far too young for me,' he snapped.

Sarah was silenced. She'd tried to be friendly, but had got nowhere. She'd leave Michael well alone from now on.

All too soon, the high school term started. Sarah was in the top class and would soon be taking exams, so this year would be hard work. Still, she'd decided that she wanted to be a nurse, and hoped to go and train in Port Moresby or Australia, then return to Kiunga and work in the local hospital.

She wasn't looking forward to being taught by Michael, and as soon as she arrived at school her classmates quizzed her about the new teacher from England. She couldn't bring herself to tell them that he was the rudest man she'd ever met, even though he was also very good-looking.

Halfway through the morning, there suddenly came a fearful commotion from Classroom 3B, next to Sarah's. There was shouting and screaming, crashes and bangs, and the whole of Sarah's class went rushing out to see what was going on. As they ran into the corridor, a very red-faced Michael dashed out of 3B, slammed the door and hared off down the corridor and out of the main doors of the school.

'Michael, Michael, come back,' yelled Sarah as Emmioni, her own teacher, pushed open the door to 3B and stood gaping.

There was a complete riot going on. The children in that class were fourteen and fifteen-year-olds, and they were throwing chairs at each other, hurling books, pencils, rulers – anything that came to hand.

Emmioni quickly recovered himself, and got 3B back to order. Meanwhile Sarah set off to look for Michael. After

The children were throwing chairs at each other, hurling books,
pencils, rulers – anything that came to hand.

searching the house and its surroundings, she eventually came across him sitting on the quay by the river, his head in his hands. He looked so dejected, Sarah didn't know whether to leave him alone or try to help. She approached him gently, sitting down beside him and putting her arm round his shoulders.

He looked up, startled. 'What do you want?' He roughly shook off her arm.

'I just wondered if I could be any help. Do you feel like telling me what happened?'

'Why should I? You'll only laugh.'

With a little coaxing, Sarah managed to find out that he had been unable to keep 3B in order, and had finally had enough and had decided to leave them to it.

'They are a troublesome bunch,' agreed Sarah. 'But perhaps Dad thought they'd be overawed by the new teacher from England and would behave decently. Everyone has trouble with them, so it's not just you.'

Suddenly Sarah remembered that she should be in lessons herself.

'I must rush back – Emmioni will wonder where on earth I've got to. Are you going to come back with me?'

'No, I'll just sit here a bit longer and get my thoughts together. But Sarah – thanks for coming to find me.'

After school, when she arrived home, her father and Michael were in the study with the door firmly closed. She could just hear the sound of their voices in fairly heated conversation.

An hour later they emerged, Michael looking subdued, her father trying to be cheerful.

The next morning when she was helping her father to wash up the breakfast dishes, he sighed, 'Poor Michael – I do feel sorry for him.'

'Why Dad? Can you tell me?'

'Well, he says he hates it here so much that he wants to leave on the next plane. I've managed to persuade him to stay until Christmas and give it a try for a bit longer, but he says he doesn't think he'll ever fit in, and he doesn't really want to anyway. Now of course he's lost his confidence, and it'll be hard for him to get it back.'

Sarah thought that he hadn't even tried to fit in.

During the next few weeks there was an uneasy peace. Mr Kerema tactfully changed round Michael's timetables so he didn't have to teach 3B again, and Michael seemed to be managing all right with his other classes. He spent as little time as possible with the Keremas, keeping himself to himself, taking long walks around the neighbourhood and only speaking to them when essential. He didn't mention the incident by the river, so neither did Sarah.

In early December came the twentieth anniversary of the founding of the high school, and great celebrations were planned. Sarah's parents were guests of honour, and old pupils and friends of the school were coming from all around, by boat, foot and plane, to join in the festivities. The day had been declared a public holiday.

Sarah had invited Michael to sit with her and her friends, thinking he'd enjoy seeing the age-old Papuan rituals. She was relieved when he actually turned up – she'd half expected him not to. They were soon joined by a happy bunch of other people – some of her friends and a couple of men she'd never seen before. They introduced themselves as Twagu and Bob, both mining engineers from Port Moresby who had come to work at the new mine in Kiunga.

Soon the festivities began, with traditional dancing. Men with crocodile drums settled in a semicircle, and both men and women dancers came forward. The women were wearing shredded-leaf skirts, boar's-tusk armlets, ornate necklaces made of boar's teeth, shells and beads, and headdresses of painted porcupine quills. Their faces were painted in bright colours. The men were similarly dressed, except their headdresses were so tall and ornate that Sarah wondered how they managed to balance them on their heads.

The dancers wove in and out, creating patterns as they sang and danced. It was a beautiful spectacle, and Sarah turned to Michael to ask how he was enjoying it.

'Oh, it's all right, I suppose. But when's the food arriving?'

She pretended it was a joke and laughed, though secretly she was furious that he was being miserable on today of all days. She decided to forget about him, and started to talk to Twagu and Bob instead. Bob soon asked her to dance, and she forgot about Michael.

'I haven't seen you around Kiunga before,' she said.

'No, I only arrived a few weeks ago. But I'll be here for a while now because I've been taken on at the mine. I like Kiunga – it's very different from Port Moresby where I come from, quieter and more peaceful. What about you?'

Sarah told him a bit about herself – he was very easy to talk to and she felt glad that she'd met someone new and cheerful.

'I thought that Englishman was your boyfriend – though I'm not trying to pry,' he said.

She explained about Michael, but was soon interrupted by an announcement that the food was ready. People were beginning to line up at the tables which were piled high with food – chickens, different kinds of fish, sago palm-cakes, yams, salads and vegetables, mounds of fresh fruit and cakes. Emmioni from the school was attempting to carve the first of the roast wild pigs, and the delicious smell of roast pork made Sarah's mouth water.

After the meal there were speeches – from the Mayor of Kiunga, several of the school's governors, and from Sarah's father, who thanked the local people of Kiunga for helping to make the school a success.

Music and dancing began again after the speeches, and it was late in the evening when Bob offered to see Sarah home.

'Would you like to come and see the next film at the Mission with me?' he asked.

Sarah was thrilled. 'I'd love to.'

It was a perfect end to a perfect day.

The Kerema family were all bleary-eyed at breakfast the next morning. Michael didn't appear, though they called him twice.

'Go and see if he's up, Sarah,' said her mother, 'Maybe he hasn't heard us calling.

Sarah knocked loudly then opened the door and stuck her head round. He wasn't there and his bed hadn't been slept in. She rushed back to the kitchen to tell her parents.

'Where can he be?', said her father, puzzled.

'I do hope he hasn't done anything stupid,' said her mother. 'We'd better have a look for him. We'll search the house and garden first, then the town. We can each go in a different direction, and meet at the quay in two hours' time.

Sarah knew that if anything happened to Michael while he was in their care, her parents would never forgive themselves.

Sarah arrived at the quay five minutes early, hoping the others had had more success in their search. She'd asked everyone she'd met whether they'd seen Michael either late last night or early that morning, but no one had.

Her mother arrived next, looking glum. Then came Mr Kerema with Bob.

'I met Bob at the bakery and he offered to help us look,' said her father. Bob smiled at her.

'Don't worry, I'm sure we'll be able to track him down,' he said.

'Hey look – our boat has gone,' her mother suddenly cried.

Most people in Kiunga had a boat of some kind or another – from one-man canoes to motor launches – but the Keremas' small dinghy with an outboard motor was missing from its mooring.

'Don't say Michael's taken it!' said her father.

'But the river's so full and fast-flowing at the moment. It's too dangerous to go out on unless you're very experienced at handling boats,' Mrs Kerema pointed out.

'Well at least we know he can only have gone downriver. The current's too strong for him to get upriver,' said Bob.

'He doesn't stand a chance,' said Sarah.

'I'll go after him,' Bob said firmly. 'He probably won't have got very far before he was in trouble.'

'But it's so dangerous . . .' Sarah's mother started to say.

'I'll take the launch from the mine. It's very powerful, and I'm experienced in handling it. And it's got several spare cans of petrol in the hold.'

So saying, he ran over to the launch, leaped in, started the engine and was off.

'Be careful,' Sarah cried, but her words were lost in the roar of the engine.

There was nothing the Kerema family could do but wait. The hours dragged past, and after four hours, Sarah's father said, 'I think we should prepare ourselves for the worst. The river's so fast running, and it's full of broken trees from upriver, piles of rocks, sudden rapids – not to mention the crocodiles. Even Bob, who seems to know what he's doing, is in danger. And as for Michael . . .' He didn't need to say the rest.

It was another two hours before they heard the sounds of a boat engine approaching. Suddenly the boat was in sight. Sure enough it was Bob. But there was no sign of Michael. The boat was making slow progress against the strong current, but eventually Bob threw out a line and was at the quay. He gave a rueful smile. 'Well, I've found him.' He waved his arm to the back of the launch.

There lay Michael, on the floor of the boat, covered in blood and dirt, his clothes torn and his shoes missing – but he was breathing.

A doctor and nurse from Kiunga hospital gently loaded him on to a stretcher and carried him off. Bob went back with the Keremas and after a cool shower, he told his tale.

He'd driven the boat slowly down the Fly river, asking at every village and settlement whether they'd seen a white man in a boat. A couple of people had heard the boat's engine, and said it had obviously been travelling far too fast in those dangerous conditions.

He had scoured the water for signs of the remains of the Keremas' boat. He had had no illusions – he had known the boat wouldn't last long in unskilful hands, and even he had had difficulty in avoiding some of the huge trees and branches that came rushing through the water at him. He had called Michael's name continually, hoping he would call back if he were marooned on the river bank.

After a couple of hours of this painfully slow progress, he had come across the remains of the Keremas' boat, half-sunk, moored to a tree that overhung the water. He had moored his own boat, jumped ashore and come across Michael, lying on the bank. At first Bob had thought he was dead because he was completely still, but when Bob had touched his back, he had slowly come round.

Michael had hit some rocks. They'd made a large hole in the hull of the boat, but somehow Michael had managed to get the boat to the shore and had tied it to the tree. Then it had slowly sunk lower and lower in the water until only the tips of the bows could be seen. He'd been so exhausted by his efforts, that he'd collapsed on the bank, coming to only when Bob arrived.

Bob had decided to leave the Keremas' boat where it was.

He and Michael had made very slow progress back in the launch, struggling against the current and trying to avoid all the obstacles in their path.

'Phew! What a story! Thank goodness you're both all right,' said Mr Kerema.

'Yes, thank goodness,' said Sarah, smiling at Bob with relief all over her face. He smiled back, and for a moment they forgot all about everything else but each other.

A very embarrassed Michael greeted the Keremas and Bob at the hospital the next morning.

'I'm so sorry to have caused you all this trouble . . . and thank you, Bob, for saving my life . . . I'm lucky I'm not dead after being so stupid . . .' Words poured out of him. Once or twice Mrs Kerema or Sarah tried to stop him, but it was as though he wanted to try to make them understand why he'd been so odd ever since he'd arrived. His whole life story came flooding out, culminating in his guilt at not having tried to fit in with them ever since his arrival. He realized how selfish he'd been, making the Keremas' lives a misery and then finally causing Bob grave danger. He told them that a part of his unhappiness was because he'd been planning to get married to a girl in England and they had been going to come to Kiunga together. But she had backed out at the last moment, and he hadn't been able to get over the disappointment.

After his long story, he lay back in bed, emotionally and physically drained.

'Oh, I forgot. I went to the post office to collect our post on the way here and there were some letters for you,' said Mr Kerema, fishing three rather crumpled letters out of his pocket.

Michael looked at them disinterestedly, then suddenly sat up in bed. 'This one's from Fiona, the girl I was telling you about,' he said excitedly.

'Well, we'll leave you to read it in peace,' said Mrs Kerema tactfully.

'No, stay please – I may need you,' begged Michael, ripping open the envelope. His hand was shaking with nervousness. 'It's the first time she's written to me since I've been out here.'

His eyes scanned the letter. His face was serious at first, then pleased, then he began to blush. 'She says she's realized she does care for me after all. She admires me for being unselfish and coming to work out here, and she says she'll wait for me to get home and then perhaps we can get married after all. If she only knew the truth – how selfish I've really been.'

'Congratulations, Michael – that's marvellous,' said Mrs Kerema.

Bob caught Sarah's eye and smiled. He took her hand and squeezed it. 'Come on, Sarah,' he said. 'Let's go for a walk. We'll leave Michael to dream about Fiona. Hurry up and get better, Michael. Your two years won't pass very quickly if you spend your time lounging in a hospital bed!'

'Don't worry – I'll be out in no time. And meanwhile, make sure you look after Sarah!'

Sarah looked at him, astonished. Then she leant over and gave him a quick kiss on the cheek. 'Fiona's a lucky girl,' she said. 'But then –' she looked up at Bob – 'so am I.'

SHADOWS ARE PEOPLE

Joyce Wilson

ON THE OUTSIDE, the hostel was a dignified grey stone mansion built in a once elegant London back street in the eighteenth century. But as soon as Mollie went inside she found herself in a close-carpeted foyer, facing a reception desk, a battery of pigeon-holes, formal lines of easy chairs – all the trappings of a modern hotel and a world of people only passing through. Later, as she perched on the edge of the divan bed in the small, first-floor room which was to be hers for the duration of the training course, she could hear the sound of other girls laughing in the shared kitchen along the corridor. The half-open glass panel above her door also let in a tempting smell of coffee. But she was too shy yet to go in search of company. The representative of the large chain-store, where she was a trainee, had informed her that the accommodation provided would be civilized, and he was right. But he had said nothing about the frightening antiseptic stillness of the bare room and its careful colours. And perhaps he had not known about the gnawing sensation at the pit of her stomach which she knew was homesickness.

Outside, the evening traffic built into a slow, crawling mass in the yellow glare of the street lamps. As it grew dark, the lamp close to her window filled the room with geometric shadows. She got up quickly, drawing the curtains closed.

The first days in the main London branch of the chain-store went very quickly. Mollie found the sessions in the office and the stockrooms interesting. She spent a tempting day in the luxurious perfurmerie department, and another in the book shop. At the start of the third week she would be able to state her preference and would receive her final training under one manager.

In the book shop she recognized another trainee as a girl who shared the same kitchen with her and the first-floor residents at the hostel. The girl was obviously bored, but just after five o'clock her face lit up when a good-looking boy of about seventeen came in. Mollie liked his rather serious face, and thought how well his trendy gold-rimmed spectacles suited him.

'Angie!' he said. 'Fancy seeing you here. I didn't imagine you were the sort to work in a book store.'

'Too right, Rich,' she shrugged. 'If you really want to buy something, ask Mollie here. See you at the disco on Saturday? Watch out, Mollie, Rich's a very fast mover when he wants to be! Don't be deceived by the bookish look!'

She wandered off in the direction of the staff changing room a good ten minutes before time, leaving Mollie blushing at the way Angie had talked. But Richard did not seem at all put out, and after a long discussion on a new paperback on the counter, to her delight he bought a book.

As he paid for it at the cash desk, Mollie watched him from a distance. He seemed very self-assured, and not at all the type she could imagine dancing with Angie and her kind.

That evening she went along to the kitchen to make some coffee, and found Angie laughing and gossiping at one of the tables with several other girls.

'Leave the kettle on again for us when you've finished,' she called out to Mollie, who nodded and stirred her coffee miserably. It would have been nicer to be asked to make the coffee for them, and join them at their table.

On the second Saturday, they were all exhausted after a long hectic day in the store. But soon after supper, Angie and another girl floated by Mollie's half open door in obviously new dresses, leaving a trail of expensive perfume in their wake. Mollie went to the door, meaning to ask them where they were going and wish them a good time. But she was too late. They disappeared down the main staircase, and she heard Angie's high voice greeting someone in the foyer. 'Rich!' Mollie was surprised to feel a little stab of envy in her heart as she heard the name of Angie's escort.

In the perfumerie department at Monday lunch time Mollie tested sample after sample until she felt sick, then wandered into the Young Set dress section and tried on a flimsy silk dress edged with lace. In the small confining space of the dressing-room she stared critically at herself in the mirror. The dress suited her. She knew she looked as good as the others. And with staff discount the price was not too high.

That night she left her door wide open, the dress a delicate splash of colour on the divan.

The bait worked, for a while. First one girl then another stopped and stood in the doorway, admiring her purchase. But no one asked her to go out to any of the events that were announced on the notice board in the corridor, and when it came to bed time, she crushed the dress in both hands and pushed it unceremoniously on its hanger into the wardrobe.

On the Friday night she made her preparations. She knew that a group of trainees from her floor were going to a dance. She took a shower, and back in her room opened the windows wide while she dried her hair and applied the new perfume she had bought that day. Then, in the half light, she dressed as carefully as if she were guest of honour at a ball, and stood looking down into the deserted street as if watching for a car.

Somewhere a phone rang, and she heard someone run to answer it. 'Coming!' It was Angie's voice.

Mollie stood looking down into the deserted street as if watching for a car.

Moments later Angie called to someone else. 'Rich has got a spare ticket for his college hop. There's folk singing. What a drag.'

There followed a hurried, whispered conversation, quite close to Mollie's door. Her pulse quickened nervously. If they were going to ask her to take a spare ticket, as an afterthought, she would have to refuse. Quickly, she took her bag from the chair, and opened her door.

'Just the person we want to see,' Angie began.

'Sorry,' Mollie blurted out. 'I'm late as it is. Ask me tomorrow.'

Before they could say any more she had reached the stairs, and moments later she found herself standing in the street, the night air touching her flushed cheeks. She knew now, that she was really attracted to Richard, and her infuriating shyness, made much worse by the loneliness she felt at the hostel, crippled her ability to let him know.

She spent the evening at a cinema, staring blankly at the screen. Tomorrow, she would ring home and tell them that she was not staying on the course. Her parents would understand. As an only child she had usually got her own way, and they had been upset at the thought of her leaving home for the first time to stay in the firm's London hostel.

But in the cold light of day she knew it was out of the question. They were almost half way through the course, and jobs were hard enough to get. It was then that she remembered that the time had come to give her preference for a department in which to take the final training. Things would not be so bad from now on, she thought, as she had decided on asking to work in the book shop.

Mollie was sorting through a pile of new titles on the book shop floor and checking the price list that went with them, when she sensed that someone was watching her. She looked up, to find it was Richard.

'Angie's not here,' she said quickly. 'She's in the make-up department.'

He smiled. 'Where else? I imagine she's bought the whole place up by now, hasn't she?'

Mollie did not know what to say. Richard's tone was kindly as he laughed about Angie, and she knew he liked going out with her. Perhaps she was not as unkind as she seemed.

'I came to buy a book, actually,' Richard was saying. She got up quickly from the floor. This was something she could handle. In no time she had found the volume he wanted; but he did not seem in a hurry to pay for it.

'Sorry you couldn't take that spare ticket,' he said. 'Angie told me you had a date.'

She bit her lip. If she was not careful she would find herself telling even more lies to make her play-acting of Friday night more convincing. Better to say nothing.

'How about tomorrow?' Richard persisted. 'We're going out in a group.' He mentioned the film she had seen.

'I've seen it,' she shook her head. At least that was the truth.

Richard did not seem to notice her confusion. 'Well, another time,' he said, almost too casually.

He must think she simply did not want his company. There was no way in which she could tell him how she felt or talk about the isolation she had built round herself, first from shyness and homesickness, and then from a sense of not belonging.

The next evening she went quickly to her room after supper. Outside in the corridor, doors slammed, voices rose and fell. She stood at her window in the dark, her own shadow filling the room behind her.

When she heard Richard's voice it seemed quite close. Another man spoke next. They were asking for Angie and her friend. 'She promised us a cup of coffee before the film,' Richard said.

For some minutes Mollie did not move. She listened as Angie came out of the kitchen and greeted the new arrivals. She heard the clatter of coffee cups, a burst of laughter. Richard seemed to like carefree, outgoing girls like Angie, in spite of his brainy looks.

The voices came nearer. 'That's Mollie's room,' she heard Angie say. 'But she's out a lot these days.'

Almost as a reflex, Mollie turned sharply, seeking cover. Her long shadow turned with her, assuming odd curves on the ceiling and the half open vent above her door. The voices died away, and she sat on her bed, her fists clenched tightly. Only two more weeks now, and she would be home.

At work next day she was white-faced and silent. She knew she had behaved foolishly, but she could not find the courage to break the pattern of her behaviour. One day she would look back on the life at the hostel as a bad dream.

It was five minutes before closing, when Richard appeared. She blushed in spite of herself, and pretended to sort through the books on a shelf.

'There's a rather unusual book I'm after,' he said in a voice that seemed to her unnecessarily loud. 'Could you order it for me?'

She fought a rush of shyness, her face turned away. 'Of course. If you can wait just a moment I'll take the details.'

Making a show of finishing her self-imposed task, she went to the cash desk and found her order book. Not until then did she look into Richard's face. And the look she found there – very serious, very gentle – made her realize that he was not in the shop to buy a book this time.

'It's about the theatre,' he maintained the charade doggedly, she thought. 'The Japanese shadow plays.'

'We need the author's name, and the publisher.' She kept her voice as steady as she could.

'Well, I'm not sure. But it's about this idea that shadows tell more of the truth than the real thing.'

'Oh?' She thought he must be able to hear the beating of her heart.

'Yes. And I've seen the proof of it, Mollie. In fact I saw such a thing last night. An empty room, peopled by shadows. But it wasn't empty, was it Mollie?'

She put the order book down very carefully. 'I wish you would go away, Richard, and just leave me alone. Please.'

'But that's exactly what you don't want, Mollie. Aren't I right? You want to belong. You want to make friends.'

'I don't know what I want any more,' she said miserably. 'Angie – she's different. It's easy for her.'

To her astonishment, Richard burst out laughing. A woman customer in a red hat looked round and glared disapprovingly. At that moment Mollie could happily have glared back.

'The Angies of this world take to London like ducks to water,' Richard said. 'But it's all an act. Dances, parties, films every weekend – it's their way – my way too, for that matter – of pretending we're not alone in the big city.'

'So my pretence is not such a bad thing after all,' Mollie spoke half to herself.

'You're wrong about that,' Richard answered. 'All pretence is bad. But it's not too late. You're in London another two weeks at least, aren't you?'

'Two and a half.' She was still counting the days.

'Well?'

'Well what?'

'How about joining the rest of us? Lots of lonely people ganged up together having a nice time?'

'But –' Mollie began.

'I know what you're going to ask me.'

'I was going to ask you if you had told anyone else. About my shadow.'

Richard shook his head, serious again. 'I don't know what you're talking about, Mollie. I honestly don't. And, even if I did see a shadow in your room. Well – shadows can't exist without people, can they?' He took up a book from the counter where she stood. This time he did not even pretend that he wanted to buy it. But as he replaced it, his hand brushed hers, and Mollie smiled at him, with new confidence.

That night in the hostel she found a letter from home waiting in her pigeon hole. There were plans for an outing on her return. Her father had re-papered her bedroom. The cat sent an inky paw mark by way of love.

When she had read the letter, she got up and went to the window in her room, firmly drawing the curtains against the night. Then she switched on her light, and opened her door.

Later, she went to make coffee in the kitchen. There was no one else there at first. But she looked up when Angie and another girl came in, and said, 'The kettle's still hot. Sit down and I'll make you some coffee.'

'Well,' said Angie with a teasing smile, 'If you've got the time.'

'Of course there's time,' Mollie said. 'I've got nothing to do tonight – except phone home and tell them everything's all right.'

TIME TRAVELLER

Jane Butterworth

JOANNA FINISHED WRAPPING UP the birthday present for her boyfriend, Neil, and then looked at her watch. Heavens! It was nearly seven o'clock and she'd promised Neil she'd meet him at seven – and he did get so cross if he was kept waiting. They were going to see a film. They'd seen it twice already and Joanna had been bored silly even the first time, because she found films about Space and intergalactic wars silly and unbelievable. But still, it was Neil's birthday and you're allowed to do what you like on your birthday.

Hurriedly, she put on her jacket and picked up the present. It was a heavy car manual. Not what she'd have chosen, but Neil made sure he got exactly what he wanted for his birthday, by giving everyone a list a month before the day, specifying make, size, even colour. He wanted a car manual so that was what she'd bought him. It did take the surprise out of birthdays but at least he'd enjoy tinkering about with the engine of his old banger. He'd bought it just after he'd passed his driving test two months ago.

It was a ten minute walk across the common to Neil's house where she was meeting him. She wouldn't cross the common in the dark, but it wasn't quite yet dusk, and there were houses in the distance, so she started walking briskly across.

She was just walking through the woods, when she heard a strange, sudden noise – a sort of electronic whirring. Then there was a blinding flash and a light so bright that she had to shut her eyes, and was rooted to the spot in fear.

The noise grew louder until she clapped her hands over her ears and cried out in terror. But then it died down as suddenly as it had come, and after a couple of seconds she tentatively opened her eyes – and gasped in astonishment. For there, in front of her, stood the most beautiful boy she'd ever seen.

He was exceptionally tall – much taller than any boy she'd ever known. He had bright golden hair, broad shoulders and strange, pale eyes. He was dressed in a shiny silver flying suit and high white boots, and he stretched out his hands towards Joanna. Fearfully, she took a step back.

'You are afraid. Please don't be,' he said, and his voice was so kind that she wasn't afraid any longer and instinctively trusted him.

'Who are you?' she breathed, clutching Neil's present, completely forgetting that she was in a hurry.

'I am Dezig, from the planet Zegoz,' he said simply. 'My planet has been destroyed, so my brothers and sisters and I are searching for another planet on which we could make our home. We each take the small craft out to discover what life is like on other planets. I have landed on Earth and you are the first Earth woman I have seen. You do not look like us.' He stretched out a hand and touched her hair. 'Your hair is soft and black and long. You are very small. And I do not think you can see into my mind as I can see into yours.'

'See into my mind?' she repeated stupidly.

'On Zegoz, we are all telepathic,' he replied. 'But I would like to take you back to my travelling craft so we may speak in private and you can tell me about life on Earth. Would you follow me?'

Dazed, she nodded, and followed him through the most densely wooded part of the common, afraid but not afraid, wondering briefly whether anyone else had seen or heard him land.

'Nobody else has heard me,' he said suddenly.

*'Who are you?' Joanna breathed, clutching Neil's present,
completely forgetting that she was in a hurry.*

She jumped. How did he know what she was thinking?

The craft he led her to was nothing like she'd imagined, and nothing like the ones in the numerous science fiction Space films Neil dragged her along to see. It was very small indeed and almost camouflaged in the undergrowth.

'This is only for travel,' Dezig explained. 'We live in a comfortable ship.' He raised his right hand as they approached the craft, and a door silently slid open. Cautiously, Joanna followed him inside, and the door slid shut behind her with a clang.

She gasped as she looked around. The craft had seemed small outside but it was vast inside: a huge shiny steel room, devoid of furniture except for a hard bench which must be where he slept. It must be uncomfortable, she thought.

'We do not sleep,' he explained. 'We merely shut half our mind away for a while to rest it. I'm sorry, I forget you do not possess our telepathic qualities.'

'Why did you pick on me?' she asked curiously.

'I thought you were a good specimen of an Earth woman,' he said.

Joanna thought about that. Did that mean he fancied her?

Dezig held out a small cup full of crystal clear liquid. 'I believe it is customary for Earth people to offer refreshment to visitors,' he said formally. 'So please take some.'

She hesitated.

'Come,' he said. 'I will drink too.'

She tasted it, and it was without doubt the most wonderful thing she'd ever tasted – like cool nectar. A warm, relaxed feeling flowed through her and she followed his example and sat cross-legged on the floor.

'Now tell me about Earth,' he said. 'Are all people black-haired?'

'Oh no,' said Joanna. 'My sister is blonde, like you. My boyfriend, Neil, has red hair.'

He looked at her in astonishment. 'Red hair?' he echoed.

'Yes,' she said. 'We all have different skin colours on Earth and hair colours and are different shapes and sizes.'

'This is an interesting discovery,' said Dezig. 'I had not read about this. All on our planet look the same – like me.'

'You mean everyone? Not just your family?' she asked.

'Family?' He looked puzzled. All people on our planet are family. Each man is my brother and each woman is my sister. All people look like me. It is the result of thousands of years of research into genetics. Once, our race were different shapes and sizes but now all are like me.'

'I don't think I'd like that,' Joanna said thoughtfully. 'It would be very boring to go out with different boyfriends who all look the same.'

'Tell me about boyfriends,' he said.

She blushed. 'Well . . . I go out with Neil, maybe for a meal, or to a film or we go to each other's houses. We play records together or perhaps go for walks. A boyfriend is someone with whom you have a very special relationship. You fall in love and sometimes if you love him a lot you get married and have children.'

'We do not have love, but do you like being with this boyfriend of yours?'

'Yes,' she said.

'You are not telling the truth,' said Dezig.

'It's really very disconcerting being with someone who can read your mind the whole time,' she said crossly. 'But . . . well, I suppose you're right. I thought I did like him very much when we started going out three months ago, but now I don't think I do. He always does what he wants – all the time. He'll be mad at me tonight because it's his birthday and I'm late. This is his present,' she added, indicating the book.

'A present? May I see please?'

She handed him the package and eagerly, Dezig tore off the

pretty wrapping paper and leafed through the manual.

'Why, this is a plan of how to build a vehicle,' he said in amazement. 'But it is so old-fashioned – it seems to run on petrol.'

'Yes,' she agreed.

'I am afraid your civilization is many years behind ours,' Dezig said apologetically. 'I don't think I can recommend to my people that we come here to live.'

'I don't think your civilization is that great,' Joanna said indignantly, 'if you don't even know the meaning of love.'

He smiled at her – a slow, lazy, dreamy smile and she felt a sudden surge of love towards him, and wanted to reach out and touch him and stroke his beautiful golden hair.

He was looking at her strangely as though he was reading her mind again and desperately she tried to block her thoughts.

'I am afraid it is time for you to go,' he said suddenly. 'I must move on. I have much to see, far to go. I do not think Earth is suitable for my people.'

She thought of how dull Neil was and how exciting life would be, travelling through space with this beautiful golden-haired stranger. 'Please take me with you,' she begged. 'I can teach you lots of things. I can teach you about love – something I know a lot more about than you do.'

He stared at her almost hypnotically, and she noticed that his clear pale eyes were almost liquid. Then he said, 'Dear Joanna. It is not possible. I cannot take you. You could not adjust to our life.'

'Don't you find me attractive?' she breathed.

'I find you beautiful. But you must go.' He passed a hand over the top of her head in a strange, almost magical way and she felt a rushing in her head and then, when it passed, a strange peace.

'I have given you a present. You will know what it is when

you are back with your people.'

'Take this.' She held out the book and he took it with a nod. She felt so attracted to him that she felt unable to leave him. She put a hand on his arm and gripped it tightly. Then, on impulse, she leaned forward and kissed him on the cheek – and drew back in horror, repulsed. For his skin was as cold and as lifeless as a corpse, and it was as if she'd laid her lips on something reptilian.

He smiled pityingly at her. 'I told you it was no good.'

Overwhelmed by terror at the awful, terrible coldness of his flesh, she turned and ran in blind panic. As if on command, the silent steel door slid open and she stumbled down the steps and didn't stop running until she had crossed the common.

She reached Neil's house and stood outside for a few minutes, panting and trembling. As she stood there, she heard distantly the same whirring noise she'd heard earlier, and spotted a bright light in the sky growing fainter and fainter. So he had gone.

Then she remembered the car manual, her birthday present to Neil that she'd given to Dezig in a fit of generosity. Whatever would Neil say? And what did Dezig mean when he spoke of a present he had given her. She looked at her watch. The hands had stopped at seven o'clock – the very moment she'd met Dezig. Goodness knows what Neil would say.

He looked sulkily at her as he opened the door.

'Do you know what time it is?' he complained. 'Eight-fifteen. You're an hour late – and on my birthday. It's too late to go to the film now. I've been waiting for you for over an hour.'

'No you haven't,' she said at once. And it was then she realized what Dezig's gift was.

'What do you mean?' Neil stuttered.

'You're a liar,' she said. 'You've only been here ten minutes yourself. You've been in the pub with your mate, John, all evening and you forgot the time.'

He stared at her in alarm. 'How did you know that?' he whispered.

'Oh . . . my brother saw you.' Well, how could she tell him that she'd been given the gift of telepathy by a golden-haired space traveller? 'Anyway,' she said, her mind made up now, 'I only came round to tell you that I'm very sorry but I lost your birthday present, and anyway I think it's about time we packed it in. After all, all we do is quarrel.'

She left him standing on the doorstep staring open-mouthed at her as she walked away. Far away in the now dark sky she could see a golden glow and she knew he was up there, watching her.

'Thanks for the present, Dezig,' she said softly. 'Now I can really have some fun.'

ROCK 'N' ROLL DREAMER

Toni Cornford

CAREFULLY, I UNROLLED MY NEW POSTER of Ricki Silver and studied it adoringly. He was fantastic – deep brown eyes that seemed to look right into mine, and thick hair, the same rich colour as his eyes. His lips were wide and full, slightly parted to show white, even teeth.

'Oh, you're wonderful,' I whispered with a sigh. 'If only . . . oh, if only I could see you for real.'

Ever since I'd heard Ricki's first record, I'd been crazy about him. Now I had every record he'd made, and my bedroom walls were covered with his photos and posters. By my bed was a bulging scrap book of newspaper cuttings and magazine articles, and I'd look through them avidly before going to sleep.

None of the boys in the tiny Irish village where I lived could ever compare with him. Next to Ricki, they were childish and dull.

I switched the radio on as I decided where to pin my latest poster. They were broadcasting a live interview with Ricki, and I didn't want to miss one single word!

'Now for the best rock show of the week,' the announcer said. 'And tonight I've managed to get, live in the studio, Ricki Silver. I know thousands of fans out there have been holding their breath for this, but now the wait's over and Ricki's right here with me.' There was a slight pause, then: 'It's good to see you again, Ricki, and welcome to the show.'

I was pinning the poster on the wall as I listened.

'Hi, Jeff, it's good to be here.'

Ricki's voice was warm and soft, and I felt my heart turn over at the sound. I lay down on my bed and looked up at the new poster on the wall, imagining that the voice from the radio was coming from the glossy print and talking only to me.

I was lost in a private world of romance as I listened, but the programme was over much too soon.

'Before you go, Ricki, I think there's something coming up you'd like the fans to know about,' the announcer said.

'Yes, I'm very happy to say we've just finalized arrangements for a tour,' Ricki replied. 'This one's only in England and Scotland, I'm afraid, but for the fans living in other parts of the country, I'm doing a full UK tour early next year.'

'That's great!' The announcer went on and on about where to get tickets and so on, but I wasn't interested. I could get all the details from the music papers at the weekend. What *I* was thinking about was how to get to England to see Ricki? I couldn't wait until he came to Ireland next year. I had to see him *now*!

I switched off the radio and lay on my bed glancing idly through my scrapbook. Somehow I had to get to one of those concerts. But how?

That was the problem that plagued me as I got ready for bed. My pocket-money, and the odd few pounds I got from baby-sitting after school, wouldn't pay for the journey, let alone the concert ticket!

My heart sank. Yet money wasn't the only problem. There were my parents to contend with, too. I sighed heavily as I turned out the light. Even if I did have enough money they'd never let me go.

'At your age, Philippa!' Mummy would exclaim. 'You're nought but a child.'

Old enough to be in love though – with Ricki Silver.

It was the following week that the idea came to me. I was standing on the harbour wall watching the men loading up a boat. It would be sailing for England on the next tide, unloading, then waiting for cargo to bring back again. All I had to do was sneak on to the boat and I'd get a free ride! It was the perfect answer to all my problems.

That night I got really excited as I went through the list of tour dates. The nearest one to the coast was in three weeks, that gave me time to save some more money and make my plans.

As the day came closer I began to feel nervous though. I'd never been far from my village before and the thought of going all the way to England on my own was scary. Yet I kept thinking of seeing Ricki, and it was enough to spur me on.

The concert was on a Saturday, so I had to leave home late Friday night. I didn't give much thought to what my parents would think when they found I'd gone, all I could think about was getting to England.

Once I was certain the rest of the family were asleep, I crept out of the house and hurried through the quiet, deserted streets to the harbour. When I saw the boats silhouetted against the moonlit sky I stopped to catch my breath and work out my next move.

I knew they'd all be going to England, but which was going tonight? Cautiously I tiptoed closer, watching for signs of one of the boats loading up with cargo.

Then I spotted it. Right at the end of the line men were carrying boxes up a gangplank – that was the one I was looking for. Now all I had to do was get on board without anyone seeing me.

Hiding behind a packing case on the dock, I waited until things quietened down and I could get to the boat without being seen. Eventually I heard one of the men say it was time for a break and a crowd of them went off to the office. That was my chance. The moment the door was shut I made a run for the boat. In a second I was hurrying soundlessly up the gangplank.

I'd been hoping to find a cosy little corner on the deck. I didn't relish the thought of being stuck down a stuffy hold for hours, but there was nowhere. Then, from the other side of the boat I heard someone whistling. I held my breath. I didn't want to be caught now so there was only one answer.

Quickly I dodged through the hatchway that led down to the hold. It was dark, and the smell was horrible, but I was too scared to care much.

Footsteps sounded overhead and stopped by the hatch. I dived behind a pile of boxes, pulling an old sack over me as I curled into a tight ball. Suddenly the whistling started again and the footsteps came slowly down the steps. I lay perfectly still and prayed hard.

It was then I felt a tickle in my nose. The sacking I'd pulled over me was very dusty and I wanted to sneeze desperately. I held my hand over my mouth as hard as I could, but it was no good. Three sneezes echoed around the confined space in as many seconds.

The whistling stopped immediately and the footsteps rushed towards me. As the sack was pulled roughly away, tears started to trickle slowly down my cheeks.

'I thought there was someone down here,' a voice exclaimed. 'I didn't realize they were pretty though!'

The remark was so unexpected, I stopped crying and stared at the guy in amazement. He only looked a few years older than me, and as he stared down his blue eyes were sparkling with fun. Then he laughed and held his hand out. 'You can't be very comfortable crouched down there,' he said, helping me to my feet. 'Come up on deck. I've got a flask of coffee and you look as though you could do with some.'

As the sack was pulled roughly away, tears started to trickle slowly down my cheeks.

I couldn't argue with him, I was too stunned. He led me up the steps and into a small room where a flask and box of sandwiches stood on the table. 'My name's Pete,' he said, pouring the coffee. 'What's yours?'

'Philippa,' I told him as I took the cup.

'So what were you doing in the hold, Philippa?' he asked. 'Running away from home?'

'No!' I replied hotly. 'At least . . . well . . . I was going to go back . . .'

Pete frowned at me. 'You mean you haven't quite made up your mind yet?'

'Of course I have,' I told him. 'I've just got to get to England that's all, but I didn't have enough money for the fare. It was only for a day or so, then I was coming back.'

It sounded funny to me, so I could understand why Pete looked so confused.

'You were going to visit someone over there?' he went on.

I shook my head as tears came very close to the surface. I don't know why, but suddenly my reason for going to England sounded a bit silly.

'Well, whatever it is, it must be important for you to risk getting into trouble,' Pete said quietly.

He came to stand in front of me, his arms folded as he looked at me carefully.

'It was – I mean, is.' I sighed shakily. 'At least I thought it was. Now . . .' I could feel the lump coming into my throat. '. . . I don't know any more.'

Before I could stop them, the tears were streaming down my face and I was sobbing uncontrollably. Pete's arms went around me and he held me gently as he comforted me.

'Oh, now it can't be that bad,' he said lightly. 'Why don't you sit down and drink your coffee? It'll make you feel better.'

I sank on to a chair by the table and sipped the coffee. It did feel good, and the warmth of it made me realize how cold and frightened I'd been down in that hold. Maybe my wonderful idea hadn't been so clever after all. Yet when I'd made my plans, it had mattered more than anything else in the world.

Gradually Pete got the story out of me, and it was strange how reluctant I felt about telling him. I honestly thought he'd laugh at me for being so stupid, but instead he seemed really surprised. 'You mean you've gone through all this for a rock star?' he asked.

I squirmed with embarrassment as I nodded.

'You must be a *real* fan – mind you, he is good,' Pete said then. 'I wish a pretty girl like you were that crazy over me though! There again I haven't got his looks or his voice.'

Something about the way Pete spoke made me want to jump to his defence. 'Oh, but you are good-looking,' I told him. 'And your voice is soft and gentle.'

My face went hot as I heard myself speak. I'd never said anything like that to a boy before. 'I'm sorry . . .' I stammered.

'Oh, don't be,' Pete said, shaking his head quickly as he grinned at me. 'It's not often I'm paid compliments and I like it! So if you want to say any more nice things, go ahead, I'm listening.'

He looked so pleased with himself I just burst out laughing.

'That's better,' he said gently. 'You should laugh more, it makes your eyes light up.'

Pete poured me another cup of coffee then he sat down on the chair next to me. 'Philippa, what are you going to do now?' he asked quietly. 'The thing is, if you're caught on the boat you'll get into a lot of trouble, and I'll *have* to tell the Captain. It's my job, you see, and . . .'

'It's all right, Pete,' I told him. 'I suppose it was a silly thing to do.'

'Especially on your own,' he said. 'And what would you have done in England? You'd have been a long way from home, and you'd have had no one to turn to if anything had happened. How would you have got a ticket anyway? The concert's sold out.'

Gently he took my hand and squeezed it. 'And besides,' he went on, 'it's much better to have a real live boyfriend than one you can only look at photos of, don't you think?'

I looked straight into Pete's eyes and my heart skipped a beat. He *was* good-looking, nothing at all like Ricki Silver, but then Pete was here, talking to me, holding my hand. Ricki Silver would never do that.

'But I haven't got a boyfriend,' I said shyly.

Pete grinned. 'Good! In that case I'd like to volunteer,' he said. 'I'll be away quite a bit, but we could write and I could phone you. I promise I'd make it up to you when I was home. Well, what d'you say?'

'Yes,' I said simply.

'Great!' Pete exclaimed. 'Now let's get you off this boat before the rest of the crew get back.'

After I'd written out my name and address for him, Pete took my hand and sneaked me along the deck and down the gangplank.

'Take care then, my little stowaway,' Pete smiled. 'You'll be getting a letter from me very soon.'

He kissed me lightly on the cheek and we went our separate ways.

I'd been really lucky that it had been Pete who'd found me. The truth was, the moment I'd stepped on board I'd been terrified, but I'd refused to be defeated. Thank goodness it had turned out well for me – although when I thought of the things that might have happened . . .

As I ran back through the still dark streets of the village, I was a lot happier than when I'd left. I wasn't going to get to see Ricki Silver after all, but by trying to, I'd found my first real boyfriend.

THE GUARDIAN ANGEL

Maureen Spurgeon

HE DIDN'T LOOK THE SORT OF BOY who desperately needed help, Linda decided. True, his brown eyes seemed dull and tired, the dark smudges underneath making him look older than she thought he was. And his jacket and jeans had a sort of 'lived-in look' – as her sister, Karen, would have said in a polite mood. Yet, his voice rang out firmly enough, much louder than the rain spattering against the grimy windows of the little hall.

Suddenly, he crashed his hands down on the upright piano, making the two other boys on guitar and drums look up like startled rabbits.

'No! We're still not getting it right. Useless, that's all we are. Useless!' The last word rose to a shout that echoed around the bare walls.

'Aw, come off it, Trevor,' the boy on guitar almost pleaded. 'Give us a chance!'

A chance. That's all Trevor wanted. That's what the girl said, earlier on when she had come into the old pram shed on the estate, where the hand-painted sign, HELPING HANDS, swung outside on a fancy hook that Sandra had screwed into place.

'Helping Hands,' Sandra had declared triumphantly. 'Now, does that sound like any dreary old advice centre?'

Linda had to admit that it didn't – more like somewhere to have a coffee and a chat and meet people who really seemed as if they wanted to help. That's what her sister, Sandra, wanted. And, being Sandra, that's what she got.

So, what with pets needing holiday homes, old people wanting shopping done and a library service to get organized, Linda knew what to expect when Sandra said quite casually one evening, 'Don't suppose you could do a few odd jobs for *Helping Hands*, could you, Linda? You know, making tea, looking up 'phone numbers – that sort of thing.'

'Yes, go on!' Mum butted in, before Linda could say anything. 'It'll do you good to make yourself useful.'

'Besides,' Sandra went on quickly, linking her arm coaxingly through Linda's, 'Mike's calling later on to take me out for a meal, and I promised I'd be early. Monday's always a dull sort of night, anyway.'

'I'll pop down later on, if you like,' Mum added briskly. 'But you're sensible enough, aren't you?'

Linda didn't bother to answer.

Soon she was confessing to one old man that she couldn't find the address of the nearest foot clinic. Sandra glanced up from handing over some leaflets to a boy wearing a college scarf and called breezily, 'It's on the list behind the 'phone books, Linda! Underneath 'H' for Health!'

The boy grinned and winked at Linda. 'Follow that! Now you know what it means to sit in the shadow of greatness!'

Linda blushed, busying herself with writing down the foot clinic address for the old man, and thinking that the boy seemed rather nice. The sort you could talk to, maybe, and laugh with, sometimes.

'Going anywhere afterwards?' He was talking to Sandra, not Linda. 'There's this new disco, just opened.'

'Sorry!' Sandra said, in a voice which meant she was. 'I've already got a date with my boyfriend!' She glanced across at Linda pretending to tidy up the filing cabinet. 'And, now I've got a new assistant, we're grabbing Monday nights for ourselves! Thanks, anyway.'

The boy sighed and turned towards the door without looking at Linda again. 'See you around.'

It was then Linda started wondering if she needed *Helping Hands*. Except that feeling lonely, being tongue-tied and wanting someone a bit special to be with, didn't seem like much of a problem – at least, not to Sandra.

That was almost a month ago, Linda had reflected that evening, looking out at the rain, and remembering her dad commenting, 'Rotten weather for May,' before she came out.

She was fiddling with her watch, and telling herself she'd wait another half an hour before locking up, when the girl came in. Just the quiet click of the door opening, and there she was, strands of chestnut-coloured hair clinging damply to her pale face, and fat beads of water dripping from the collar of her jacket. She was painting painfully, as if she'd been running for a long time. Her brown eyes stared anxiously into Linda's.

'Can – can I help you?' Linda offered rather feebly. 'Come and sit down.'

'No, I – I don't have much time.' Maybe she'd be two or three years older than Sandra, Linda guessed, but she spoke more like a woman. 'You see, there's someone who needs help desperately – the sooner the better!'

'What's the name?' asked Linda, automatically reaching for the message pad.

'It's Jameson – Trevor Jameson. He runs *Branchline* – you know, at the back of Hillfield House. And someone's got to give him a hand before it's too late. Simply got to. All he needs is a chance.'

For a moment, Linda wished Sandra was there. But then, she was scribbling on the message pad, and hearing herself saying, 'All right, I'll call and see what needs doing.'

'Oh, thanks! Thanks a lot!' Whoever she was, she sounded

grateful enough to make Linda feel quite proud of herself. 'I knew you wouldn't let me down.'

'Best leave a note about where I've gone,' Linda went on, still scribbling. 'Can you tell me . . .?'

But the door was already closing, and there was nothing more than the swish of rain and traffic in the distance.

'Wasn't kidding about being short of time, was she?' Linda murmured aloud. 'Lucky I've even got a name and address!'

Hillfield House was easy to find, being near Hillfield library, which was just past the new Civic Centre. *Branchline* proved rather more difficult, because the sign pointing the way was smeared with dirt, and there was no light along the narrow path leading to what might have been a garage or a bike shed in the dark.

Linda could just about read a handwritten notice inside one of the windows: BRANCHLINE THEATRE COMPANY. NEW MEMBERS WANTED. The faintly dismal sound of an old piano, with a guitar and drums in the background, drifted up through the broken skylight.

And, now? Well, here she was, walking slowly towards the small platform where three pairs of eyes were squinting at her through the gloom.

'I'm Linda Hunt,' she announced, racking her brains to think of an excuse for calling. 'That – that notice outside says you want new members.'

There was an awkward pause, before the guitar-playing boy said, 'That notice has been up some time. Things've changed.'

'What Steve means,' Trevor said quietly, 'is that we're ready to chuck it in. We're just not good enough, not any more. And it's mostly my fault. I can't seem to concentrate, like.'

So, that was it. That was what the girl meant about Trevor desperately needing someone. As soon as she'd noticed the lines on his face, and the way his shoulders drooped, she knew she felt sorrier for him than she'd ever been for herself, even though she didn't quite understand why.

'No wonder you can't concentrate when you can't even see properly!' she remarked with some feeling. 'Couldn't you get some stronger light bulbs, and maybe a few lamps and things?'

'Yes. . . .' Trevor didn't seem exactly half-hearted, but he didn't look too enthusiastic, either. 'Only, there's more to it than that.'

'If I cleaned the windows, that'd let more light inside,' Linda continued eagerly, starting to enjoy herself. 'Then you'd be able to practise much better!'

'Yes. Well,' began Trevor, after another pause, 'it's not that easy. Time's running a bit short.'

Time was running out. That's what the girl had said.

'What Trev means is that we've only got another fortnight to get our act together for the Arts Festival competition,' the drummer explained patiently.

'This time last year we'd have made it. No sweat!' Steve informed her. 'Since then – well, we've hit a bad patch. Nothing seems to be going right.'

'So – won't you be wanting any new members, now?'

Linda must have looked as disappointed as she felt, because Trevor managed a weary smile as he said, 'What could we give them to do?'

'Look,' Linda let out a deep breath, 'I've already offered to smarten this place up a bit. And, my sister says . . .'

'Your sister?'

Tina debated whether to explain about *Helping Hands*, then decided against it. After all, she reasoned, Trevor might not like the idea of someone else interfering. Besides, Sandra already had plenty of boyfriends.

'My sister, Sandra – she – she's quite a bit older than me, and she's always talking about sorting out one problem at a time. Wouldn't do any harm anyway, would it?'

She was glad when Steve added his opinion. 'Nothing to lose, is there, Trev? You know me and Andy, we're always right behind you.'

'And we might still make it!' said Andy, with the first touch of lively conversation Linda had heard all evening.

'Okay.' Trevor sounded too tired to be either pleased or fed up. He turned to Tina. 'You can start tomorrow night, if you like. Do you have to come far?'

'Not really – only Highcroft Estate. It's a fairly straight walk.'

'Quicker by the single-decker bus from the clock tower!' Trevor announced, taking Linda's arm. 'Come on. I'll walk you through the shopping precinct, then you'll miss most of the rain. There's a bus due at half-past, I think.'

He pushed open the rickety door and guided her out into the narrow lane. The dim light glinted in the puddles that led away from the shabby little hall.

'Quite a night,' Trevor remarked, looking up at the sky. 'You must have been dead keen to join *Branchline*, I must say. How did you know about us?'

'Er, someone told me, a little while ago.' Linda wished she could sound more convincing. 'I've always been interested in music and things like that.'

Fortunately, she didn't need to say anything else, because Trevor remained silent until they'd walked through the deserted precinct and out into the High Street.

'Look at that! A bus actually on time for once!' Linda couldn't help being rather disappointed. 'Well, see you tomorrow, then.'

'Got your fare?' he asked.

'Just about.' Linda grinned, and he smiled back, making his mouth crinkle at the edges.

'See you tomorrow night, Linda,' he said, turning up the

collar of his jacket. 'Must dash!'

'Yes . . . all right. 'Night, then, Trevor.'

It was only when she'd got home and struggled out of her wet anorak, that Linda remembered. She still didn't know who the girl was. Only that she'd been right about Trevor needing a friend. Somehow, the thought made her want to start skipping around the bedroom.

By the time Trevor arrived at *Branchline* the following evening, all the furniture had been neatly stacked, with the lights winking brightly on the freshly polished windows.

'Hey! Some improvement!' he exclaimed joyfully, rubbing his hands together. 'This gives us more space for practising stage routines, and everything!'

Linda swept some more dust from the platform on to the floor with a proud flourish. 'Thought you'd be pleased. And I found an electric kettle, so maybe we can even have a coffee break!'

She wondered afterwards if he might have smiled again, or said something else, if Steve and Andy hadn't come in and started to set up the drum kit. And yet, it didn't seem to matter too much, not when the first song was judged by Trevor to be 'not too bad, to start with'.

She started humming to herself, feeling happy even when Trevor waved goodbye to her at the bus-stop. After all, hadn't he called her a great help, and said they couldn't have managed without her? Nobody had ever said that before.

'I'd watch out if I were you.' Sandra advised later on, after Mum had ordered Linda to strip off her dirty clothes and take a hot bath. 'Sounds to me as if someone's getting you to do the donkey work, so's they can claim all the credit.'

Linda stopped singing just long enough to picture the girl's brown eyes clouding anxiously. And the way Trevor smiled. She couldn't believe it. Not really. Even if Sandra was so much more clever, as people were always pointing out. But – Trevor hadn't said anything when she'd mentioned she was interested in music. Girls at school thought her voice wasn't bad at all.

It was almost a week before Linda felt like singing again, after lots of rehearsals and run-throughs, as Trevor called them, with snatches of music hastily written on scraps of paper, and practised until they were as near perfect as he could make them.

He hardly seemed to notice Linda fetching and carrying, sweeping and dusting, waiting for him to walk with her through the shopping precinct, and secretly hoping he'd say something more than, 'Thanks for everything, Linda. See you tomorrow.'

So, she didn't really know why she started singing. It wasn't even a song she knew or had ever learned. Maybe it was the rain clattering down again, making her think the girl might appear from nowhere, still with a wet face and damp hair, but her brown eyes now glowing warmly.

'*He's a real nowhere man. Going through his nowhere land.*
Making all his nowhere plans for nobody. . . .'

Linda wasn't sure she'd got the right words, but she seemed to remember the tune.

'*Doesn't have a point of view.*
Knows not where he's going to.'

She didn't know whether she heard the door being pushed open, or not.

'*Isn't he a bit like you – and me?*'

'Okay! That's enough!' It was an order, flung viciously across the hall as if she were hated.

'I – I was only singing, Trevor.'

'Well, you can shut up!' His voice was thin and piercing now, each word seeming strangled. 'Just shut up! Leave us to do the stage work – got it?'

Leave us to do the stage work, he said. So, Sandra had been right about him only wanting her for donkey work. Nobody but Linda Hunt would be stupid enough to think anything else.

She bit her lip, and untied the scarf from around her hair, thinking of catching the bus back home, and never seeing Trevor again, never being friends with him.

It didn't exactly seem a good time to start singing again. Yet, maybe, the song suited him.

'He's a real nowhere man. Going through his nowhere land.
Making all his nowhere plans, for nobody.'

'Linda – that song.' Steve interrupted quietly. 'Hazel, Trevor's sister, that's the one she always used to sing. We were rehearsing it for last year's competition, when . . . well, when . . .'

Steve's words faltered to a stop, although his mouth was opening and closing as if he was trying to think of some way to tell Linda something which, from the look on his face, she already knew.

'How – how did she die?'

'Killed in a car crash. I kept the bit I cut out from the paper, because – well, sometimes, I still can't believe it. It was Hazel who got us together to start with, see? She was always behind us, pushing us further on. Losing her, hit us all pretty hard. Trevor most of all.'

Linda stared at the newspaper cutting she held in her shaking hand. The long hair was printed black, the eyes only a shade lighter, instead of the rich, deep brown that Linda remembered, sparkling with hope when she'd promised to see Trevor.

There was an awkward tap on her shoulder, making her stand quite still, not wanting to turn around and see his face.

'Sorry I yelled at you, Linda, but I don't have to explain, do I? About Hazel, I mean. My sister.'

244

Linda still couldn't turn round, not until he took her hand, and said in a husky sort of voice, 'Would – would you like to see the photo that press picture was printed from? I always carry it around with me.'

Hazel's brown eyes were as lovely as she remembered. But her smile was brighter, Linda thought, as if there might be a candle burning deep inside, bursting into light.

'I haven't been able to talk about her,' Trevor was saying shakily, 'not until just now, really. You – you'd have liked her, Linda. Everyone did.'

Linda began stroking the photograph lightly with her finger. 'Maybe I never got to know her, Trevor. But she was still the best friend I ever had.'

'Eh? What did you say, Linda?'

'Nothing. It doesn't matter.' She handed back Hazel's photograph, feeling a delicious shiver of happiness to see Trevor smiling, and holding out his hand towards her.

'Like to run through *Nowhere Man*? Don't forget, we've still got the competition to win!'

They laughed softly together, as if they were enjoying a precious secret. A secret which, Linda knew, Hazel would always share.

They laughed softly together, as if they were enjoying a precious secret. A secret which, Linda knew, Hazel would always share.

GREEN EYED MONSTER

Toni Cornford

DALE WAS LEANING against a fresh bale of straw, looking thoughtful as he watched me clean out Lady Midnight's stall. 'Pamper her, Sally,' he said with a faraway look in his eye. 'I want her in a good mood for the race tomorrow.'

'Don't worry,' I said with a smile. 'The race is important to *all* of us. She'll be on top form, I promise.'

'With you looking after her I know she will be,' Dale went on with a grin. 'And like all nice ladies this one loves the gentle touch!'

Dale was teasing and I knew it, and when I turned to answer him I was laughing. Then I saw Chuck standing by the stable door and I stifled the friendly retort that came so automatically to my lips. Instead, I assured Dale in an efficient voice, 'She'll be happy and ready to win tomorrow. So don't worry, you'll be riding your first winner for the stable.'

The sudden change in my voice warned Dale that Chuck was watching us and he responded instantly. 'See you then, Sally,' he said as he turned to leave. Then, 'Hi, Chuck. All ready for the big day?'

'Naturally,' Chuck replied curtly.

Dale walked past him and out into the yard, but Chuck hadn't looked at him once, he was staring at me in that jealous way I'd come to dread lately. 'What was he doing hanging around you again?' Chuck demanded irritably.

'He wasn't hanging around me,' I replied with a sigh. 'He was just checking on Lady Midnight, that's all.'

'Huh. It looked like it,' Chuck muttered. 'I'll get even with him one day, Sally, you can bet on that.' Without another word he turned and stomped out.

I could understand Chuck's resentment towards Dale, but I couldn't condone it. In the beginning, I thought it was something which would pass, but as time had gone on, Chuck's anger and hatred had grown out of all proportions.

The problem had started when Mitch Murphy, the owner of the stables where we both worked, had taken Dale on as an apprentice jockey. Chuck had been confident that he'd be Mitch's first choice as apprentice when the job came up. He'd been a groom for a couple of years, and to everyone at the stables he'd been the obvious one to get the apprenticeship. So there'd been a lot of raised eyebrows when Mitch had taken on Dale Burton, someone from outside.

Chuck had been bitter and angry. When he'd heard the decision he'd blown his stack and gone straight into Mitch's office to ask why. The reason Mitch had given him was that he wasn't happy about Chuck's attitude to the horses. He could be rough and impatient with them, and that didn't conform with the policy of the stables.

There'd been a fierce argument, but Mitch wouldn't budge from his decision. Chuck had no option but to go along with it, although he made it plain from his attitude to Dale that he wasn't going to let him forget the opportunity he'd snatched from him.

As the weeks passed and Dale became popular with the rest of the staff, Chuck's resentment towards him started to smoulder. Then Dale gave Chuck another reason to be bitter – me. Unfortunately Dale didn't know that Chuck and I were dating, but he soon found it!

I was working in the stables one morning when Dale came back after exercising one of the horses, and I automatically went over to make a fuss of the horse.

'You love horses, don't you, Sally?' Dale asked quietly. 'I've watched you around them and you're so gentle and caring.'

I shrugged, feeling a bit embarrassed. 'My father used to ride,' I told him. 'He was pretty good in his day, too. I suppose I inherited it from him.'

'Did he used to race?' Dale asked with interest.

'No, he was into showjumping,' I replied. 'When I was little I remember sitting in the kitchen with my mother and polishing his trophies and cups.' I smiled at the memory. 'There seemed to be hundreds, all different shapes and sizes. I used to polish them till my arms ached, but I didn't mind. I was so proud of my dad. I was determined even then, that when I was old enough I was going to work with horses.'

'I'm glad you did,' Dale said, 'or we'd never have . . .'

'Sally!' Chuck's voice seemed to boom around the confined stable, and I jumped, startled by the sudden sound.

'Hi, Chuck,' I said, my voice sounding guilty even though there was nothing to feel guilty about. 'You scared me – I didn't see you come in.'

'That was obvious!' he snapped. 'Mitch wants to see you, so you'd better get going. Anyway I want to have a quiet word with the jockey here. There are a few things he should know!'

Chuck had never shown any signs of jealousy before, but at that moment his eyes were flashing with anger and his lips were set in a narrow line.

Neither of the boys said a word until I'd left the stable, but I didn't go straight to Mitch's office, I stood outside to hear what Chuck wanted to say to Dale. It was very short – and very unpleasant!

'I'll say this once,' Chuck snarled. 'Stay away from Sally. I've seen you cast your wandering eye over her, but forget it. She's my girl and she stays that way. Find someone else!'

'Hey, hang on,' Dale protested. 'I didn't know you were going out together. Anyway, I was only being friendly. Sally's a nice girl.'

'You're right, she is,' Chuck interrupted. 'And she's mine!'

As he turned to come out of the stable, I ducked around the corner so he wouldn't see me. I was furious with Chuck. He had no right to behave like that, and he certainly had no right to be talking about me as though I was a piece of his property!

I was so angry I deliberately avoided him for the rest of the day. The scene that morning had confused and upset me, although I wasn't sure what to do about it. Dale and I had always been friendly, and while we laughed and joked together there was nothing in it, but Chuck plainly thought otherwise.

When I saw him that night I couldn't just let the incident pass without saying something, yet Chuck had a very plausible reason all ready for me. 'It's got nothing to do with me being jealous or anything else,' he said with a disarming smile. 'It's just that the guy's keen on you, everyone knows that, Sal, and I don't want to lose you. You're very special to me and I just don't want Dale taking liberties and embarrassing you.'

He looked deep into my eyes and as he leaned forward to kiss me I had no reason not to believe him.

Yet after that night, my feelings for Chuck began to change until I wasn't sure how I felt any more. Most of the time he was sweet and attentive as he'd always been, but his sudden flashes of anger showed themselves more and more often.

Nevertheless, I made a point of going on being friendly towards Dale, if only to prove to him that Chuck didn't own me. Yet whenever Chuck was around we both seemed to become cautious. It was a really crazy situation. Dale was far too nice a guy to steal someone else's girl, but there was no way I could convince Chuck of that.

As the weeks passed, my relationship with Chuck started to go wrong. We began to argue, not much, but enough to leave bad feeling between us after a date which meant we had to do a lot of making up.

Then Mitch announced that Dale was to ride in the Silver Bowl Trophy, one of the biggest races in our area. It was an important race, not just for Dale, but for Mitch, too. If one of his horses won, the Murphy stable would become well known and mean a lot more business for Mitch.

We all hoped Lady Midnight would win – even Chuck, which I must admit surprised me. The night before the race, he took me out to dinner and naturally our main topic of conversation was the Silver Bowl.

'Oh, I really hope Dale wins tomorrow,' I said excitedly. 'Everyone's really keyed up about the race, and it would be such a boost for Mitch. Since he took over from his uncle he's worked so hard to make it a success – this would be exactly what he needs.'

'That's true,' Chuck agreed.

'Just think of all the extra business we'd get,' I went on. 'People would want Mitch to train and stable their horses, and mothers would be queuing up for their darling little children to be taught at the riding school. Maybe he'd even expand!'

Chuck nodded, yet he seemed miles away, lost in a world of his own. Suddenly he turned to me and smiled. 'Sally, darling, let's forget about the race, the stables, and Mitch Murphy,' he said softly. 'It's all I've heard for weeks. So for tonight, can we change the subject? I want to talk about you – us. We haven't been getting on too good lately, and I know it's been my fault. I want to make it up to you – show you I'm not such a bad guy after all.'

That evening was the happiest we'd spent together for a long time. Chuck seemed so anxious to please me, just as he had when we'd first started going out together. The subject of my friendship with Dale wasn't mentioned either, which was a relief, and when Chuck gently took me in his arms to kiss me goodnight, I honestly thought he'd finally got over his bout of jealousy.

Next morning, everyone was at work extra early and the stables were buzzing with excitement. Mitch and Dale spent hours closetted in the office going over all the details of the race, while the rest of us concentrated on getting everything ready.

The saddle and bridle were polished until they gleamed, and Lady Midnight was groomed to perfection. When she was led into the horsebox, I'm sure she knew that all our hopes were pinned firmly on her winning.

I didn't see Chuck to talk to until we got to the racecourse. As chief groom, he'd gone on ahead in his own car. When I finally arrived, he was standing by the rails of the paddock staring at the starting post.

He'd been quiet all morning, hardly speaking to anyone, but I'd been too busy to bother about why. Now I felt uneasy. His mood was a complete contrast to the night before, and as I watched him stroll over to Lady Midnight to give her a last brush, I couldn't stop my growing suspicion that Chuck was up to something.

Dale looked marvellous in his racing colours, and Lady Midnight pawed the ground, making it plain she was raring to go. I laughed as I went up to wish him good luck, then I stood back to admire the horses circling the paddock before leaving for the starting post.

Suddenly Chuck went over to Dale, his hand outstretched. I watched in amazement. After all he'd said about Dale, and the threats he'd handed out, I couldn't really believe Chuck was prepared to forget their differences so easily. Yet that's exactly what was happening – or *appeared* to be happening.

Dale took Chuck's hand and shook it, but I was staring at Chuck's other hand as it rested on the back of Lady Midnight's saddle. While he was adding his good luck wishes to ours, Chuck was pushing something under the saddle!

My heart started to beat frantically. He was going to sabotage the race. He was going to stop Dale winning, and get his spiteful revenge on Mitch at the same time. Chuck hadn't forgiven or forgotten. On the contrary, the resentment he'd been harbouring all this time had finally boiled over.

What had he said to me about getting even with Dale?

As Chuck sauntered back to where I was standing, he was smiling to himself – a smug, secret smile that made me almost hate him.

'You put something under that saddle, didn't you?' I demanded furiously. 'How could you, Chuck? How could you be so malicious?'

Chuck tilted his head back and looked at me defiantly. 'He had it coming,' he replied with unnerving coldness. 'We both know I should be up there now, Sally. He's got no right to all the glory!'

I was so angry I couldn't speak. Chuck had shown the sort of person he was and I didn't like it one bit.

Out of the corner of my eye, I saw the horses start to move out of the paddock towards the starting post. Without another thought I turned and ran to where Mitch was standing. Quickly I told him what had happened, and that Chuck hadn't denied it when I'd challenged him.

Mitch heard me out then swung around and glared at Chuck, his face a mask of anger. But his first concern was for Dale and Lady Midnight. Only it was too late. Before we could warn Dale, the horses were already lined up waiting to go into the stalls.

'Oh, no!' I gasped as the stalls opened and the horses began to surge forward.

'Don't blame yourself, Sally,' Mitch said. 'We'll just have to hope for the best.'

I could hardly breathe as I watched the horses gallop towards the first turn. Any minute, Lady Midnight could rear,

*While he was adding his good luck wishes to ours, Chuck was
pushing something under the saddle.*

throwing Dale, and causing nasty injuries to the other riders, too.

How I hated Chuck right then, and how I felt for Dale. He was such a nice person, he didn't deserve to be the victim of Chuck's viciousness.

'He's gaining on the leaders.' Mitch looked at me, a puzzled frown creasing his forehead while his voice rose with excitement.

'But he can't be.' I whispered. 'Surely . . .'

Mitch was right though. Lady Midnight was steadily catching up with the first three horses, and a minute later she was neck and neck with the leader of the field. My heart was thudding in time to the hoofbeats on the hard ground, and I crossed my fingers tightly.

As Lady Midnight pulled slightly ahead to take the lead, I forgot about Chuck and started urging Dale on. With only a furlong to go to the finishing line, Lady Midnight moved into a clear lead. She couldn't lose – not now!

Tears were streaming down my face as Dale cleared the finishing line well ahead of the others. Mitch grabbed me and hugged me, then we ran to welcome them back.

'Congratulations, Dale,' Mitch called out as he patted Lady Midnight. 'That was a faultless ride.'

Dale slid out of the saddle and grinned. 'It might not have been,' he said, handing something to Mitch, 'but it's lucky I've got a suspicious mind.'

Mitch opened his hand and studied the small, sharp edged piece of stone lying in his palm.

'I knew Chuck was up to something when he wished me luck,' Dale went on. 'And when I checked, that was under the saddle.'

Mitch closed his fist around the stone. 'I think it's time I dispensed with Chuck's services,' he said grimly. 'We can do without his sort at the stables.'

When he'd gone to find Chuck I turned to Dale. 'You were fantastic,' I told him. 'I'm only sorry Chuck did what he did. I feel awful about that, Dale, as though . . .'

'Stop right there,' he said with a smile. 'None of this is your fault, Sally. Chuck's always had it in for me, something like this was bound to happen sooner or later.'

'Maybe,' I sighed. 'But when I realized what was going on, there wasn't time to warn you. Oh, Dale, I wish there was something I could do.'

I felt so helpless, and somehow responsible.

'There is,' Dale said seriously. 'Have dinner with me tonight to celebrate.'

Suddenly his lips curved into a smile and I felt my heart lift. Even if Chuck had been staying on at the stables there was no way I could have gone out with him again. I couldn't forgive him for what he'd tried to do to Dale.

When Dale came back from being weighed in, he put his arm around me and I felt proud and happy. I'd made a mistake over Chuck, but it wasn't the end of the world. I was only glad I found out what he was really like in time, and I knew I'd enjoy a lot more of Dale's company.

FALLEN HERO
Toni Cornford

'RIGHT, HERE'S THE HAT, MANDY,' Karen Barker, the editor of *Pop-In* magazine, said, holding out a huge cardboard top hat filled to the brim with postcards. 'We had a terrific response to the competition, and now it's up to you to pick the person you'll be going to dinner with.'

As I reached out my hand to pick the winning card a flashlight went off.

'Hold on, Cindy, my film's jammed!' Mike, the photographer quickly put in a fresh film. 'Okay, let's do it again.'

My hand had been resting on one of the cards, and at Mike's instruction I moved it slightly and picked up another one.

It had been my manager's idea to hold the competition in conjunction with some articles the magazine were doing on me and the band. We'd had a lot of success with our first album and two of our singles had got into the charts. Now we needed to promote our forthcoming tour, and that's when our manager, Dave, had come up with the idea of a competition.

'How would you like an evening out with Cindy, the singer with Apple Blossom? Pop-In Magazine can make it happen for you! Try our competition today and you might be the lucky one . . .'

The band and I had been thrilled at the coverage the magazine had given us. They'd done an article on each member of the band, finishing the series with the competition. It had been a lot of fun, and now the competition had been judged and we were all in the magazine's offices to pick the winner.

–'Ready now?' I laughed at Mike.

'Say cheese,' he said with a cheeky grin.

As he spoke I turned to look at him, laughing at the old-fashioned phrase, and holding up the winning card. The flashlight went off again and everyone cheered.

'Who's the lucky person?' Karen asked excitedly.

I glanced down at the card while the others crowded round.

'Come on, Cindy,' Dave urged. 'Don't keep it to yourself. Read out the name and address.'

For a moment I could hardly speak, then I shook my head. No, it couldn't possibly be him – entering competitions to meet a singer just wasn't his scene at all.

'Gavin Samuels,' I read. 'He's from Selbury.'

Karen took the card from me and scribbled down the name and address.

'Selbury . . . Isn't that your home town, Cindy?' she asked suddenly. 'What a coincidence!'

'It certainly is,' I agreed.

'This will make a terrific story!' she went on. 'I'll contact him today and make all the arrangements.'

While the others were discussing the publicity angle, I wandered away to the far end of the office, lost in thought.

Gavin Samuels . . .

My heart started beating a little faster just thinking of him, and my mind went back to my schooldays when I'd been crazily in love with the handsome sixth former. I'd been two years younger than him and couldn't hope to compete with the older girls, so I'd had to love Gavin from afar.

When he'd played in the school football team I'd gone to every match, cheering him from the sidelines and wishing it could have been me who'd comforted him when he'd been injured. At the end of term disco I'd refused to dance with anyone, content just to sit and watch Gavin, hoping against hope that before the night was over he'd notice me and come and sweep me off my feet.

Of course none of that had happened. Gavin had always had his pick of beautiful girls and I hadn't stood a chance.

After he left school and went to college my heart broke and I was convinced I'd never recover. It was agony going to school day after day and knowing he wouldn't be there. Yet in time I did get over Gavin – or so I'd thought until I'd seen his name on the postcard.

'Hey, Cindy, what are you doing over there on your own?' Dave called out. 'We're making plans here.'

'Coming,' I called back.

Quickly I pushed my memories away and put a bright smile on my face. Anyway, it might not even be him, just someone with the same name . . .

Karen arranged everything for the following week. I was to arrive at the restaurant at seven o'clock where I'd meet the prizewinner. We wouldn't be alone, though. Mike, Dave and Karen would be with us for the first part of the evening while we had drinks, to get publicity shots and comments from Gavin. In fact the only time Gavin and I *would* be alone was during the actual meal.

I was trembling with anticipation as I got ready. What if it *was* him? I'd thought of nothing else since I'd picked that postcard out of the hat. Yet it had to be my Gavin. How many Gavin Samuelses lived in Selbury?

Those old memories came flooding back again and my heart was suddenly beating faster, almost taking my breath away. Would he realize I was the skinny fifth former who'd had such an enormous crush on him?

When the car came to collect me I took a last look in the mirror.

'Well,' I said out loud. 'This is it, Cindy. Tonight you

finally get to meet your hero . . .

Dave came to greet me as I stepped out of the car, and Mike started taking pictures.

'You look fabulous,' Dave said admiringly. 'Our prize-winner's going to be bowled over, believe me.'

'Is he here yet?' I asked nervously.

'Oh, he's here all right!' Dave laughed. 'He was half an hour early, and Karen's been bombarding the poor guy with questions ever since!'

Dave took my arm and led me towards the lounge, where a section had been cordoned off for our exclusive use. Mike ran on ahead to take more pictures.

'Oh, yes, I almost forgot,' Dave said suddenly. 'Gavin mentioned something about you having gone to the same school. It might just be a ploy, of course.' He laughed. 'You know how people love to be able to say they went to the same school as a star. But if it's true, it'll make a terrific story. Do you remember him at all?'

I couldn't answer straight away, and I felt stupidly light-headed. Eventually I shrugged.

'There was a guy with the same name at school,' I said carefully. 'But he was older than me. I won't know for sure till I see him.'

Dave stopped to let me go in front of him.

'Well, take a look,' he said quietly. 'He's over there with Karen.'

I glanced in the direction Dave had indicated, and my heart seemed to stop beating. When it started again I could actually hear it pounding. He was more good-looking than I remembered, and his hair was lighter, bleached by the sun. His face was leaner, too, and had a more mature look about it. But there was no doubt – it was the same Gavin Samuels I'd been in love with at school.

As though he'd felt me staring at him Gavin suddenly looked

up, his eyes meeting mine. For a full minute he just sat, transfixed, then he was on his feet and coming towards me. He might have looked older, but his broad, tantalizing smile was still exactly the same.

'Cindy,' he said softly as he took my hand. 'I can't believe it's really you.'

I was vaguely aware of Mike dodging around us taking photos from all angles, but my whole attention was focussed on Gavin.

'Oh, it's me all right,' I said with a shaky laugh. 'And *I* couldn't believe it when I picked your postcard out of the pile of winners. I didn't think this sort of competition was your style, Gavin.'

He laughed. 'It's a long story,' he said, taking my arm and leading me over to Karen. 'I'll tell you over dinner.'

Karen was enthralled by the fact that Gavin and I had been to the same school, and kept saying what a wonderful, romantic story it would make for the magazine. I didn't tell her the truth behind it though. Right then, I didn't want anyone to know how I felt about Gavin – especially Gavin himself!

As Karen scribbled away in her notebook I kept wishing she'd hurry up and finish the interview so Gavin and I could be alone. And by the look in Gavin's eyes he was feeling the same.

'Okay, that's all for now,' Karen said as she snapped the notebook shut. 'I suppose you two have got some catching up to do, so I'll leave you to it.'

Suddenly Gavin and I were alone. I'd been so looking forward to this moment, but now it had come I didn't have a clue what to say.

Dave had instilled in me that I was the star of the show, and therefore would have to make the opening moves to put Gavin at ease. Yet as I searched around frantically for something to say to open the conversation, Gavin did it for me.

'Cindy, this is incredible, isn't it?' he said. 'I never thought we'd meet again this way.'

'You were going to tell me how you came to enter the competition,' I reminded him.

'Oh, it was my sister, Petra,' Gavin explained. 'She gets the magazine every week and was reading the feature about you. She was jumping around like a two-year-old when I said we'd been to school together, and she kept on at me to have a go.'

'I'm glad you did,' I smiled.

Gavin nodded and smiled back in his charming way.

'I'm glad I did, too,' he said softly. 'In a way it was my last chance to . . .'

Before Gavin could finish what he was saying the waiter came over and opened an enormous bottle of champagne.

'Here's to you, Cindy,' Gavin said, raising his glass to me. 'And every success in your career.'

We drank a toast, then waiters were fussing around serving dinner and I didn't have a chance to ask Gavin what he'd been about to say.

During the meal we reminisced briefly about our school-days, but Gavin was much more interested in my career. He wanted to know all about the recording sessions, who wrote the songs, and even where I bought my stage clothes. They were odd questions, and the intent way Gavin listened to my answers made me feel a bit uneasy.

'What an exciting life you've made for yourself, Cindy,' he said wistfully. 'A lot better than those end of term discos. Weren't they the pits?'

'Oh, I don't know,' I said in a slow, teasing voice. 'You seemed to enjoy them. But maybe that was because you were always surrounded by beautiful girls!'

Gavin was quiet for a moment, then he looked deep into my eyes.

'Yes, but none of them was the *right* girl,' he said seriously.

My heart started to pound at the way he was looking at me

and I began to feel embarrassed under his gaze. Just then the waiter served our coffee and I was able to change the subject.

'What did you do when you left school?' I asked evenly. 'I know you went to college, but what did you take there?'

Gavin looked strangely uncomfortable at my question, but he quickly recovered his composure.

'Oh, things didn't quite work out,' he began cautiously. 'But to be honest I had second thoughts. I dropped out at the end of last year and decided to get a job instead. I was lucky, too. I'd got to know this guy at college whose father had a small advertising agency, so I got him to take me on. I did some photographic work for him, but . . . well, that didn't work out either . . .'

My feeling of unease was growing rapidly. I kept thinking back to the Gavin I'd woven romantic daydreams about for all those years. At school he'd been so self-assured and was always talking about the future. Gavin had known exactly what he wanted from life and that was one reason why I'd loved him. Yet after all the things he'd been telling me over dinner I couldn't help wondering how much of his talk at school had just been showing off.

As I watched Gavin he didn't seem quite so attractive any more, and as I listened to him I began to feel slightly *suspicious*.

'So what are you doing now?' I asked.

'At this precise moment – nothing at all,' he said candidly. 'Oh, I've written off for loads of jobs, but none of them are what I really want.'

'What do you really want, then?' I asked.

Gavin smiled. 'What I'd really like is to get involved in the music industry. It's something that's always interested me. Travelling all over the country, meeting new people, and being a part of all that glamour. Cindy, you're a very lucky girl, do you realize that? You've got it all!'

Slowly pieces were beginning to fall into place, and I didn't like the picture that was building up. At the back of my mind something Gavin had said earlier was nagging at me.

'Gavin, before dinner you were saying something about it being your last chance,' I said cautiously. 'Last chance for what?'

He hesitated, looking a little unsure of himself. Then the charming smile was back, curving his lips and making his eyes sparkle; only this time I wasn't dazzled by it, I just waited patiently for his next carefully planned move.

Gavin reached out and covered my hand with his, squeezing it gently.

'My last chance to meet you again, Cindy,' he said evenly. 'When we were at school I always wanted to get to know you. There was a quality about you even then – before you got involved in all the glitter of show business.'

'So why didn't you?' I asked him innocently. 'You had five days in every week to walk up to me and say hello.'

Gavin nodded and sighed.

'I know, and I've regretted not doing just that ever since,' he said. 'The thing is I didn't have the nerve. I was too shy.'

As the last piece in the puzzle fell neatly into place I stopped feeling suspicious and uneasy. I also stopped loving Gavin – if I ever really had loved him.

The one thing Gavin had never been was shy, and from our conversation it had become more and more obvious that Gavin wasn't interested in me so much as the glamour of my new life. No doubt he'd shown as much enthusiasm in advertising and photography when he met someone who was able to get him a job without Gavin having to put himself out too much.

Suddenly I felt very annoyed. Gavin was trying to *use* me.

Oh, his winning the competition had been pure luck, there was no doubt about that. If Mike's film hadn't jammed and I hadn't moved my hand ever so slightly, I might have been sitting here with someone totally different. I was also willing to bet that when Gavin had been notified he'd won the competition he started making plans to turn his prize into the chance of getting himself a nice cushy job.

It was a nasty shock to realize suddenly that Gavin was an opportunist as well as a shallow, self-centred person, but in a way it was a relief, too. For the past week I'd been reliving all my dreams about him. Now it was time to put those dreams away forever.

'Cindy,' Gavin was saying, 'you don't know how thrilled I am to see you again. Don't let's end it here. I'd love to see you again – only without the cameras and publicity. We've got a lot of lost time to make up. So what about dinner tommorrow? Just the two of us . . .'

I glanced up to see Karen and Dave coming towards us. Mike was standing by an empty table putting a new film in his camera and I smiled to myself. I'd waited a long time for this moment, only now it was too late.

'Gavin, I'm sorry,' I said, shaking my head. 'But the answer's no. Our schooldays are over now, and that's really all we have in common . . .'

AN AUSTRALIAN DREAM
Jane Butterworth

DAVY GAZED OUT OF THE WINDOW of the smooth, luxurious coach and sighed heavily as he watched the countryside speed by. Suddenly he felt overwhelmed with loneliness and longed to return to England – he seemed to have been away such a long time.

It had been weeks since the actors and film crew had arrived in Australia and they'd been filming in Adelaide and Perth; now, however, they were heading out of the city and into the outback to finish filming the series.

It was a funny thing, but television companies always seemed to film the first part of the series last, and *The Currie Pioneers* was no exception. The main part of the tale of one immigrant family's struggle to build a life in Australia during the last century had already been filmed, and all that remained was the first couple of episodes.

Most of the other actors and actresses had returned home. The only people left besides Davy were Jason and Gary, who were playing his brothers, and Joseph Riley and Mary Minter, who were playing his parents. Davy had quite enjoyed his time in Australia while they'd been based in the cities because there was always plenty to do, but where they were heading now was so far from anywhere that they were going to have to live in caravans for the next fortnight.

He cheered up when they reached their destination – a log cabin nestling on top of a hill surrounded by dramatic countryside. He gazed at the land – it was lush and green, not at all as he'd imagined. Just like England really. There were acres of forests and fields, and not another house in sight. The caravans were luxurious, air-conditioned and so big they might as well have been houses.

He started to unpack his case and noticed that Jason and Gary were having a mock fight outside. He'd be glad to see the back of them – being in such close contact for so long with people he didn't particularly get on with got him down.

Sometimes he wished he'd never landed this part, although his agent had told him that it was the best thing that had ever happened to him, and that since the production was co-sponsored by an Australian TV company it would make him a star on both sides of the world. Not that he wasn't already a star in England – since he'd started making regular appearances in the country's favourite soap opera he'd become a household name. And he wasn't sure he liked that too much.

'Whose land is this?' he asked the producer, Warren, as they ate supper round a makeshift table outside. It would have been quite fun if they hadn't been bombarded by flies and other insects.

'It belongs to a farm a couple of miles west of here,' Warren replied. 'So we're not entirely on our own, even though it seems like that. We've got radio contact with them. Tomorrow the guy's arriving with the horses so you can take a ride over there if you want.'

Horses! Davy felt a thrill of pleasure when he heard about them. He adored riding. One of the reasons why he'd landed the part of Jed Currie against fierce opposition was because he was such a good rider, and Jed spent the first couple of episodes in the saddle virtually the whole time. Davy had grown up in Cornwall, and although he lived in London and hardly saw his family now, he still sometimes remembered what it had been like when he was a kid and used to ride his pony along the sands in the early morning. But that was before he'd auditioned for a

TV talent contest, just for a laugh, at the age of thirteen. He'd not only won it, but he'd been signed up by an agent shortly afterwards.

He had gone to live with his agent and her husband in London, and soon he had been appearing regularly in television adverts; gradually he had lost touch with his Cornish background and even a little bit with his parents, but every time he felt lonely he'd long for the freedom of the countryside.

The next morning the sky was blue and gold and the sun shone brilliantly. When the trainer arrived with the horses that were to be used in the filming, Davy knew he just had to have the little grey mare to ride.

'Please Joe,' he pleaded with the director. 'I know she and I are going to get on.'

The horse nuzzled him as he stroked her velvet ears, and the director said, 'Oh all right. But don't you disappear on her just yet – we'll be starting on scene three in ten minutes and you'd better know your lines. Come on everybody, settle down now!'

Davy knew that Bridie was the right horse for him. They seemed to have a special relationship, and she knew it too. When they came to film the scene where he was supposed to break her in, the trainer wasn't needed as she did everything Davy told her. He wished he could take her back to England.

During a break in the filming, he couldn't resist it any longer – he saddled up Bridie and rode off, into the open land.

They rode through forests and fields, out on to rolling grasslands. The wind whipped through Davy's hair, which he'd grown long for the series, and he felt a wonderful happiness grow within him as he rode.

Then, almost out of nowhere, a figure seemed to appear in front of them. Bridie was so startled that she reared up, and Davy tumbled to the ground.

Dazed, he shook his head then looked in alarm for his horse

in case she'd bolted. But Bridie was standing there quietly, her reins held by a pretty young girl.

'Why on earth did you do it?' Davy demanded angrily. 'Jumping out on me like that – I could've been killed.' He tried to get to his feet but suddenly felt dizzy and sat down again.

'Don't get up. Sit there for a while,' the girl said, in a soft voice with a light Australian accent. His head soon started to clear and he looked at her properly – he thought she was the most beautiful girl he'd ever seen. She had long reddish-blonde hair, a sprinkling of freckles on her nose and she was tanned a light brown. But what was different about her from most of the girls he knew was that there was no trace of make-up on her open, fresh face – he liked that very much.

He smiled. 'I'm sorry I shouted at you,' he said.

'I'm sorry I startled your horse,' she replied. 'I didn't mean to – I saw you riding by and wanted to say hello. We don't often get visitors here. Are you from the English film unit?'

He nodded. 'And you must be from the farm whose land we're renting.'

'That's right. I'm Lizzie Carter.' She extended her slim hand and he grasped it and heaved himself up at the same time, keeping hold of her hand a little longer than he need have done.

'I'm Davy Stuart,' he said.

'Are you an actor or one of the technicians?' asked Lizzie.

He flushed. It had been a long time since he could go anywhere without being recognized.

'I'm an actor,' he admitted. 'But don't let's talk about me. Tell me about you. How do you manage, living out here in the middle of nowhere? You must feel very isolated.'

She laughed. 'I guess it seems pretty remote to you,' she said. 'It does get a bit lonely sometimes – we were really pleased when we were contacted by your television company. I used to have my school lessons over the radio. Mind you, I go into town once a week so life doesn't get too lonely.'

'But town's a couple of hours away,' said Davy, aghast.

She shrugged. 'I've never known any different. Do you feel better? How about coming back to the farm for a drink?'

He nodded cheerfully, and walked Bridie to the farmhouse. It was a large wooden building with a pretty verandah, and it looked friendly and inviting.

He tied up the horse outside and followed Lizzie indoors.

'This is my mother,' she announced, and the small, fair-haired woman looked up and smiled.

'Nice to meet you,' she said.

'How about some barley water, Mum?' asked Lizzie. 'And do you think you could have a look at Davy's head? He just came off his horse.'

'Oh no,' Davy protested, but Mrs Carter came over and explored his head with sensitive fingers. She found a tender spot and put on some ointment which she promised would soothe any pain he felt. Lizzie poured out barley water from an earthenware jug.

'Davy's from the television people,' she said.

'Fancy! I expect you find it very quiet here,' said her mother.

He didn't say that he'd been dreading coming here, because he'd forgotten that he had. Suddenly he knew he didn't want to go home any more. He felt strangely drawn to this wild, dramatic country and wanted to explore it, to get to know more about it.

He said simply, 'I love it here.'

He and Lizzie went to sit outside on the verandah, and he listened quietly while she told him about her life on the farm, the hard yet enjoyable work and the rigours of the changing seasons.

'Don't you ever want to get a job and move to the city?' he

asked.

She smiled. 'Why should I? I work here. Since Dad died I've helped Mum run the place.'

He stared at her in amazement. 'You mean you and your mother run the farm?'

'Ah, we have some farmhands,' she said. 'But Mum and I do all the work!'

He was silent for a moment, then he said, 'This place . . . the life you lead . . . it's so similar to the series we're filming. I suppose that's why the producer chose to film here.' He reached out and took hold of her hand. 'But I'm glad he did,' he added.

'So am I,' she said softly.

He told her about his life in England; about his smart new flat in London and his childhood in Cornwall, and how he couldn't walk down the road without someone asking for his autograph. She listened with wide eyes as he talked about how his acting had made him a public person, and how nice it was to be in Australia where nobody knew him.

'My grandfather was a pioneer, just like the Curries in your series,' she told him. 'He used to – whatever's the matter?'

A look of horror had come over his face, and he jumped to his feet. 'I'd completely forgotten the time. They'll murder me! I sneaked off during a break in filming and I only meant to be half an hour or so. They'll be sending out search parties – I've got to go.'

Her face drooped in disappointment and he added quickly, 'But I hope I can see you again.'

'Would you like to come to supper tomorrow?' she asked shyly. 'Mum would love it – we don't get too many visitors.'

'I'd love to. Until then.' Self-consciously, he bent over her and brushed the top of her red-gold hair with his lips. He had untied Bridie and was cantering off before she could say any more.

He was lucky; when he returned to the film set, production had been held up because a stunt on horseback had gone wrong and the director was trying to work out another way to do it. They'd hardly noticed he'd been gone, so he unsaddled Bridie, gave her a quick rub down and slipped unnoticed back into the midst of things.

So began the happiest period of Davy's life. During the day he'd concentrate on filming, and so enthusiastically did he throw himself into the character of Jed Currie that he heard Warren telling the director that it was the finest thing he'd ever done. He almost became the character – perhaps it was because in the evening he'd ride over to Lizzie's farm and eat supper with her and her mother, just like Jed would have all those years ago. They'd talk and then he and Lizzie would sit on the verandah hand in hand, sometimes saying little, just listening to the sounds of the night or watching the beautiful sunsets.

Then, when he rode back to his caravan to bed, he'd feel like Jed would have felt after meeting his sweetheart . . .

However, soon the day Davy had been dreading arrived. Filming was finished and the following morning the team would be packing up. They would drive to Perth and catch a plane back to England. He should have been looking forward to going home, but he was dreading it.

That night at the farm, he grasped Lizzie's hands almost desperately and said, 'Please come back to England with me, Lizzie. We could get married. I know we only met two weeks ago, but I feel like I've known you forever.'

She smiled wanly, but her clear blue eyes were sad as she replied, 'You know I wouldn't fit into your world. I'd stick out like a sore thumb in my cotton dresses at your posh film star parties and restaurants. Besides, I don't want to live in that world. I'm happy here on the farm – and what would Mum do without me?'

Impulsively he said, 'If you won't come with me, then I'll stay here with you! I'll give up acting. You're right, the life here is so much better, so much more real! Now I know why I found the part of Jed so easy – it was *me*! We'll get married, and I'll help you run the farm. Oh, please say yes!'

She looked up at him for a second, then nodded delightedly and he hugged her.

'But Davy,' she said, 'you must be very sure. You mustn't rush things.'

'I'll have to go back to England,' he said, 'to clear up a few things, do post-production work on *The Currie Pioneers*, sell my flat and tell my agent I'm giving it all up. I'll return in three months. You'll never want for anything again – I've got plenty of money.'

'Are you sure you'll be happy here?' she asked anxiously, but he hardly heard.

'Oh, I love you, Lizzie,' he said happily.

When they said goodbye he saw a glimmer of tears in her eyes, and he felt a lump in his throat as he turned from her for the last time . . .

He was strangely quiet during the flight home. He felt drained of all energy, with a sort of emptiness inside. Every second meant that he was being taken a little further from Lizzie and he couldn't bear it.

When the plane had eventually touched down at Heathrow airport and Davy was being driven towards his flat in London, his heart gave a funny little leap. The car sped through the crowded streets. It was a spring day – cold and sharp, but with lots of sunshine, and everything seemed bustling and alive. He had a sudden pang at the thought of turning his back on all this forever . . .

He unlocked the door of his flat and smiled when he saw that his agent had been round to air the place for him and had left him something in the fridge to eat. She really was more like a mother to him. There was a large pile of mail on the table and he was just about to sit down and look at it when the telephone rang.

He picked up the receiver. 'Hello?'

'Davy? This is Alison, Alison Cartwright.' She was a friend of his who worked as a disc jockey on the local radio station. 'I heard you were back today so I thought I'd give you a call. I'm having a party tonight and I'd really like you to come.'

It was on the tip of his tongue to say that he was tired and jet-lagged and anyway, what was the fun in going to a party when the girl he loved wouldn't be there? However, he decided on impulse to go. He might as well enjoy life while he could – he'd be leaving it all behind soon.

His tiredness left him when he arrived at the party, and he enjoyed being the centre of attention – after all, he'd been away for two months and everyone wanted to ask him about Australia and the television series. But he didn't tell anyone about Lizzie – he couldn't bring himself to. He knew no one would understand. By the time he left he'd talked to practically everybody at the party and danced with nearly every girl – he hadn't had so much fun for ages.

A brief image of Lizzie flashed into his mind before he fell asleep, then was gone.

The next morning he'd hardly opened his eyes before the phone rang. It was his agent.

'It's Saturday,' Davy said in horror. 'What do you want?'

'That's a nice welcome!' she said. 'I work weekends as well! Just wanted to say hello, welcome back and to tell you I've put you up for a part in the BBC dramatization of *The Mill On The Floss*.'

He was just about to tell her not to bother as he was giving up acting for good, when something held him back. Well, if he won the part he could probably fit it in before he left for Australia. So he took down the details, promised to read the book, and felt a slight feeling of guilt after he'd put down the phone.

He looked out of the window. It would be late in the evening in Australia and Lizzie would be feeding the horses. He wondered if she were thinking of him. He found it hard to picture her face . . .

When her first letter arrived nearly a week later his heart leapt with pleasure, and nostalgia swept over him.

In the next envelope he opened that morning there was an invitation to a film premiere and he put it down, thinking hard. He adored film premieres. Would he really be able to give all this up? Wouldn't he miss it? The idea of life in the outback, the same sort of life that Jed Currie had once lived, had seemed so appealing when he was actually in Australia. But now that he was back in London, leading his normal existence, it seemed a remote dream. Suddenly the thought of giving up his friends, his work and his pleasures for a life of isolation in the outback didn't seem so attractive to him. It was almost as though he had become Jed Currie while he'd been in Australia – but now he was back in England he had turned back into Davy Stuart. And it had been Jed Currie who had fallen in love with Lizzie, not Davy Stuart . . .

Two weeks after his return he realized he'd never really intended moving to Australia. He'd just been captivated by Lizzie and the beauty of the country around her. He felt a sadness when he thought of her gentle, pretty face and of the happiness they'd shared, but he knew that it would be impossible to recapture that happiness.

The following day he started to write the most difficult letter he'd ever written in his life.

My dear Lizzie,

I can hardly bear to write this, but I have to force myself. Now that I am back in England I've realized it would be impossible for me to come to Australia to live . . .

He tried not to visualize her tears when she read on. He wrote how much he'd loved her, trying to let her down as gently as possible, and told her he'd realized that he was deluding himself – he could never give up his city life. Finally he sealed the letter with a heavy sigh.

He hoped she would understand . . .

STEPS TO STARDOM
Toni Cornford

I'D BEEN WAITING FOR THE PHONE CALL for five long days. Now, as I listened to the voice on the other end, Mum stood anxiously beside me.

'Yes . . . yes . . . I'll be there,' I said finally.

Slowly I replaced the receiver, letting the news I'd just received sink in.

'Well?' Mum prompted impatiently. 'Did they offer you a part?'

Excitement bubbled inside me. I longed to be able to find the words to make this moment really memorable, but in the end I just blurted it out.

'Not *a* part, Mum,' I told her. '*The* part! They've asked me to play Tara – the starring role!'

For a moment Mum and I stared at each other.

'Oh, Gayle . . .' she said tearfully. 'Oh, darling, I'm so proud of you.'

The next moment she was hugging me and we were laughing and crying at the same time . . .

I belonged to a small local ballet company, and it had been the choreographer who'd told me auditions were being held for a new ballet, *Girl from Another World*. He'd more or less pushed me into going, at the same time brushing aside my protests that I wouldn't stand a chance. At the most I thought I'd danced well enough perhaps to be offered a part in the chorus, but I was convinced the part of Tara would go to someone with far more experience.

The company putting on the production was very well known, and at the audition we were told that if the ballet was a success it would be taken on a tour of the continent. I could hardly believe all this was happening to me. It was the most wonderful moment of my whole career – or it should have been. There was just one cloud on my otherwise sunny horizon – my boyfriend, Sam.

We'd been going out together for almost a year, and while Sam had always seemed interested in my dancing I'd always had the sneaky feeling he didn't really take it too seriously. I'd noticed it most strongly the night he'd come to the company's performance of *The Minstrel*.

I'd had a small part with a complicated solo, and I'd put my whole heart into it, determined to dance well. The show had been a huge success and on the last night there'd been a small party afterwards. Sam had stood quietly at my side as people came up to congratulate me on my performance.

'I hope you realize what a gem you have here,' the producer had said to Sam with a smile. 'We have high hopes for Gayle, you know. Look after her, Sam, she's going to go a long way.'

Sam had smiled politely and said all the right things, but there'd been no pride in his voice and my euphoric feeling of success had slowly faded.

On the way home he'd been very quiet.

'What's wrong, Sam?' I'd asked.

He had been silent for a moment, and I had been surprised to find I was holding my breath.

'Do you really want to be a professional dancer?' he'd asked suddenly.

'Yes, of course I do,' I'd replied immediately. 'You know how much I love dancing.'

A heavy silence had fallen over us, and I could feel a strange tension building up.

'Why, Sam?' I'd asked carefully.

He'd slowed the car and pulled in to the side of the road. In the darkness he'd turned to me and taken my hand.

'Because I love you, Gayle, and you know I want us to get married,' he'd said softly. 'Call me stupid if you like, but I've got this dread that if you go on with your career one day you'll dance right out of my life, and I couldn't bear that.'

Tenderly I'd reached up and touched his face.

'Oh, Sam, that's silly,' I'd told him fondly. 'You know I love you, and there's no reason why I couldn't combine my career with being your wife.'

'Yes, but I don't want to be married to someone who leaves for the theatre the moment I get home at night,' he'd continued. 'And I certainly don't want to be the sort of husband who trails along behind his wife. Gayle, I've got a good career, too. Oh, I admit being an accountant isn't glamorous, but it's safe and secure and it would give us a good life.'

I hadn't realized Sam had felt that way about my career, but my ambition was too strong for me to give it up. Somehow I had to make him see that.

'Sam, let's leave it for a while,' I'd said eventually. 'We're both young, and there's no reason to rush into anything. I've worked hard to be a dancer and I want to use all that hard work and training, even if it's only for a short time.'

I'd eventually managed to persuade him that there was plenty of time for us to think about getting married and the subject had dropped. Yet now I'd accepted the part of Tara, I couldn't avoid it any longer.

When I'd told Sam I was going to audition for *Girl from Another World* he'd wished me luck and I was sure he'd genuinely meant it. Looking back now I couldn't help feeling he'd been sincere because it was a big production and he didn't think I stood a chance. How was he going to react when I told him I hadn't just been accepted – I'd been offered the lead role?

Sam had been away on a course for the past two weeks and was due home the following day, and in the evening I was going to *have* to tell him.

'Just be honest with him, love,' Mum said as I was getting ready. 'I'm sure he wouldn't want to stand in the way of your career. He knows how much it means to you.' She put her arm around me. 'Whatever happens, Gayle, you know I'm on your side.'

What she was really saying was that if things didn't work out between Sam and me she'd help me over the heartbreak. Yet there was no reason why it should come to that, provided I could make Sam see how much this part meant to me.

I was pleased to see Sam when he came to pick me up, but I couldn't help feeling apprehensive as well. On the way to the restaurant Sam told me all about the course and how it would help him in the future.

'You should have seen the hotel they put us up in, Gayle,' he went on. 'It was luxury, pure luxury. I only wish I'd had more time to look around the town. It was one of those old harbour towns, full of history. In fact I thought it would make the perfect place for a honeymoon!'

He went on and on about it, but he never once asked me how the audition had gone and I got the awful feeling he was deliberately avoiding the subject. I sighed to myself. Well, if Sam wasn't going to bring it up I'd have to. The tricky bit would be finding the right moment.

The opportunity didn't arise until we'd finished our meal and the waiter had brought our coffee.

'This isn't fair,' Sam said with a laugh. 'I've done nothing but talk about myself all evening. It's your turn now, darling. What have you been up to while I was away, and did you miss me?'

He looked deep into my eyes and smiled lovingly.

'Of course I missed you,' I said, returning the smile. 'And

I've been up to quite a lot in the past two weeks.'

'Tell me,' Sam encouraged.

I took a deep breath.

'Well, the important part was going for the *Girl from Another World* audition,' I began. 'Remember me telling you about it? It's the new ballet that . . .'

'Yes, I remember,' Sam interrupted, nodding impatiently.

A flicker of something like annoyance made his smile fade briefly, but I didn't take any notice. I carried straight on.

'The audition went very well,' I said enthusiastically. 'So well, in fact, that they offered me the part of Tara.'

Sam was watching me intently.

'Tara?' he queried. 'What's that? One of the smaller parts?'

I shook my head and took another deep breath. This was the moment I'd been dreading.

'No, Sam,' I said evenly. 'It's the leading role. It's going to mean a lot of hard work, but I'm really thrilled about it.'

He picked up his coffee cup and drained it in one go, then he forced himself to smile.

'Well, congratulations,' he said. 'How long's it on for?'

'At least four months,' I told him, and then came the part I knew Sam wouldn't like. 'And if it's a success here we'll be going on a tour of the continent.'

He studied me carefully for a moment, then he laughed harshly.

'Well, this is a surprise to come home to,' Sam said, a sharp edge to his voice. 'What you're really trying to say is now you've got this part there's no room in your life for me. That's it, Gayle, isn't it? I should have seen this coming months ago. I knew you'd leave me one day.'

'Hey, if you carry on like that I just might!' I laughed lightly. I was teasing, but Sam didn't see it that way. Quickly I went on. 'Oh, darling, you know how much dancing means to me, and I don't see why it should interfere with us. Anyway, I won't let it.'

'And what about when we're married?' he demanded angrily. 'What then? Do I stay quietly at home like a dutiful husband and happily watch you wandering off all over the world?'

'That's not fair,' I said crossly. 'We're not even engaged yet and I think you're taking far too much for granted.'

'Maybe you're right,' Sam muttered coldly. 'Well, I won't any longer, Gayle.' He stood up, almost knocking over his chair. 'Come on, I'm taking you home. There's no point in carrying on this conversation. You've obviously made up your mind and what I think doesn't matter!'

He threw some money on the table to cover the bill then looked down at me, his eyes glinting with anger. I picked up my bag and stood up. I'd never seen Sam in such an angry mood before and I didn't quite know how to handle it. He turned on his heel and walked quickly from the restaurant. I followed more slowly, trying desperately to think of a way to calm him down.

'Please, Sam . . .' I began as I got into the car. 'It's not worth quarrelling about. Can't we talk this over properly?'

The only reply was a roar as the car's engine burst into life. As we turned into the road there was an angry screech when the tyres spun on the gravel, then we were speeding along the road, Sam urging the car to go faster and faster. I sat stiffly, clutching the sides of my seat as I struggled to control my panic.

'Slow down, Sam,' I begged after a moment.

My heart was pounding, and I was terrified. Sam, who was usually such a careful driver, had suddenly turned into a maniac. I closed my eyes and gasped as he threw the car into a bend, narrowly missing the curb.

'Sam, *please* . . .' I whimpered. 'You'll kill us both!'

Ahead of us was a bridge. It was only wide enough for one

car to cross at a time and Sam was approaching it much too fast. Suddenly headlights blinded me and Sam spun the wheel to avoid the oncoming car. He managed to turn just in time, but he was going too fast to stop. Before I even had time to scream the car was ploughing into a tree at the side of the road . . .

The next thing I knew I was waking up in hospital. A nurse was sitting by the bed, and I was surrounded by machines making weird mechanical bleeps.

'Don't worry, love,' the nurse said with a warm smile. 'It looks much worse than it is. It's nice to see you awake at last. We've been worried about you. How are you feeling?'

'I . . . I'm not sure,' I replied slowly.

My head felt fuzzy and my mouth was dry.

For a moment I couldn't remember a thing, then it all came flooding back. Sam . . . his terrible anger . . . and finally the accident.

'Sam . . . ?' I asked.

'He was lucky,' she said. 'Just a few scratches. Now, no more talking, and I'll go and get the doctor.'

It was the doctor who told me what had happened after the car had crashed. Apparently my head had gone through the windscreen and on arrival at the hospital I'd slipped into a coma. That had been *a week ago.*

After the doctor had examined me thoroughly, he sat on the edge of my bed, his face serious.

'Well, Gayle, the good news is that there's nothing broken,' he said with a quick smile.

'And the bad news?' I asked nervously.

'Maybe it's not so bad,' he said. 'Besides the cuts on your face, you were heavily bruised in the accident, and unfortunately most of the bruising was to your legs. What worried us was the coma. You see, we couldn't be sure just how much damage had been done until you were awake and we could test your reflexes properly.'

Tears sprang to my eyes.

'Are you . . . are you telling me I can't dance any more?' I whispered.

He pursed his lips.

'Gayle, we just don't know yet,' he said quietly. 'We know you can move all right, but you may have lost some flexibility. For anyone in an ordinary job it wouldn't make any difference, but for a dancer . . . Anyway, don't start worrying about it now. I want you to get a good night's sleep and tomorrow the physiotherapist will be in to see you. We'll know more then.'

It was a frightening moment – almost worse than the car crash itself. When the doctor had gone I lay back on the pillows and let the tears come. I thought about Sam a lot right then, but it was with bitterness, not love. What if I couldn't dance again? My whole career would be in ruins, and all because of his jealousy.

When my tears eventually dried I knew I never wanted to see him again. In that one night of rage he'd lost my love completely, but he wasn't going to deprive me of my career, too. If there was the slightest chance of me dancing again I was going to grab it with both hands. I'd worked hard before and I'd work hard again. All my life I'd wanted to be a dancer, and now I was more determined than ever.

In the weeks that followed I refused to see Sam. He came to the hospital several times, and phoned Mum, begging her to persuade me to see him. My answer was always the same – I couldn't find it in my heart to forgive him.

All I wanted to do was concentrate on getting well and making sure I was fit enough to play Tara.

It wasn't easy, but with the help of the staff at the hospital I did it. I exercised for hours every day, refusing to stop even when I was exhausted, but when I danced on to the stage on the opening night every second of pain had been worth it.

There was only one sad moment. When I arrived at the theatre I found a huge basket of flowers waiting for me in my dressing room. Attached to the basket was a card.

Good luck on your big night and every success with Tara. Please believe me, Gayle – I'm so sorry.

It was signed: *Sam.*

I knew it was his way of trying to make up for what had happened, but for me it was too late. When I stood with the rest of the company to take the final bows I had my first taste of real stardom. I wasn't going to give it all up for someone like Sam.

One day I might fall in love again, but until then all I want to do is dance . . .

WORD OF A SONG

Maureen Spurgeon

NOBODY WOULD EVER BELIEVE, Paula told herself wearily, that she had been earning a living as a songwriter for the past eleven months. Recently the same tune kept coming into her head, spreading itself around the studio, even before it reached her fingers tapping out notes on the piano. Yet she had written at least thirty successful songs, all completely different. Why did this one song stay in her memory?

Any minute now, and Jake Priest would be sure to wander in, clicking his fingers absent-mindedly and saying something like, 'Paula – that sounds like the number you were putting together just after Herbie Benson's TV talent show final. Memories play funny tricks, I guess. Especially on an old song promotions man like me . . .'

Paula sighed, and shutting the piano lid, reached for her holdall and glanced at the clock. Too early for lunch. A bit too late for coffee. But she had to take a break, before that melody began haunting her with its unwelcome magic, yet again.

Outside, life seemed to be going on as usual. There were children playing, busy shoppers, and impatient motorists jostling to get past the road-works in front of the newspaper offices – near the exact spot where she had stood, proudly watching Barry and the rest of his group, just over a year ago.

'Let's have a nice big smile!' She could almost hear the press photographer's voice, yelling to make himself heard above the din of clapping and cheering from excited admirers. 'Not every day we get a local group winning top place on Herbie Benson's

Stars of Tomorrow television show, eh?'

'Suppose not . . .' That was when Barry had started impatiently clicking a button on his new digital watch, Paula remembered. 'But we've got a couple of agents to see about recording contracts this morning, so if we've answered all your questions . . .'

'I understand you've already got Buddy Marshall handling your work,' the reporter had persisted, scribbling hard. 'He manages most of the top pop groups, doesn't he? Is that why you called your group The Buddies, after him?'

'No, how could we? That was our name when we had just started and were playing at the Soda Fountain at weekends.'

The Soda Fountain . . . Paula debated whether she should go there now, just to sit outside at the red and white tables and convince herself that some things hardly changed at all. The place would still look the same as it had when Barry first began strumming his secondhand guitar, smiling at her because he could tell she liked his playing, his voice. Liked him, too.

After that, they had had coffees together, and she had told him that she'd written a few songs – which was just what Barry needed then, because he wanted to get together and form a band with a few lads from technical college, and, he said, there was a limit to the number of golden oldies they could play in one evening.

Even the name The Buddies had been her idea, Paula reminded herself, sitting thankfully on the wooden bench in the town square. And, later on, she'd pushed the band to do an audition for Herbie Benson's television show. Barry could hardly believe it when they were actually accepted, not even when rehearsals began, and the whole group had their hair trimmed by make-up girls, with discussions going on around them about their costumes, and the right sort of stage set.

'I-I always knew you would win, Barry.' Paula remembered the words she had spoken to him as the results of the finals were televised to millions of viewers from a giant screen. 'You had everything you needed to make it to the top . . .'

Whether Barry ever heard what she said, Paula never knew. Next minute there seemed to be thousands of people, all wanting to meet him, clamouring for interviews, for photographs, souvenirs, handing over cards, forms, telephone numbers – always, so it seemed, with someone from the television company to take charge. Paula had loved every minute as much as Barry did. Especially when the fuss was at last beginning to die down, and he'd spotted her standing alone, watching all the bustle and excitement.

True, there had only been time for a quick kiss, and a hurried whisper. 'Thanks for everything, Paula. We'd never have done all this if it wasn't for you. Remember that, honey.'

Paula did remember. But the next day, when Barry chose not to mention to the press about her naming the group the Buddies, or even entering them for the Herbie Benson *Stars of Tomorrow* show, she had begun to wish she could forget what he'd said. That was what had made it seem so unfair at the time . . .

Two or three weeks later, when the recording contract had been signed, Barry's name was on the lips of every disc jockey, every presenter of every pop music programme on radio and television.

That one particular tune kept coming back to her now, after she had written at least thirty songs for Jake Priest and Merlin Records, all reasonably successful, all completely different.

Paula was hardly aware she was humming the tune again, letting the words fall into place with every note, just as she wrote it for Barry.

> '*I want you to know, I'll always love you.*
> *I'll be right there, whatever you do –*
> *Wherever you go, I'm waiting for you . . .*'

It was only when the ache came back into her throat that she realized she had been remembering the song at all.

The first time Barry had heard her playing it on the dusty piano in the basement rehearsal room at Merlin Records, he'd smiled.

'Might have known I'd find you hidden among the rubbish!' he had joked, his brown eyes glowing warmly, as they always did when he wanted to make her laugh. 'How long have you been down here?'

'Not too long . . . Well . . . you know, ever since we got here, this morning . . .'

'It's nearly three o'clock now! So, what have you been doing with yourself while we've been working on our first album?'

'Only this song . . .' And the first few notes tinkled rather mournfully among the clutter of fading boards and broken scenery. 'You know . . . You were saying that you needed some new songs fairly soon, and I thought . . . as I've helped you out a bit before . . .'

'Please yourself, honey!' A swift peck on her forehead, and he was dashing towards the door. 'Just thought I'd better tell you that we'll be staying on for quite a while yet, so you might as well go home. Okay?'

Paula had wished then that she could slam down the piano lid and march straight past him without a word, without even looking at him.

Instead, she had stuffed the half-written song into her bag, trying hard to ignore the laughter and the loud voices which floated down the stairs from the studios overhead, the sound of synthesizers, and the warning 'Recording session in progress. Do not enter,' illuminated outside the door.

She'd imagined she could see Barry there now, playing a new guitar, and clearly enjoying himself. A youngish man wearing a sweat-shirt with 'Radio City' printed on it was standing by, holding a microphone – he was probably a radio reporter, waiting for an interview, Paula had guessed. Just about everyone wanted to talk to Barry those first few weeks. That was, she corrected herself, everyone who mattered at all.

She had waited most of a long, painful week after that, wondering if Barry might find time to telephone her, or maybe call round, the same as he always had. Then she had gone back to the studios, to the forgotten basement, the dusty piano, and a song which was never far from her mind.

At about lunch-time that day, a girl she had thought was Buddy Marshall's secretary had poked her head round the door.

'Oh . . .' There was an uncomfortable pause, as if the girl was trying to think what to say. 'It's you, back again. Wondered who it could be, tinkering away on that old relic.'

'Sorry . . .' Paula had waited for the girl to answer her, before she added timidly, 'Any chance of me seeing Barry today?'

'Wait upstairs if you like!' Paula watched her walk away briskly, her heels clicking smartly across the tiled floor, as she called back, 'The album's nearly finished now, I know. There's still some photographs to be shot for the music magazines, and Barry's got to see some designers about record sleeves and stage costumes for the group's tour. That's the lot, I think!'

Eagerly, Paula had followed her up the stairs, preparing to make herself comfortable on the familiar leather couch in the reception area, when the studio doors swung open and Barry came out.

For one terrible moment, Paula had thought he was going to walk past her without even noticing she was there. Then, he'd jerked his head at her, his brown eyes bright and hard.

'H-hello, Barry . . .' She wished she could think of something else to say.

'Hi. What are you doing here?'

'I only came to tell you I've finished your song. You know,

the one I was working on, last time. I-I think you'll like it . . .'

There had been just the trace of a thin smile on his face.

'Thanks for trying, kid. But the songs I sing have to be something special these days!'

'B-but, Barry . . .' Paula was almost running after him, along the carpeted corridor. 'Barry, if I could just play it through for you . . .'

He had swung round angrily, brushing the sheets of music to the floor.

'Look, just quit trailing around after me, okay? I've a lot to get through, right now. Anyway, Buddy doesn't think that having any kind of a girlfriend would be good news for my fans. Get the message?'

So, that was it. She no longer fitted in. Barry had told her.

The doubts she had been trying to pretend weren't there, and the excuses she had made for him, made it all a bit less of a shock. But there were still lonely, silent tears to be shed. She rushed into the now-deserted recording studio, anywhere to be alone.

When the doors of the studio were suddenly pushed open, she had dried her eyes, thinking he might have come back . . .

'Waiting for someone, sugar?'

And that was the first time Paula had ever seen Jake, the chubby-faced Song Promotions Manager, who, she discovered, also managed to look older than he really was.

'No . . . I only came to bring in a song for Barry and The Buddies . . . But, they've . . . I-I mean, he's gone . . .'

Jake dragged a chrome stool towards the studio piano, making a lot of noise.

'Okay, then,' he said, making it sound like a command. 'Let's hear it.'

'I want you to know, I'll always love you.
I'll be right there, whatever you do . . .'

There were still lonely, silent tears to be shed.

Paula only knew she was singing for Barry, wherever he was. But Jake must have thought it worth listening to, because he had said, 'Hmmm, that's not bad. Have you written anything else?'

He had sent out for lunch for both of them, from a fast-food take-away, and had listened to all her songs. He'd then offered cash for five of the numbers from the days spent in the Soda Fountain.

'That first song I heard you playing, Paula,' Jake said at last. 'Hold on to that for a while. Might have been okay for the new group we've had in here. Now what was their name, you know,' he clicked his fingers for inspiration. 'That's it, Barry and The Buddies. But I think their album's been sorted out. I'll let you know.'

As it happened, the song was hardly mentioned again. And if anyone at Merlin Records remembered that Paula had been Barry's girlfriend, that was never mentioned, either. With Jake behind her, and one successful song following another, Paula was glad to work, telling herself each day how lucky she was because of the way things had turned out, and that at least she was no longer a struggling songwriter.

It had only been a chance remark at the studios that morning which had begun rubbing at the sore place in her heart, making it seem as if it all happened only yesterday, instead of a whole year ago.

'Heard the news?' One of the sound engineers had been calling across the canteen. 'Barry and The Buddies are splitting up after the next album. Old man Marshall tried to talk Barry out of going solo, but the band wouldn't have it. Cancelled the rest of the contract between them, there and then!'

'Merlin Records won't let Barry go without a fight, though,' Jake's hearty voice boomed all around. 'Matter of fact, I was thinking of asking young Paula to write some material for him to try out. What do you think?'

It was hard to believe that a song could be almost forgotten, then remembered so easily, word for word, note for note.

Paula decided to walk on towards the Soda Fountain. Its red and white canopies looked like part of a stage back-drop, false and unreal.

'I want you to know, I'll always love you.
I'll be right there, whatever you do . . .'

As she opened the door she heard the words of her song again, but they no longer seemed to be inside her head. They were being sung in Barry's voice, and on his old guitar he was playing the accompaniment she had written.

And yet, she thought, the ripple of enthusiastic applause could hardly be wishful thinking. Nor the sight of the brown, curly hair which Paula had always thought matched his eyes so perfectly . . .

It was him! 'Barry! I-I thought it was you singing. But I couldn't be sure . . .' she stuttered.

'Back where we started!' He smiled at her, and held out his hand. 'Great to see you again, Paula. Reckon we've got a lot to talk about.'

'Y-yes . . .' She hoped that she wouldn't begin sounding angry, or bitter. 'Jake Priest did mention that he wanted me to write some songs for you . . .' She drew in a deep breath, watching him steadily. 'Is that what you wanted to talk to me about?'

The finest actor who ever lived, she decided, could never fake the look of mingled unhappiness and discomfort she saw on his face.

'So, you've heard The Buddies and I are splitting up. But we wouldn't have lasted long together, anyway. Everyone knew that. As for you writing me some songs, well – you were the real success, weren't you?'

He took her hand and held it tightly, his voice almost dropping to a whisper.

'I never did forget the last song you wrote for me. Jake showed it to me. You know, he could have sold it a hundred times over? He told me so himself.'

Paula swallowed hard. 'I think,' she said quietly, 'he knew all the time that I had written it for you. Nobody else, Barry.'

'Paula . . . I-I'm sorry . . .'

And, watching the sadness which clouded the brown eyes, she had to believe him.

'Guess I had to find out the hard way how much you mean to me. How much I really needed you.'

'And now?' she asked.

'Now, I'm starting all over again,' he told her firmly, gently pinching her cheek in the way she used to love. 'Do you think a great songwriter like you could give a helping hand to a struggling singer like me?'

She laughed, lifting up her face to his, and wondering how it was that life could suddenly seem so good.

'I could try,' was all she said. 'But, Barry . . .'

'What, Paula?'

'How did you know I'd come here today, to the Soda Fountain?'

He began smiling again, his eyes glowing warmly.

'Maybe I took the time to learn your song properly, Paula. Remember how it goes?'

> '*I want you to know, I'll always love you.*
> *I'll be right there, whatever you do . . .*
> *Wherever you go, I'm waiting for you . . .*
> *Want you to know, I'm thinking of you . . .*'

Away from the television cameras and recording studios, the song still sounded wonderful, the way Barry was singing it, to her.

Paula always knew it would be something special – once Barry really understood the words.

DANCE TO THE MUSIC
Jane Butterworth

'COME ON, JULIE – WE'RE HERE!' Julie looked up vaguely and wondered why her friend Michelle was standing over her impatiently.

'I know you don't like school, but this is ridiculous!' Michelle said jokingly.

'Heavens, I hadn't realized where we were,' Julie said in alarm as she grabbed her bag and raced off the bus just as it started to move off.

She'd been unaware that she'd arrived at the school bus stop because she'd been in the middle of a daydream all about her favourite rock band. This had been sparked off after she'd noticed a small advertisement tucked away in the corner of her favourite music paper:

'WANTED – EXTRAS FOR ROCK FILM.'

She'd read about the film *Dance to the Music* countless times because it starred her favourite band, Loose Change. It was a film about a rock band – their life on the road and eventual climb to stardom. Some parts were being filmed in a disused ballroom only a few miles from Julie's home town. For several scenes the makers of the film wanted boys and girls to come along and dance, while the band was filmed playing. Julie was dreaming of going along and being spotted and signed up for stardom . . . but come what may, she was going along to see Loose Change next week!

'You're miles away,' Michelle commented as they hurried through the school gates.

Julie smiled distantly, but said nothing. She certainly wasn't going to tell anyone of her plan to go along and try for extra work on the rock film – her friends teased her enough about being star-struck. They thought she was mad because she dreamed of a career on the stage, dancing, singing or acting, and teased her because she had pictures of Loose Change's lead singer, Gary Harris, all over her bedroom wall.

Fortunately school was due to break up a couple of days later although, Julie told herself, she was so keen to see Loose Change she'd probably have taken a day off.

The advertisement had said go to the Ritzi Ballroom at midday the following Friday, but she wasn't taking any chances. When the day came she left home extra early, hoping to be the first in the queue.

Before she'd left she had looked at herself critically in the mirror, and had been pretty pleased with the result. The shocking pink pants and tight black top would give her the freedom to dance and they were trendy, too. She made up her face with theatrical fantastic make-up and then set off, her heart thumping with anticipation . . .

But although she arrived at the ballroom long before midday, there was already an enormous queue which snaked right round the building. Her heart sank. What's more, everyone there looked very trendy indeed, much more than she did. She felt sure they'd be much better dancers than her. Suddenly she felt depressed – she'd felt good before she'd arrived and seen everyone else.

Lots of people were still arriving so she patiently joined the queue and prayed she wasn't too late. At midday the doors were opened and people started shuffling in, under the watchful eyes of a couple of rather bored looking young men – obviously members of the film company.

Julie held her breath as she got nearer the doors. They let her pass and she felt sick with relief as she followed the others into the ballroom, especially as they closed the doors shortly afterwards, leaving hundreds of disappointed people outside.

Julie looked around the magnificent ballroom; people were milling round the dance floor, and on the stage were bright lights, cameras and little knots of people looking worried or rushing about with technical equipment. Her heart gave a leap when she saw the members of Loose Change sitting casually on the edge of the stage chatting to each other – she'd never been so close to them before.

A young actor, whose face she recognized, was chatting to the singer of Loose Change. Julie tried to push her way through the throngs of people clustering around the stage, to get a better view, when a young, good-looking man with a mass of fair curly hair leaped up on the stage and shouted through a microphone, 'Can we have a bit of quiet, please?'

Everyone stopped talking and looked at him expectantly.

'First of all, can I say hello and thanks for coming,' he said. 'My name's Mike Shepherd – I'm the assistant director of *Dance to the Music*. The scenes we're shooting today are all set in the ballroom. In the story the band are playing here and they get spotted by a talent scout. Later on we'll be shooting a fight scene, but at the moment all I want you to do is dance. We'd like to have a look at you dancing before we start filming so we can select some of the better dancers to appear in camera range at the front of the stage. If you could start dancing when the boys start playing, I'll come round and have a look at you.'

'They'll never notice me,' Julie thought dispiritedly. She was in the middle of the ballroom and had little chance of getting to the front as the band were already starting to play. People began to dance, swaying and leaping this way and that, and some of them looked as though they were professionals. Julie decided to forget about her surroundings, and she imagined she was at the local disco with Michelle, enjoying the music.

She was astonished when she felt a light touch on her arm and she spun round to see the assistant director standing behind her.

'Get down to the front of the stage, love, will you?' he asked.

Too excited to think straight, she made her way to the front of the stage and joined about two dozen other girls and boys. The band laid down their instruments and looked bored, while the assistant director jumped up on the stage again, and started telling the band what to do in the next scene.

Julie watched the band as they sat around, tuning their guitars and only half listening to what Mike Shepherd was saying. Then she turned away in embarrassment because she realized that her favourite, the singer Gary Harris, was looking straight at her!

The director started pairing people up and he suddenly grabbed hold of Julie and pushed her towards the young actor she'd spotted when she'd arrived. 'You partner Louis, love. You look good together. Louis's playing Gregory, the boy who has been sacked by the band and is now out to make trouble for them. In this scene he's dancing with you – okay?' He started pushing people this way and that, and said, 'When the music starts you must stay in the position I've put you in, and dance as naturally as possible.' Suddenly he looked hard at Julie. 'What's your name, love?' he said.

'Julie,' she replied nervously.

'You've got nice hair, can you let it down?' he asked, flipping her pony tail with his fingers.

Julie flushed in embarrassment and undid her hair so that it flowed over her shoulders in a long, golden sheet. She looked up and saw that Gary Harris was still gazing at her with rapt attention. The next time she caught his eye he winked boldly. She grinned at him.

'Okay, let's run through the next number,' said the assistant director.

Loose Change started playing 'One More Chance', the title track of their last album, and everyone began to dance.

'You'll have to forgive me,' said Julie's partner disarmingly, 'I'm not much good as a dancer. I'm an actor and when it comes to dancing I've got two left feet.'

'You're doing fine,' said Julie, beginning to relax.

'Okay, that was great,' said the director after the band had finished playing. 'We'll roll this time. Start the lights off, please.'

A variety of coloured lights started to flash on and off, rippling backwards and forwards and sprinkling the dancers with vivid colours. It looked weird and magical.

'Okay, let's get on with it,' said Mike Shepherd. 'When the music starts – dance, and give it all you've got.'

Half a dozen times the band began to play and everyone started to dance, but the director stopped them because something wasn't right. Julie began to think that perhaps acting wasn't such a great idea after all.

'Is it usually like this?' she whispered to Louis, her partner.

'It's usually worse,' he replied with a smile.

Eventually the director was satisfied and started preparing for the next number when suddenly there was a commotion from above, and someone shouted, 'Look out!' Julie glanced up and at that moment Louis gave her a shove which sent her flying to the ground. As she fell a heavy light hit the ground with a crash inches away from where she'd been standing.

'Good grief! Are you all right?' asked the assistant director as he rushed to help her up.

Ashen-faced, Julie nodded. 'Thanks to Louis,' she said.

'It was lucky I saw it coming,' Louis said. He and the director gently helped her to her feet. She winced with pain as she stood up and her worse fears were realized – the light had hit her foot a glancing blow and she could hardly stand on it.

'I think I've broken my foot!' she said, and burst into tears.

'Someone call an ambulance, quickly,' said the director. A crowd of people clustered round her sympathetically. 'Are you all right apart from that?'

She nodded but felt she might as well be dead. If her foot was broken her big chance was over. Ruined. She wouldn't be able to dance in the film and she hadn't even had a chance to meet her favourite group. Someone brought her a chair and she looked at her swollen ankle. What bad luck!

Everyone was relieved when two ambulancemen ran in carrying a stretcher. They picked her up and put her on it – the last thing she remembered as they carried her out of the ballroom was Gary Harris's face, looking at her in concern . . .

The kindly hospital doctor who examined her foot smiled at her sympathetically.

'I'm pretty sure nothing's broken, but we'll pop you down to X-ray just to make sure,' he said. 'I think it's just badly bruised – you're a lucky girl.'

'Does that mean I can dance on it this afternoon?' Julie asked hopefully.

He laughed out loud. 'Heavens, no! It'll be stiff and sore for a few days yet, and you'll have a job walking on it. No chance of doing anything energetic.'

'Oh,' said Julie in disappointment.

Sure enough, no bones were broken, but that didn't make her feel any better. She still couldn't appear in the film.

A red-haired nurse came hurrying up and said, 'All done, Julie? You can go now, then. We'll get an ambulance to drop you off.' She helped Julie down the hospital steps. As Julie was just about to climb into the ambulance, a uniformed chauffeur jumped out of a sleek, black car and came running up.

'Miss Julie Woodville? I've been sent by Mr Shepherd and the film company to collect you,' he said. Julie gaped in astonishment as he helped her into the luxurious car and draped a sheepskin rug over her knees. She felt like a film star!

'Mr Shepherd asked specially that I bring you back to the film set at the ballroom,' said the chauffeur after Julie had asked him where they were going.

She brightened up. At least she'd be able to watch the filming for the rest of the day, even if she couldn't take part.

The chauffeur drove Julie to the stage door of the Ritzi Ballroom and helped her into the building. She found herself backstage, only a little way from where the band was playing, their heads bent over their instruments in concentration.

'I'll tell Mr Shepherd you're here,' promised the chauffeur.

Julie saw with a pang that the actor Louis was dancing with a new partner.

She heard the director shout, 'Cut! Okay everyone – go and have a cup of tea and be back in half an hour.'

He came backstage and smiled at Julie.

'How are you, love?' he asked.

She smiled wanly. 'Better, I suppose. But I won't be dancing for a week.'

'Look,' said the director, 'I've had an idea. The band were very taken with you – and so am I. You've got a lovely face and all that beautiful blonde hair! Anyway, the band have quite a big say in what goes on in this film and Gary, the singer, suggested we use you for a dream sequence which takes place later in the film. I'll explain it in greater detail if you agree, but the main thing is a shot of a girl's face with her long fair hair blowing in the wind. Gary thinks you'd be perfect – how do you feel about it?'

She opened and shut her mouth but no sound came out. Eventually she said, 'I'd love to!'

'We'll be shooting that scene next Thursday in the studios,' he said. 'I'll send my production assistant to see you to get your address and arrange for a car to pick you up on Thursday morning in case your foot's still giving you trouble. Anyway, I hope you'll stay and watch the filming for the rest of the day, but if you want to go home the car will take you any time you want.'

Overwhelmed with happiness, Julie nodded. This exceeded her wildest dreams!

At that moment Gary Harris walked up to her and smiled. This time she looked straight at him and smiled back.

'Hello,' he said, 'I've been wanting to meet you.'

'I've been wanting to meet you too,' said Julie, and all of a sudden she forgot all about the pain in her foot . . .